# The
# Fighting Pride

## Darren Cairns

The Fighting Pride

Published by Amazon KDP

M0D2085744657

Copyright: Darren T. Cairns, 2025

All rights reserved

**Author's contact information**

Email: tommydan2210@outlook.com

X: @dazzler1921

**Link to book on amazon:**

https://amzn.eu/d/eJw9Vb6

## Part 1

## For I am about to fall

# Chapter 1

Shamrock Hills was a modest town in the North-West of Ireland. The year was 1996. The people did okay there. Cobbler's End once employed seven hundred factory workers. Most of the factories were now gone. The town had seen better days, but it was still a worker's town. Tough. Stubborn. Prideful.

The Church of the Resurrection was in its one-hundred-and-thirtieth year. It overlooked the town like a watch tower. Father O'Dowd was already in the vestry, leafing through his sermon notes. He looked up as the morning light illuminated the stained-glass window.

#

Danny Breen was a boxer. He was deep into his roadwork, keeping a steady pace and enjoying the crisp morning air. His morning jogs had long been a feature of life by the Drumferry river. No matter the weather, spotting him in his grey hooded sweater and white running shoes was as sure a bet as any, and the Shamrock faithful knew their betting. Many men's wages went on Danny Breen, the 'Shamrock

Express', a former amateur standout in the prestigious middleweight division, and the last in a proud lineage of Shamrock fighters.

The storied careers of national champions, European belt holders and top ten contenders were captured in paint and immortalized on gable walls. One man, Luke 'Quick Hands' Gibson, was celebrated more than any. Everyone, from the layman to the scribe, knew they would never see his like again. But the town had not given up on blooding another world champion to add to its boxing tapestry. It only took one fighter, and Danny Breen was the heir apparent.

He cut through the park and sprinted all the way to the Gibson statue. He filled his lungs with the cool autumnal air as shafts of light cut through the sycamore trees. His body felt good bar a pulsating sting from a cut lip. Every fight took something from the body, and the last also took his unbeaten record. His ledger now read twenty-five wins and one defeat. He'd beaten Peter Simmons twice in the amateurs but was second best over twelve rounds in the pros.

Across town, his sister, Dee, pulled back the blinds and angled the radio antenna to silence the static. She had a busy day ahead. First, she had to ready her twin sons, Aiden and Alex, for school. Their father, Ivan, used to do the school run, but he worked in the Netherlands now. Before her shift at the Harbour chip shop, she would tend Da's grave. Monday also meant a visit to Serenity House, and she hoped it would be one of Ma's better days.

# Chapter 2

Growing up, Danny Breen idolized Roberto Duran. Known as 'Hands of Stone', the Panamanian fighter infamously piled on fifty celebratory pounds between his two fights with the great Sugar Ray Leonard. The rematch took place in November of 1981 and was one of the most anticipated fights in boxing history…

But Duran quit in the eighth round, turning his back on Leonard and telling the referee, 'No mas.' Leonard couldn't believe his luck. Duran had taken him to hell and back seven months prior, but the second time around, the weight cut had left his opponent weak as a kitten.

Danny Breen cried himself to sleep that night, though he learned a valuable lesson. Once the boxing got serious, his enduring breakfast was two poached eggs on whole wheat toast, a small bowl of porridge and a banana.

He stepped into the shower. His skin took little time to replenish after the fresh sweat of his morning run. He was over a week removed from his last fight. His forehead and temples showed signs of battle though the swelling had receded. His face was lean and the skin stretched tight across his brow and cheekbones. As a boxer, it left him susceptible to cuts.

Fighting with a cut eye was the first big test of his professional career. It came in his tenth bout when a clash of heads opened a deep gash over his left brow. His trainer, Fitzy, was not only a master tactician but a very capable cut man and was able to stem the flow of blood with a shot of adrenaline and a healthy smear of Vaseline. It kept the ring doctor at bay while Danny jabbed and danced his way to the final bell. In boxing anything could happen, and Dermot Robinson of the Shamrock Gazette was particularly impressed with the fledgling Breen.

*Breen shows again what a classy boxer he is. Well ahead at the time of the cut, the Shamrock Express showed a fine array of punches, mixing combinations to head and body and controlling the tempo with an educated left jab.*

*Breen employed superb lateral movement, gracefully gliding left and right, landing stinging jabs and working in feints that kept Collins frustrated and at bay. At 22 years of age, Breen has it all ahead of him.*

It was his tenth bout, and it was a decade ago. Danny stepped out of the shower and eyed himself in the mirror. Physically, he looked as good as ever. His abs and torso were sculpted as if from granite. His shoulders were evenly rounded and his forearms lean and wiry. Standing at six feet, he was perfectly built for the middleweight division.

He'd lived the fighter's life and was now a fighter dealing with defeat. He knew a perfect record wasn't the mark of a great fighter. Winning great fights was. Thinking that, he momentarily felt unsure of the fighter looking back at him. His sister, Dee, would have plenty to say on the topic. He couldn't avoid her forever.

#

Dee was at their father's grave, and it never ceased to surprise her how quickly weeds grew. Removing them, she checked her watch and made her way into the Church of the Resurrection. She quickly blessed herself and slipped into the nearest seat. The acoustics carried the sermon to every corner and crevice, rising high above the altar where it mingled with the artwork of heaven.

'Praise be to the God and Father of our Lord Jesus Christ, the father of compassion and the God of all comfort…'

Father O'Dowd kept the sermon short. While a capable orator on his day, he preferred a more laconic style of speaking, mindful that upping the verbosity would lower congregation numbers. As it was, Dee was one of fifteen people to accept communion. When the service concluded, she approached the candles. Lighting one, she remembered her father and mother during happier times… during visits to the seaside and summer walks in the Applecross glen. She remembered Danny winning his first pro fight.

She recalled the panic Ma felt when he took his first power shot, a hard left hook that thundered off his jawbone and shook him to his boots. It was an early scare and just what he needed to find his edge, stopping his opponent at the end of the second round. Danny ran to his corner, hands aloft, where Fitzy, his trainer of twenty years, embraced him.

Ma still hadn't looked up from the first hook. The sound pierced her ears like a gunshot and struck terror in her heart.

The candles flickered as the door to the vestry opened. Father O'Dowd ran his thick hand over the pulpit as he looked to the ceiling. He was an imposing figure, but he had a gentle way about him. He saw Dee ahead of him.

'Was my service that bad?'

'Father?'

'Don't be coy, Dierdre. I even bored myself this morning.'

Dee redid her hairband and straightened her posture. She was thirty-one years old. She'd known him all her life, yet a tinge of shyness persisted. Dee feared no one, but she'd forget her age around Father O'Dowd. He peered again at the ceiling. His balding back crown was prominent despite the dim lighting. The lines on his forehead bunched together in deep grooves, and only a sprinkling of ginger remained on his beard.

'It's a sight, isn't it? They say it took the painters four months to finish. It will need redoing at some point. I couldn't imagine painting over it. I'd sooner make peace with those yellowy patches there.'

Dee looked up. 'I never noticed.'

'I'm surprised. You studied it long enough this morning. I can see it all from up here, my child. Your lips don't move as your mind broods.'

'I have been brooding, Father.'

About Danny's first loss? You said it was coming.'

'Aye, but to Simmons?'

Dee checked the anger in her voice as Father O'Dowd looked down from the ceiling and to the rosary beads in his hand. 'For I am about to fall, and my pain is ever with me. I confess my guilt. I am troubled by my sin. Psalms 38. Would you like to take confession?'

'Yes, Father.'

# Chapter 3

Eileen Breen's birthday dress lay across the foot of her bed. Her makeup sat ready for use on a dressing table bordered with pictures of family and friends. She'd been a beautiful girl in her day, tall and shapely with thick chestnut hair and plump, blushing cheeks. She had been a fine dancer. Rarely a month passed without her name making the papers, and throughout, she remained delightfully self-effacing of her gifts.

After finishing school in 1961, she found work as a dinner lady. Opportunities were limited then, and for young ladies, serving lunches was an efficient way of scanning the town's bachelors. Eileen had no shortage of offers and rarely turned down an invitation to a dance. That was until she rolled her ankle doing the jive. Beatlemania, her boss lamented, had a lot to answer for.

Eileen and her roommate, Christine, rarely had visitors and were surprised to hear the buzzer go at 8pm the following Saturday. Chrstine made for the front door as Eileen rubbed the crease of her skirt and pulled a sock over her swollen foot. Straining, she could hear a man's voice. After a moment, Christine returned with a gift bag and a bouquet of daffodils.

As her roommate searched for something imitating a vase, Eileen looked inside the bag. Rowntree's Dairy Box were her favourites, and she couldn't help but indulge. She quickly snaffled a hazelnut log before turning her attention to the card.

*Dear Eileen,*

*I learned of your injury only yesterday afternoon. As you may have noticed, I only eat in the hall on Mondays and Fridays, and I did not see you on either day. I hope your ankle is mending well and that you are back on your feet soon.*

*Dancing can be hazardous, not that I have much experience in that domain, though I do enjoy music. You will probably know that the Swingin Chords are coming to Shamrock Hills two weeks tomorrow. They are playing in the Blue Note Club which I believe you are familiar with.*

*I would be delighted if, health permitting, you would accompany me.*

*Sincerely yours,*

*Arthur M Breen*

On the night, the band did not disappoint. Eileen's ankle held up, though she was careful not to push it, limiting herself to slow dances with Arthur Breen who, if he was nervous, hid it well. A local photographer had set up in the adjoining hall. It was fitting that Arthur Breen paid only for a single print of himself and Eileen.

He later had it fitted in a walnut frame, and it sat above their mantlepiece for thirty years. It now resided in Room 14, Serenity House, taking pride of place on Eileen's dresser. Beside it were pictures of their four children, Jimmy, Danny, Dee and Connor. She wore olive green that night. It was still her colour.

#

Danny Breen was running late as he made the thirty-minute walk to Serenity House. He crossed at Ashbourne Hollow and remembered to buy his mother a birthday card and a box of toffees. Riley's Paper and Post stocked a decent selection. Leaving without Riley having seen him, Danny was glad of the local anonymity that a close shave and a smart denim jacket afforded him. Since his loss to Peter Simmons, he wasn't in the mood for talking.

He didn't look forward to this day. The week on which it fell reminded him of things he'd rather forget. His childhood sweetheart, Ela, had left years ago. Dublin was calling, and Danny assumed she'd be back… for visits if nothing else. Things were left to drift, and somewhere along the way, it became the past… but not this week. Ela's birthday fell on the following day.

That wasn't his mother's fault, and he doubted if she'd even know it was her birthday. Still, he made the effort for his sister, Dee. Family was everything to her. Reaching Serenity House, he set down the toffees with the rest of the gifts. Dee was tying a knot in the last of the balloons. Jimmy, their big brother, sat cross-legged on the armchair, leafing through a week-old newspaper. Danny reached for the pen on the coffee table.

'Keeping busy, Jimmy?'

'Yeah, you know me, working hard. You?'

'I started running this morning. I'll be back in the gym tomorrow'.

'I reckon Peter Simmons hasn't left the pub yet', replied Jimmy. 'But I suppose he earned it'.

Danny nodded half-heartedly and tongued the envelope closed as Jimmy raised his palms to Dee's murderous glance. She didn't like that side of Jimmy. Nobody in the family did, and only Jimmy knew whether he purposefully straddled the line between drollness and condescension. Danny walked to the window as Dee rearranged the cards. Jimmy returned to his paper, oblivious to the tension that had gathered in Danny's shoulders.

They hadn't noticed their little brother, Connor come in, the rustling of his sweet wrappers taking the place of words. His eyes peered vacantly at the pen on the coffee table.

'Where's mum?' asked Dee.

'The nurse said we can try again tomorrow. She's having one of those days'.

## Chapter 4

The wind whipped in hard as Fitzy undid the padlock of the Celtic Fist Boxing club. His face was red from the merciless shellacking of rain and hail. He lived only minutes away, but running was out of the question, and a car was beyond his means. Coaching didn't pay much, or if it did, the cost of running the club kept him living week to week. The gym was in its twenty fifth year. From the carpark it looked like a glorified tool shed. There were no windows, and the tin roofing was browned and crumbling.

All Fitzy knew was boxing. He understood what it took to be a fighter. As a young man, he had over a hundred fights in the amateur ranks, competing in Ireland, Britain, America and Germany. His come forward, uncompromising style won him more fights than he lost, and he was never dropped or stopped.

He fought through cracked ribs and perforated ear drums. He once won a fight with a broken jaw. He had slow feet and a short reach so often took two shots to land one. Inside fighting was his style; it was how he earned his boxing moniker, the 'Irish Pitbull'. He'd more than deserved his mural in Shamrock Hills. It was painted on the side of the Cloverhill flats where he lived next to Danny.

Turning pro as a nine-stone featherweight in 1964, he tore through his first twelve opponents. He was then set to take on Archie Buchannon for the British title. Ten thousand roaring Glaswegians had no effect on Fitzy who went at Buchanan from the opening bell, winning the jab exchanges and holding the centre of the ring.

In the second, he dragged Buchanan into deeper waters, tying up one arm on the referee's blind side and firing off three, chopping right hands. The third dislodged Buchanan's mouthpiece. Two rounds in the books. And then a third and a fourth. 'Keep breaking him down. It's your fight!' screamed Fitzy's trainer as he ran a cooling iron over a welt below his right eye. 'He's drowning, Fitz!'

The bell went for the fifth and Buchanan fired off a five-punch salvo. He tied Fitzy up and wrestled him back to centre ring. It was an act of defiance that sent his Tartan army into raptures. The two fighters circled each other with fearsome intensity. In the sixth, Buchannon let fly with a lightening flurry of punches to head and body, the last one landing flush on the jaw and momentarily stunning Fitzy. The Glasgow faithful rose to their feet. A cacophony of noise shook the arena as Buchanan pumped his fist in acknowledgement. They snarled at each other at the bell. Six rounds were scored, and they had six more to go.

#

Fitzy recalled the night like it was yesterday. Every look. Every feint… and every gasp for air as the ring lights burned above him. He wiped dry his glasses and held them to the office light, inspecting them through his one good eye. He could live without his right, and he never thought about the British title belt, yet decades on from that night in Glasgow, the fire still burned. But it was no time to dwell. His fighters had returned from their roadwork. One was Danny Breen. The other was a young welterweight, Paddy Hughes. The Celtic Fist coach approached them.

'All done? Four circuits and no slacking?'

'All done, coach', they replied.

"Good. Get ready for sparring.'

Fitzy kept a watchful eye on Danny. He had a couple of fighting years left. Fitzy had about the same time as a trainer. He was no longer a fledging featherweight. His once carved abdominals were lost under a boulder of soft fat. His career would end with Danny's. It could be four fights down the line. It could be half a dozen. It could be none. It depended on Danny.

Paddy Hughes was a pressure fighter. His bulging back and torso were built for power punches. Standing at five foot eight, he was a hard man to budge, his hefty thighs supporting his low, squatting stance. He was a headhunting fighter with a solid chin. He lived in the Celtic First gym having previously trained out of Ballywell, the provincial rival of Shamrock Hills. He was just the kind of fighter Fitzy needed. Boxing was a young man's game, and the Celtic Fist gym needed young blood.

Danny Breen was in the ring and ready to spar. He bounced on his toes and shook out his arms as Paddy slid between the second and third ropes. Fitzy leaned on the turn buckle and reset his stopwatch. 'Alright…. six rounds, fellas, so pace yourselves. Paddy, work your feet and cut the ring off. Don't follow Danny about. Step across to cut the distance and keep it midrange. Place your punches. Touch, touch bang! No loading up.'

'Christ! Are we sparring or not?' snapped Paddy.

'Mind your tongue, or I'll get in there and drop you like a bad habit! Time!' shouted Fitzy.

Danny Breen wiped the grin off his face and got down to work. He used every inch of the canvas. His shifts in weight flowed like water. It was balance and grace that could not be bought. Danny boxed from the legs up and always had. After three rounds, Fitzy had seen enough and called an end to the spar. Paddy Hughes stormed off to the changing room having failed to land a single clean shot. The first rule of boxing was patience, and Paddy was stretching Fitzy's .

## Chapter 5

Leonard and Vincent Grant were the last of their kind. Ireland was changing, and they were smart enough to see it coming. The evolution came naturally to Leonard who gladly traded his knuckle dusters for Ted Baker suits. Doors that were once barred shut were now held open for him, to council meetings, black tie dinners and five-star hotels.

Vincent was different. To look at, he was the spit of his older brother, also tall and well built, with a thick head of brown hair neatly combed back. He too wore fancy suits and owned a big house in Cedar Heights… but deep in his soul there remained a wildness.

It might have been the whiskey that made Vincent goad Robbie Flyn, a man 40lbs heavier and handy with his fists. Vincent reeled from the first punch. He tasted the blood filling his mouth and tongued the sting of his lip. In a violent lust, he charged at Robbie Flynn and left him draped over the bar like a forgotten coat, blowing claret bubbles of his own blood.

For that, Vincent got a five-year sentence in the summer of 1980, and the resulting bad press killed his brother Leonard's run for office. Some said it was no less than the Grants deserved. They may have been regular churchgoers and were known to help families through hard times, but people remembered where they came from. They were traditional fighting men. An attack on one was treated as an attack on all. The family code was simple.

*Never start what you can't finish, and not an inch will you give*

The words echoed through every fibre of Vincent's being as the cruel heels of imprisoned men rained down on him. Vincent sunk his teeth into the calf of the nearest denimed leg. He clamped down hard as he was dragged across the slick tiles of the gymnasium floor. He felt his ribs begin to cave when the guards burst in, sweeping their batons in tidy arcs and breaking up the gang of four.

Vincent spent a week in the infirmary. It was the easiest time he served such was the strength of the painkillers they fed him. Once he was able to walk unassisted, a decision was made to move him to block B.

'It will not happen again. Not on my watch. I'll tell you what I tell everyone, Vincent. Be fair to me and I'll be fair to you. My name is Arthur Breen. Best you call me 'boss.'

Vincent grunted his acceptance and slowly eased himself into the bunk. Despite the returning pain of three cracked ribs, he breathed hard through the anger of knowing his attackers were safe from him. As sure as shit was brown, he would, given half a chance, hit them back twice as hard.

He never did get revenge on the 'Gymnasium Four', but he'd learned to live with it, realizing that his freedom was a price not worth paying. On a beautiful spring morning in 1985, with the air cleansed by overnight rain and rich with the songs of swallows, he embraced his brother, Leonard, at the prison gates. Vincent's face burrowed into the expensive fabric, his brother's scent drawing tears of refreshment and hope. He looked back one last time and nodded his thanks to Block officer Breen.

There was much to discuss that day as Leonard's BMW powered along the back roads, slicing through blue pools of rain water. The concrete was slick and shimmering as the sun continued its climb. Leonard was planning another run for office. Having just been released, the press would have a field day if his little brother wasn't seen to be paying a social penance. They pulled up outside the Church of the Resurrection. Vincent ambled towards the church door. He didn't recall it being so big, and as he dipped his hand in the baptismal font, he felt more boy than man. Confession was brief. Father O'Dowd suggested that his counsel be given during a walk of the church grounds.

'Forget the former things; do not dwell on the past... now it springs up... I am making a way in the wilderness and streams in the wasteland. Isiah Chapter 43. Consider it, Vincent. Consider where the wellspring of renewal is found.'

#

Outside the shutter door of the Celtic Fist Boxing club, the sharp pops of padded gloves were heard. Early rounds were for finding rhythm, measuring range and finessing form. The gym prospect, Gary 'Thunder' McGinty, had come on well in recent weeks. He made full use of his five-inch reach advantage, peppering Paddy Hughes to head and body.

'Work him out, Paddy! Cut the distance!' counselled Fitzy, leaning over the ring post and stroking his week-old stubble. The stopwatch rang to end the third round. Danny Breen worked McGinty's corner. He reached for his gum shield before shooting water in his waiting mouth.

Across the ring, 'One Shot' Hughes blew hard through his nose. He refused Fitzy's offer of water. He kept his eyes on the opposite corner and strained to hear what Danny was muttering in McGinty's ear. When the bell went, he raced to centre ring where McGinty caught him in his tracks by a beautifully-timed uppercut. He got up immediately, more embarrassed than hurt.

He again charged at the prospect and drove in three spiteful uppercuts, splitting McGinty's guard and sending a spray of blood across the ring. Danny Breen quickly entered the ring and pulled Paddy away while Fitzy took McGinty's weight, sparing him the indignity of collapsing to the canvas.

Paddy shrugged off Danny. He then tore at the Velcro of his gloves. He breathed deep and bull-like as Danny shoved him in the direction of the changing room. Fitzy rinsed off McGinty and examined his nose. No break.

Just cracked cartilage. Cheekbones fine. Orbital bones good. He was smiling. He'd fight another day.

'You did well, son. You got your feet under you now?'

'Aye coach. He rung my bell but I'm fine.'

'Good lad. Shower and get yourself home. If you throw up this evening, head to the hospital just to be safe.'

Fitzy stayed in the ring and took a moment to decompress. He surveyed his gym, silent but for the hum of ventilation fans. Heavy bags hung still and solemn, uniformly lined along the mirrored wall. Skipping ropes lay in an impossible tangle. The fight posters of Tyson, Holyfield and Hearns were warped and bubbled from the heat of hard sessions. The ring light tripped out, leaving a dim glow coming from the office. He cast a long shadow across the canvas as the ring of the telephone sliced through the gym, shaking him from a rare moment of solitude.

'Celtic Fist Boxing club.'

'Fitzy… it's Vincent Grant. Something's in the works. How are you fixed for the next three days?'

'Depends. What's in the works?'

'Hard to say, but it could be good for the club. And it could be very good for Danny.'

# Chapter 6

If England had a home from home for the Irish, it was Liverpool. Once the greatest port city in the British Empire, it provided homes and jobs for thousands of Irishmen and women fleeing famine. As Liverpool itself faced harder times during the war years, there developed a shared identity between native and immigrant. Over time, family names that were once indicators of the blow-ins, the Murphys, the Kellys and Nolans, became synonymous with the social and cultural fabric of the city.

There were plenty of Breens in Liverpool, and Danny Breen of Shamrock Hills was visiting for the first time in a decade. As the ferry pulled out of the docks, the smoke and steam mixed with the mist and the damp. Danny and Fitzy buried their noses in their fleeces. They leaned into the railing as the Belfast lights grew dimmer.

'You know what I know, kid. The Grants were asked if you wanted sparring,' said Fitzy. The old trainer cupped his hands and exhaled hard, jiggling his legs to fight off the cold. 'Maybe we've plateaued for too long. Some good sparring will tell us what we need to know, and then we'll see what's next.'

Danny looked across the water. His breath quietly hissed through chattered teeth. He'd heard it from Fitzy already, that had he been fresher he'd have seen the shot coming. Had he followed orders, he would have tied Peter Simmons up till his head cleared. Then he would have got back to boxing smart and proven that he was a class above and ready for the big fights.

But Danny never recovered, and the manner of the defeat raised questions. Was Peter Simmons just too good on the night or was Danny in decline? It was supposed to be a 'stay busy' fight, but for Simmons, it was an opportunity to take the scalp of an unbeaten fighter. Boxing could be the cruellest of sports. One loss could derail the best-laid plans. Years of training camps, of building a fanbase and working the media, and all to watch it dissipate under the lights when it counted most.

Rebuilding a fighter was a subtle art. Perception was everything in the fight game, and a comeback fighter needed fresh momentum. Most important of all, he needed to put on a performance that reestablished his value as a major commodity in the boxing economy. The next fight was crucial. It was about getting the right name at the right time… the right calculation of risk versus reward.

Danny's backer, Vincent Grant, had warned him that he couldn't afford another slipup. Vincent was a good manager. He paid Danny's stipend and arranged his fights,

More importantly, Vincent was a generous patron of the Celtic Fist gym. Had he not been, the gym would have closed years ago. After his prison release, he bought a 30% share and a stake in Danny's career. He still believed Danny would be champion of the world.

#

The ferry was quiet. Danny and Fitzy sat in the lobby and played cards. They had a flask of black tea to see them through the night. Fitzy was beginning to nod off as Danny yelped, 'Gin!' The trainer cursed under his breath. He gathered the cards and slid the deck to Danny. He then lit a cigarette.

'It's *no smoking* in here,' said Danny, pointing at the sign.

'Sod it. Bloody freezing out there.'

'Then quit.'

'Never'.

'How old were you when you started?'

Fitzy playfully blew a plume of smoke in Danny's direction. 'Did I not tell you about my stint as an altar boy? That was my punishment for getting a taste for these.'

'You're winding me up, Fitz.'

'Dead serious. I was once an altar boy. Ask your ma if you don't believe me…'

When Fitzy thought of Eillen, he still saw her as she was. It didn't feel that long ago, but the sight of the hand holding his cigarette, the veins bulbous blue against papered skin, reminded him that life went quick. He attempted to lighten the mood.

'You know who was an altar boy with me? Father O'Dowd.'

'Our Father O'Dowd?' asked Danny.

'Yes, Father O'Dowd of the Church of the Resurrection. He also got into a spot of bother.'

'What did he do?'

'They were his cigarettes.'

Fitzy's snorting laugh echoed through the empty lounge. The hour hand passed four in the morning. He regaled Danny on what life was like at the real Dunhaven School for Boys, back when straps and canes were a teacher's best friend. The boys learned to endure the strikes such was their frequency, but the loss of liberty to the church, every Sunday morning, was the cruellest punishment of all.

'I remember that first Sunday. By God, O'Dowd was angry with me... roaring his head off all the way home. Then he clobbered me to the ground, and I got up and went at him like a man possessed. Always be mindful of the little man, I told him. We were good mates after that.'

They were three hours out from Liverpool and in an unspoken pact, lowered their heads. They didn't raise them again till the captain's voice boomed over the intercom. Danny and Fitzy both yawned as they crossed the gangway, the great city of Liverpool welcoming their return with a grey sky and light drizzle.

## Chapter 7

Amateur clubs were the lifeblood of boxing. Hidden away in forgotten corners, the whipping snaps of jump ropes and the booming cracks of punch bags endured.

They offered sanctuary and belonging. Fellow boxers became brothers and the coaches their substitute fathers. Boxing was life, and the fighters' bread and butter were the small hall shows. They travelled the length and breadth of the country for a purse that covered the next month's rent. They were the true journeymen boxers. No representation, sponsors or stipend. Just a readiness to bite down on the gumshield and come out fighting at the bell.

On a given night, maybe the right people would take notice. It could lead to better training, bigger shows and fatter purses. That was the allure, but for most it would remain a cruel mirage. It was called prize-fighting, a reminder that boxing was a business first and a sport second. From the days of the bare-knuckle code to colour broadcasts and satellite tv, it was always about the money... and promoters preferred hungry fighters.

Liverpool had ample hunger, yet it hadn't produced a world champion in twenty years. To the local scribes, it came down to the London promoters running professional boxing like a cartel. They controlled the venues and the dates, had contacts in every major club, scouts in every county and the backing of the TV networks.

Someone needed to tear up the script. What the city needed was one of their own, a local promoter with deep pockets and an eye for talent. It needed a salesman with the necessary bombast to compete with the London promoters and bring major boxing back to Liverpool. That man was Francis 'Big Daddy' Nelson.

He had his sights fixed on Mersey Gloves ABC. It was run by Tommy Brown. Tommy was a prolific coach having produced countless regional champions. Big Daddy Nelson was impressed, and he wondered just how far Tommy could take his two middleweight prospects, Kevin 'The Canon' Neary and Davey 'The Hitman' Hibbert.

Neary was thick-boned and rugged. He led with a stiff jab and packed a left hook to the body that drew groans from opponents. Hibbert was lithe and deceptively rangy. He won fights on activity but tended to get greedy. Those in the know thought he had a suspect chin. They weren't world beaters and they didn't need to be. Ultimately, styles made fights, and that's what most concerned 'Big Daddy' Nelson. He didn't have the big draw names to impress a television network, but with some clever matchmaking, he was convinced he could sell a good product. He trusted his instincts. There was an appetite for something fresh... something dynamic.

First, Nelson needed to measure his prospects against a seasoned professional. Tommy Brown suggested reaching out to Barney Fitzpatrick. 'He has a middleweight. Danny Breen. Excellent amateur. Clever boxer-puncher. I have the details written down somewhere. Fitzy will be on board.'

When the offer came, Fitzy did not hesitate. He needed to examine his fighter closely. Top fighters measured range to the millimetre, and every mechanic of boxing, drilled over thousands of hours, had to synch, blend and snap like the flash of a camera. The slightest miscalibration could be the difference in winning or losing.

When Peter Simmons handed Danny his first professional loss, the Shamrock Hills man cut a bemused figure. Dermot Robinson of the Shamrock Gazette commented that Breen, for whatever reason, appeared too accepting of the defeat. Defeats were meant to hurt, no more so than the first. That's what concerned Fitzy most. Where was the pain of defeat? Where was his fighting pride?

#

He pondered this as he wrapped the gauze around his fighter's knuckles in Mersey Gloves ABC. Danny breathed evenly through his nose. His lips protruded from the addition of his gum shield. Fitzy spoke softly through his tried and tested instructions. 'Just another spar, Danny. The only difference is it's their gym, so they'll want to impress you. How do your hands feel?'

'Yeah, fine.'

In the ring, Danny and Kevin Neary kept it mostly mid-range. Danny elected to hold his ground. He needed the conditioning, and midway through the second round he began to walk Neary down, inviting him to unload heavy shots to head and body. In the third, both fighters mixed it up, trading body shots on the inside and fighting out of the clinches. It was a good pace, staying just on the safe side of a real fight. When the buzzer went, they bumped gloves in appreciation of the good work they'd shared.

Hibbert watched on. The next three rounds were his. Fitzy rinsed Danny's gum shield and massaged his neck. Danny pushed at his protective cup, a difficult task with laced gloves. He drew deep breaths through his nose and closed his eyes. Good sparring required a clear head. No distractions, just 100% focus, and no tension… for tension was the enemy of rhythm.

What rhythm he'd built soon escaped him as Hibbert, fresh to the ring, landed double jabs and combos before smothering Danny's counters. Danny was forgetting to breathe, his fighting instincts were off, and his legs felt stiff and leaden. Hibbert kept the pressure on. Danny tucked up and tried to watch for openings but couldn't set himself to punch. Hibbert dictated the terms, limiting his visitor to one moment of success, a well-timed right cross that brought praise from both trainers.

Fitzy fanned Danny down with a towel. 'Come on. Get your head out of your shoulders, son. You're letting yourself down.' He sprayed water on Danny's chest and rubbed grease across his reddened nose. 'Last round kid. Show some fight.'

Hibbert was feeling the pace and had come off the balls of his feet. Danny feinted a jab to his body and pounced with an arcing left hook followed by a full-bloodied right cross. Hibbert's legs buckled as the shot rippled through him. Both men were gassed as they elected to plant their feet and exchange heavy leather. For the first time, Hibbert ceded ground. Danny stepped across him. The toes of his lead foot dug hard into the canvas. He measured his man with a wide, winging right hand that crashed off Hibbert's temple.

The timer went. Danny slumped in his corner, head down and panting hard. Fitzy unlaced his gloves. The trainer was satisfied. His fighter had shown he still had some fight in him.

## Chapter 8

Refreshments were offered at the reception of Nelson Ring Promotions. Danny had a mineral water, and Fitzy had his first ever latte. They peeped through the glass doors and counted twelve well-dressed professionals tapping diligently on keyboards and glancing at monitors through designer-framed glasses. On the surrounding walls hung paintings of boxing's most iconic fights. There was the 'War' between Hagler and Hearns, and 'The Rumble in the Jungle' between Foreman and Ali. There was also a pair of trunks worn by John Conteh and a robe once worn by Frank Bruno.

'Mr Fitzpatrick? Mr Breen? Mr Nelson is ready now. If you'd like to follow me, please.'

Danny sported a scruffy beard, and his floppy brown hair was swept to the side. He was generally care-free when it came to social graces but was taken aback by the soft burgundy carpet. His wide eyes absorbed the rich décor, of upholstered leather and varnished mahogany. Francis Nelson was a huge man in the flesh, all of six foot five and 230 pounds.

He was fresh-faced with receding blond hair and an easy-going smile. His left wrist was fitted with a Rolex Daytona that caught the light of the chandelier. He offered them the sofa. Beside it sat Leonard Grant. He looked like he'd been there a while and was very much enjoying his gin and tonic. Danny and Fitzy had not been expecting him. Vincent, perhaps. But not Leonard. When all the men were seated, Francis Nelson began his pitch.

'Fellas, I like to be frank when it comes to business. When I reached out, I had more on my mind than a couple of days' sparring. We are new to the boxing game, but we're investing heavily. I was talking with Peter Harrod of GBT Sports before you fellas came in. My apologies for keeping you waiting.'

He reached for his most expensive bottle of Remy Martin and a quartet of tumblers. 'I've been saving this for a while.'

He continued to lay out his grand plan to bring big nights back to the North-West. Leonard Grant sat relaxed while Danny's interest grew. He liked what he was hearing. Fitzy lightly drummed his fingers against the arm of the sofa, patiently waiting for his moment.

'Where's the money coming from to stage these shows? There's the site fee, security, medical, and that's before the cost of the promotion. That won't come cheap, especially without tv money.'

Francis gave Fitzy a quick nod of respect before downing his drink. The old man knew the game. 'GBT will offer me a TV deal. Don't worry about that. First, and this is where Danny comes in, I need fighters on my roster.'

'What's your offer, Francis?' asked Fitzy.

Francis and Leonard exchanged a quick glance. 'We want to sign Danny to an exclusive promotional contract, initially on a three-fight deal. If all goes well, we see him fighting for a world title.' Nelson passed a document to Fitzy.

'The Universal Boxing Federation?'

'Correct. Newly formed and keen to crown their inaugural champions. All my middleweights will be ranked and eligible to fight for the belt.'

'How many?' asked Danny.

'I'm hoping four by the end of the week, and I want you to be one of them. I want to put on a four-man tournament to crown a world champion. That's my vision. And you'll back yourself to make the final, won't you, Danny? You've already shown you're a class above the competition.'

Danny looked at Fitzy and then to Leonard. If Hibbert and Neary were the opposition then he was as good as champion already. Nelson refreshed everyone's drinks. Danny was sold. Later, the receptionist saw them to the elevator. The thought of the UBF belt strapped around his waist added bounce to Danny's step. He had felt in his bones that there was more to the trip than sparring, and Fitzy was quick to remind him that there were more rounds to come. Back in the office, Nelson's mood, was less jovial.

'Seems a bit frosty between you and his trainer.'

'We've had our moments', replied Leonard. 'Vincent knows him better, and he'll do right by Danny.'

'But you're less sure about Fitzy. Why? He's just a trainer'.

'Trainer-manager.'

'Contractually?' asked Nelson.

'Yes', replied Leonard.

Francis returned to his desk and poured himself another shot of cognac. He'd been in business his whole life but was beginning to realize, as all fresh promoters did, that boxing was more complex than it seemed.

## Chapter 9

Bubble and squeak with bacon was Thursday night's dinner. Aiden and Alex were in their bedroom, whispering out their best course of action. First contact was crucial. It was the difference between a stiff telling off and Christmas being cancelled. Their mother, Dee, attacked the potatoes. The cabbage and bacon fizzed and spat as the kitchen filled with a thick steam. She plated up and served it with bread and butter. Her sons were in all kinds trouble, but they were still growing boys.

They closed the door gently and slid into their seats. The scent of bacon filled their nostrils... but their stomachs remained tight with nerves. They exchanged glances, neither wanting to be the first to reach for a fork. Dee had already started, taking methodical bites of a meal devoid of enjoyment. Alex was kicked under the table. He was the oldest by seven minutes, so naturally it fell on him to break the silence.

'Mammy?'

Dee didn't look up from her dinner, and the boys signalled silently to each other, determining whether it best to proceed. Alex tore at the crusts of his soft white bread, buying himself precious seconds.

'We're really sorry, Mammy.'

Dee set down her fork and pushed the plate away. Her appetite was spoiled for the evening. Aiden's eyes began to water while Alex's remained on his bread. 'Drawing a beard on the Virgin Mary... what under God were you two thinking? In my day they'd have broken a cane over your backs! What am I to say to the headmaster tomorrow? Eh boys? How am I to look that man in the eye?'

'Sorry Mammy...' they replied in unison.

'Just eat.'

Without uttering another word, they cleared their plates, left them in the sink and returned meekly upstairs. Dee typically kept smoking outside the house but chose to open the back door and let the fumes drift of their own accord. The phone rang as she lit her second. It was her big brother, Jimmy.

'Dee, I got a letter from the care home. The four of us need to meet up.'

'Right. We'll do it on Monday when Danny's back. I take it you haven't told him about Ela?'

'No, I didn't see the point. It's Shamrock Hills. He'll find out soon enough.'

#

Danny was tired from sparring. Twenty rounds in three days had taken their toll, and he looked forward to stretching out in his cabin bed. Despite the bruised rib, the Shamrock Express was happy. Contracts had been drafted and three good paydays lay ahead. It was the break he'd been waiting for, but despite matching him beer for beer, Fitzy's joy was noticeably less pronounced.

'Something bothering you, coach?'

'Nothing is bothering me, kid, I'm just thinking over the last few days.'

'What's to think about? It's a hell of a deal.'

They touched cans and took a deep drink. The foam from Fitzy's spilled onto his beard. He leaned in close, not wanting to shout over the noise of the returning football fans. 'What would your dad have made of Big Daddy Nelson?'

Danny pursed his mouth like he'd bitten a lemon. 'I don't think he'd have liked him.'

'But would he have let you sign?'

'For a shot at the title? Aye. He'd have been sold from the start.'

It would be another six hours before the ferry docked in Belfast. Fitzy was second to the bathroom. He brushed his teeth and scratched an itch just south of his cotton white briefs. It was a sight Danny could have lived without. Fitzy's front side was just as unpleasant. His belly protruded like a hot air balloon as he knelt by his bedside to pray. 'Wipe that grin off your face, Shamrock. You'll be my age one day.'

Fitzy was out as quick as the light, but Danny grew restless as the alcohol slowly wore off. He tossed and turned, his mind working its way through his twenty-five-and-one pro record, fourteen stoppages, regional and national title belts to his name... but no world title.

He used to dream of headlining Madison Square Garden and making the cover of Ring Magazine. Now, as the sun crept over the Belfast lough, it dawned on him that his prime fighting years were nearly done. His last eleven fights spanned almost nine years. They should have secured his legacy as the best since Luke 'Quick Hands' Gibson, and the fighting pride of Shamrock Hills. That's what his father had prophesised.

*Danny, you're going all the way. You've got the best feet in boxing. A natural mover, built in rhythm, never rushed, fast and fluid. You're dedicated to your craft. You're going all the way.*

'Eleven fights...' Danny thought to himself. Fights were how Danny measured time, and his father, Arthur Breen, had been gone for eleven of them. For ten wins and one loss. His father's voice still lived within Danny... in every morning run, in every round of shadow, and with every punch thrown. It could still be heard despite its ebbing and fading through time, and its distant echo now haunted Danny as Fitzy rose to relieve his bladder.

#

The sun was breaking through the Belfast clouds, and the ground was dusted with overnight frost. Fitzy brought out his checkers board as the train slowly pulled out from the station. Danny spun it around, giving him blacks and the advantage of first move. Half an hour passed, and Danny's losing streak extended to three.

'Balls!'

A nearby child let out a giggle, and it cost him a nip on the arm from his mother.

'When are you teaching me chess?' asked Danny.

'Now that's a game' replied Fitzy. 'A game of strategy. Disguising your attacks, probing, creating openings, adapting and reacting…'

'Sounds like boxing', Danny commented.

Fitzy mused over the board. He could see the win but chose not to set the trap, instead playing a simple block. 'It's about showing it on the night, kid. And that isn't just a matter of mindset and strategy. When the fight gets hard, the warrior spirit comes from in here.' He patted his chest.

'You showed it against Archie Buchanan, didn't you?'

Fitzy shook his head. 'I showed it in every fight I ever had. I wasn't blessed with your talents. All I had to bring was heart, and I never lacked it in the ring.' He removed his glasses and closed his good eye. 'Detached retina. Long before the eye swelled shut, half the world blacked out, but I could see enough of Archie. Seeing the white towel come in... it was the worst feeling of my life, kid. I'd have beaten Buchanan with one eye and he knew it. But he got the win. And that's life. Things get taken from you. We can't control that. All we *can* do is keep fighting. Your move.'

They arrived in Shamrock Hills a little before noon. Danny decided to visit Connor. It had been a while since his last visit, and his little brother didn't get out much. He was welcomed at the front door by his two housecats, Lyano and Panthro. He looked around the side and spotted steam funnelling from the vent by the kitchen window. Connor was lowering a hearty portion of chips into the fryer. He waved Danny in with his free hand.

Connor lived on his own, in the same three-bedroom house they'd all grown up in. Simple dinners, the company of his cats and the stimulation of daytime television sustained him. He learned to stretch his money and was able to hold down part-time hours at the local shop.

Danny cringed as he watched him butter the bread inch-thick. Connor still tucked his bottoms into his socks. Some things never changed, and Danny liked that about him. The house was just how Ma left it. The family coat of arms still hung above the sofa, and a framed picture of the family remained on the window sill. It was still home to Danny. It's where he and his father watched tape after tape of Fitzy's boxing collection.

He recalled his father watching Sonny Liston pummel Floyd Paterson for the heavyweight championship of the world. Danny and Connor were tiptoeing down the stairs. Their dressing gowns trailed behind them, and their hands were gloved inside Dee's winter socks. It was a short bout. A nine-year old Dee cleared away the gowns and the makeshift gloves as Da took the belt to Danny. Connor, his nose bloodied, promised his mother he'd never box again. For Danny, his love of the sport had just begun.

He stood up to leave, jingling the loose change in his pocket and giving the living room a quick scan. Fifteen quid remained in the electric meter, and there was plenty of coal in the bucket. On the coffee table, good progress had been made on a 500-piece jigsaw. He saw himself out, flicking a foot at Lyano as he closed the door behind him.

#

In the Celtic Fist gym, Paddy Hughes was ripping into the heavy bag, denting its sides with full-bloodied shots. Sweat ran off his back and poured from his brow. Fitzy knocked on the main light but the welterweight didn't flinch, continuing his assault on the bag like it had stolen from him.

'Easy lad. You'll break your hands.'

Fitzy walked gingerly over. His hip was still cramped from the cabin bed. He gripped the bag from behind. 'Let's see a bit of finesse on those hooks, Paddy. Pick your spot.' The force of the blows travelled through Fitzy's gut. The boy hit like a mule.

'Are you listening, son?'

Paddy ceased punching and leaned his forearms against the bag.

'Is that it, Fitzy? I don't listen? Is that why I was left here while you headed off to Liverpool with Danny?'

Fitzy released his grip of the heavy bag. He usually didn't look people square in the eye... not since that fight with Buchannon.

'Have you forgotten what you did to your last sparring partner? You don't get rewarded for taking liberties in that ring. That's not how this place works!'

Paddy unwrapped his hands. The skin of his knuckles was reddened and torn. He leaned over the spit bucket and cleared his throat. He dabbed himself down with a towel and flexed his fists. The nerves in his wrists twitched from the trauma of the shots.

'I should have been there too.'

# Chapter 10

The Shamrock Gazette was a bi-weekly newspaper, and Connor Breen always bought the Monday edition. That's how he started his week. A short walk to the shop for a paper and a fresh loaf of bread. Then he'd feed the strays. They were beginning to tire of dry kibble. Perhaps word had spread that their indoor pals got fed from the can.

For his own breakfast, Connor had cornflakes as usual. He scraped the remains of the bowl onto the lawn for the birds. He returned to the warmth of the kitchen and made himself a cup of tea. The cats purred by his feet. They rubbed their well-fed sides against his shins as he scanned the paper. 'Breen making green?'

*Local fighter Danny Breen, the 'Shamrock Express', is poised to sign a three-fight promotional deal with emerging boxing promoter, Francis 'Big Daddy' Nelson. According to boxing insiders, Breen and his team spent last week in Liverpool where Nelson is based.*

*Nelson was not available for comment, although his representatives have confirmed that he is working hard on delivering a series of fights that will bring major opportunities to Ireland's top fighters. The Gazette did manage a response from Leonard Grant- Breen's manager and local businessman- who said that 'a number of opportunities are being explored.'*

*Breen, the former national champion and amateur star, boasts twenty-five wins in the professional ranks with his sole loss coming at the hands of old amateur rival, Peter Simmons. Said Breen on his first defeat, 'It was an off night, but I make no excuses. We had a good camp and I felt strong all week. Credit to Simmons. He was the better man tonight.'*

*Breen has not fought since, and unfortunately, such long spells of inactivity have come to characterize his professional career. Now, at thirty-two years of age, the Shamrock Express needs to hit full speed and secure his financial future. Francis Nelson has certainly been bullish since his introduction to the sport, decrying what he sees as 'paltry purses and second-rate shows' holding back Liverpudlian fighters from fulfilling their potential.*

*There is no doubt that Nelson has the required financial muscle to breathe new life into Liverpool boxing's ecosystem, but how the likes of Danny Breen stand to benefit remains to be seen. Might the Shamrock Hills native cross the water for the big fights that have so far eluded him? According to Leonard Grant, we will find out 'soon enough.'*

#

Vincent Grant's copy of the Gazette lay scattered over the back seat of his Alfa Romeo. Its well-dressed owner cursed at the sky as he paced back and forth. He patted both breast pockets in search of his lighter. Failing to find it, he started up his vehicle and waited for the temperature to build. The yard was quiet. Only crows perched on the phoneline bore witness to the blasphemy. His brother, Leonard, hadn't mentioned going to Liverpool.

Vincent nodded through clenched teeth and put the Alpha into first. He sped out of the yard, sending loose chippings spattering. The engine's growl startled the crows on the phone line. He stopped at the lights and peered left over the Drumferry river. The waters were choppy, and fat drops of rain began splashing off his windshield.

His prison cell didn't have a window, and watching the weather change was one of the things he'd missed most. The thought calmed him as the lights turned green. He turned off the bridge and towards the power station.

#

Dee was on kitchen duty. Tuna and sweetcorn. Egg and onion. She had already vacuumed the floor and beat the dust off the cushions. Connor was working on his jigsaw in the living room. Danny was first to arrive and joined his little brother. 'Whenever you're ready, Dee. Two sugars for Connor. Just milk for me.'

'A boot up the hole for you' she replied as she came through with a tray packed tall with sandwiches. Her tea never disappointed. It was well-brewed and piping hot. She was in her work apron, freshly washed but still smelling faintly of chip fat. The doorbell rang at two minutes to twelve. Jimmy Breen was never late.

'I read your piece in the Gazette, Danny. Sounds like a done deal.' Danny took a moment to swallow his bite. 'Aye. It all moved very quickly.' Jimmy raised his brow and nodded. 'Well, let's hope the money is as good as the paper says. Mum's care costs have shot up.'

'By how much?' asked Dee, the edge of her bum perched on the arm of the sofa. 'I'm already living hand to mouth. Ivan's wages are gone before I touch them.'

'It depends, and that's why we are here. They want her moved to Dementia care.'

Dee's hand clasped her mouth, muffling the pain that rose in her chest. She got to her feet as her eyes darted from one brother to the other. 'Would someone bloody take this cup from me?' Danny reached first, noticing the quiver in her hand.

'We're looking at a 40% increase,' continued Jimmy. 'What can you swing, Danny?'

'I've no money right now, but the next three fights will pay well.'

'I don't think that will cut much ice with Serenity House. I can't tell them to hold off on the bills while my little brother dreams of world titles.'

Danny set his tea on the mantlepiece and swallowed the insult for his sister's sake. 'I need to feed the cats', said

Connor. His slow steps crossed the living room floor and into the kitchen. Danny shook his head at his elder brother. 'My first fight will be early February. It will soon come round.'

Connor returned from the kitchen. 'I'll take care of her here.' Dee squeezed his arm. 'And she'd love that, Connor, but she needs the nurses looking after her day and night.'

'There is something you can do for her', added Jimmy. 'You can refinance the house. I can do all the paperwork. I'd just need your signature. That would free up some money in the short-term and buy us a few months… at least till the 'Shamrock Express' starts making bank.'

Before taking time to blink, Danny had his brother pinned to the wall. Dee shrieked at him to let his big brother go. 'No Dee, I won't let him go. I've taken enough digs. What is your problem, Jimmy? I'm a boxer. It's all I know.'

'It's not the boxing I have the problem with.'

'God forgive you, Jimmy! Danny, he doesn't mean it', cried Dee.

'Don't I? I don't care about the boxing, Danny. I'm passed caring.'

#

In the power station carpark, the Grant brothers made a dash for the Land Rover as the rain continued to lash hard. Sleet gathered at the base of the windshield. Leonard turned on the heating and rubbed his hands while Vincent watched the wiper blades swipe left and right. 'Will you ever learn to think before you act? Those are big players in there. You embarrass me when you pull shit like that.'

Vincent rolled his eyes. 'Now you know how I felt reading the Gazette.'

Leonard's look of vexation gave way to scorn. 'So, this is about Liverpool? Francis Nelson called and said he wanted to talk business, so I packed an overnight bag.' Vincent drew hard from his cigarette, and his head shook with what remained of his rage. 'I'm the kid's manager, Leonard, not you. I'm the one who got him a national title shot, but according to the Gazette, you're *exploring opportunities* for him?'

'God save us, Vincent. It's a bit of hype for the kid, and the Gazette owed me a favour. Danny got some press and a hell of a fight deal, if he wants it. That's good. But no, you fly off the handle and gatecrash a meeting. Have you forgotten I'm your brother?'

'You're the one who needs reminding, Leonard... keeping me in the dark like that...'

'And maybe that's for the best, coz I'll tell you this for free, if you'd blown a gasket with Nelson, there wouldn't be any offer for the Gazette to write about. Have a bit of faith, for God's sake. Nothing goes ahead without your signature. You know that.'

Vincent's face started to soften. He was Leonard's match in looks and size, but he couldn't stand up to a berating from his big brother, especially when he was right.

'It's not just business when it comes to Danny', he said. Leonard cradled the back of his neck. 'I know, brother. You're just like Da, God rest his soul, getting all worked up over nothing.' Vincent let out a deep sigh, and Leonard playfully batted him across the head. 'Dinner at my place tonight. Bring Leanne and the kids. We'll comb over the fight deal. It's your baby, Vincent. Alright?'

'Aye, alright.'

#

In the town hall square, finishing touches were being made to the tree. The snow had begun to fall hard and would settle thick on the pavements, gardens and rooftops of Shamrock Hills. Snowflakes landed on young, buttoned noses as the town lit up with the magic of Christmas. For that, it was worth braving the elements even if it meant cars losing grip on the narrow sloping streets.

Dee would miss it for the first time in years having taken an extra shift at the Harbour chip shop. Every pound mattered, now more than ever.

## Chapter 11

The thermostat was in the office, and only Fitzy had a key. Only he knew the true costs of running the gym, and keeping an equitable temperature for his fighters was low on his list of concerns. A few minutes jumping rope and a vigorous stretch was all that was needed to get the blood warm.

In the back room, Paddy Hughes slept with his socks on and his body wrapped under two heavy blankets. He liked the mornings. Hot water, less stink and no gym noise. Fitzy had seen to his basic needs, fitting his room with a fridge and a 13-inch television. It was better than the streets, and it was good enough for Paddy.

He was not a son of Shamrock Hills but of Ballywell, and home had been the St Mark's Orphanage for Boys. He hadn't seen his mother since the age of eight. She was 'afflicted'. That was the term they used at St Mark's, and the eight-year-old Paddy hoped she'd overcome it… whatever it was.

As he slipped into his tracksuit and laced up his boots, he heard the shutter door go up. He looked at his hands. His knuckles were white and calloused, and thick veins ran up the sides of his sinewed forearms. He could hear the rhythmic slap of the speed rope.

'Morning Paddy' shouted Danny Breen. 'Roadwork in fifteen. You feel up for the Applecross Glen? It's no colder there than in here.'

'Aye', Paddy replied.

#

The fighters jogged across the St Columb's bridge. Scratchcard Jonny was outside O'Reilly's, rolling a cigarette and eyeing passersby. He'd be there till lunch, hoping for chat and a win on the cards. The dole queues were long again. Everyone took a hit in January, the removal of lights marking a sobering return to reality on the Hills.

The town's Christmas tree had come down, and the last few families were removing theirs. Dee always kept hers up till January seventh. It was a Breen family tradition just like Christmas lunch in the family home. Dee always cooked too much, but not even the bones went to waste, much to the satisfaction of Connor's cats. Jimmy hadn't attended, marking a break from tradition that bothered her greatly.

The fighters ran by the fabled Cobbler's End. It was a sad sight. In recent years, another attempt had been made to regenerate it. It should have been a beehive of bourgeoise activity by now, but the funding dried up in 1992, and the project was abandoned. In a way, the whole saga epitomised Shamrock Hills. It was a good town but a nearly town.

As a result, there were no bistro bar dwellers or monied mocha drinkers on the land of the old factory quarter. Just the same old winos and nuisance teens tearing up the gravel in their second-hand dirt bikes. Cobbler's End remained 'Beggars' bend'. And life went on as Danny and Paddy entered Cedar Park.

The lawns were typically sparse. The sub-zero temperature kept most walkers at home, but it was a pleasant cold for running as Danny and Paddy broke into sprint. Upon reaching the foot of the Luke Gibson statue, they leaned on their knees and fought for air. The steam from their breaths billowed around them. 'I can't help it, Paddy. I see 'Quick Hands' and I have to hit full speed.'

They extended their quads, and their groans mixed with the clicks and clacks of nearby starlings. The trees were as dry as old bones, and the grass was greyed and brittle with frost. Even the statue showed signs of mid-winter with Gibson's face slightly more silvery than usual. Danny had been there for the big unveiling. On that wet Friday morning in 1979, he caught a glimpse of the real 'Quick Hands' Gibson. It was the last time he set foot in Shamrock Hills. He had a thirty-acre ranch in sunny Arizona that he called home.

Paddy eyed the statue. 'Was Gibson really that good?' Danny stepped back and took in all ten feet of it. 'He was. I was there when he beat Alfonso Rodrigues for the title. Can you imagine that? Rodrigues coming all the way here for a title defence?' Danny shook his head in wonderment, no longer retelling a story but reliving his happiest childhood memory.

'I was there with Da and Fitzy. Half the town was there… all packed into the Pavilion. That's where all the big events happened years ago. The atmosphere that night, Paddy… when Gibson stopped him in the tenth, I thought the roof would blow right off the place.'

Paddy looked away from the statue and to his stablemate. Danny's eyes were transfixed with nostalgia. Excitement coursed through his veins. His face looked suddenly fresh and boyish with glee. As he watched him, Paddy felt a longing like a shot to the solar plexus.

'They thought I was the next one', Danny continued. 'Well, if I get the UBF title around my waist and a mural downtown, I'll be happy with that. Anyway, we have five more kilometres and then we'll stop for brunch. Fitzy's treat. You hungry?'

'If Fitzy's paying then aye, I'm starving.'

#

Dana's kitchen did the simple things well. Favourites included the Shamrock fry with locally sourced sausage and the steak and ale pudding with chive onion mash. They were fine options but too calorie-rich for professional boxers.

'We'll start with the champion's porridge and black coffee. You see this fella, Dana? Remember the face and remember the name. Paddy Hughes. Future champion of the world.'

The years had been kind to Dana. Her thick auburn hair and creamy skin complimented her winning smile and affectionate charm. Paddy looked around restlessly as Danny scratched at his stubble and waited for his coffee to cool.

'Have you got a fight date, Danny?' she asked.

'February the twenty-fourth. I'm fighting Ricky Murray, the Clydebank Destroyer.'

'And what about you, Paddy?'

The Ballywell brawler shook his head. Dana, feeling like she'd said the wrong thing, wished them both luck and returned to the kitchen. Paddy nodded. His frowning eyes flitted left and right. His head sunk into his huge shoulders. Danny knew that look.

'Fitzy knows what he's doing, Paddy. It's tricky in the pros, but you'll have a date soon. Just keep grafting.'

'I've done nothing but graft, I need a fight, Danny. I've waited long enough'.

Danny nodded. 'And Fitzy will make you wait longer if you don't watch the backchat. I guarantee you, Paddy, if you show some respect in the gym, a fight date will soon follow'.

They made short work of the porridge and ordered more coffee. Danny weighed up whether to order the grilled chicken pitta or the steak and pepper panini. He eventually opted for both and had Dana split them with Paddy. It was the best meal Paddy had eaten in a long time.

The last two years had been lean ones for the boy from Ballywell. That was the price one paid for the gambling affliction. He worked off his debt in a welder's yard, and by the time he was back in the black, Ballywell was dead for him. He'd attracted the wrong kind of attention and the best his old coach, Sammy Stewart, could do was find him a club somewhere else.

Sending Paddy to Fitzy had not been his first thought, but it just so happened that the Celtic Fist owner was looking to bolster his stable. After doing his homework, Fitzy decided to take a punt on Paddy. Other than his obvious fighting potential, Fitzy understood that the soul of boxing was about saving young men like Paddy from slipping through the cracks. That said, a trainer could only do so much.

Fitzy had tried being Paddy's coach, psychologist and substitute father. Paddy had the talent, the athleticism, the spite and the rage, yet there was something missing. Something was stopping him from harnessing his true potential… and it was something Fitzy knew all too well. It was also something Fitzy never talked about.

#

In the Church of the Resurrection, Dee sat in the confessional box. She tucked her hands inside her sweater, shielding them from the cold draft circuiting the church. She had been to see her mother. Eileen Breen was clean and well-dressed. She had eaten well over the festive period. In body, she was doing as well as expected, but the woman who made her Eileen Breen was steadily slipping away. The grille slid left.

'In the name of the Father, the Son and the Holy Ghost. Begin when you're ready, my child.'

'It's been six weeks since my last confession.'

Father O'Dowd could hear her stifling the pain, swallowing the warmth that filled her chest and gathered in her throat. 'Cry my child, and when ready, confess your sins.' Hot tears ran through the gaps in her fingers. 'I have been a neglectful daughter and a bad sister. I'm sorry, Father. I'll compose myself.'

'My child, you are too hard on yourself. Matthew Chapter 11, verse 28. You remember it?'

'Come to me, all of you who are wearied and burdened, and I will give you rest.'

'That's right. Now, what of your brother, Connor?'

'We left him alone in that house, just him and those cats. What kind of a life is that? We promised Ma we'd take care of him.'

'And Jimmy?' asked the priest.

Dee wiped her nose, and her breathing gradually returned to normal. 'It's like he isn't part of the family anymore. He does all he can for Ma, but that's all that keeps him connected to us. He hides it well, but he's the angriest person I know.'

'I will pray for him. And for Connor.'

Father O'Dowd closed with the Lord's prayer. 'Shall we speak more by the candles? There's a lovely big radiator there.' Dee could detect a grin cross the old priest's face. 'Aye, Father. I'm in no rush.'

'Good. January is tough on a priest.'

They lit candles and warmed the backs of their legs on the radiator. A tickling cough had been working on Father O'Dowd, adding a dry crack to his voice. He cleared his throat. 'As I said Dierdre, January is tough on a priest. We never got talking about Danny. I read about him in the Gazette a few weeks back.'

'Yes, he'll be fighting next month. That Nelson fella from Liverpool is promoting it. I am happy for Danny, but... God I don't want to say it, Father... he's drifted since Da died.'

'That's understandable. Arthur was the driving force, and you were a great support, keeping Danny focused on boxing and taking care of your mother. It was terrible what happened Eileen. Such a strong, healthy woman. And Arthur...well... he never quite came to terms with it.'

'No, he didn't. He left me and Jimmy to come to terms with it while he took care of the boxing. Anything else he cured with drink. And God forgive me, Father... I sometimes look at Danny and wonder if he has any idea what sacrifices were made for his boxing. It's not too late to turn his career around, but I don't think the fight is still in him. He fought for his Da, and Da died.'

'He fought only for Arthur? That's certainly not my recollection. I know Ela's back. Believe it or not, I get out of this place from time to time.' Father O'Dowd turned to look at Dee. 'You can't avoid her forever.'

'I know, Father. I should have said before now. It's been years since I've seen her. There are things we need to say… about Danny, Da… everything.'

The priest thumbed the rosary beads in his hand. 'I wonder, Dierdre. I wonder if all the guilt you shared today stems from what you have kept from Danny and Ela. I speak not just as your priest but as someone who knows you and your family. Be kind and compassionate to one another, forgiving each other, just as in Christ, God forgave you.'

#

Danny Breen lay in bed and flicked through his old boxing pictures. He had some great ones of the All-Ireland junior championships. He also had pictures of his pro debut. Fitzy was a good fifty pounds lighter. His father looked sombre but proud. There was a picture of the whole team. Da, Fitzy, Vincent, Dee…. and Ela. She was holding his mother's hand.

Danny stopped at his favourite picture. Ela was perched on the back of a chair next to him. Her lilac cardigan fell past her knees. Her wavy blond locks lay softly over her shoulder as she held her guitar and serenaded her man. He had just been crowned the Irish amateur champion for the first time. He was the Fighting Pride of Shamrock Hills.

## Chapter 12

The Grants enjoyed Irish coffees. Their bellies were full from another of Leanne's signature roasts. This Sunday's had been lamb and mint sauce, red cabbage and garlic roasted potatoes. The children had already escaped to the game room. The Sony PlayStation had barely cooled since Christmas morning.

The holiday period passed peacefully by Grant standards. Christmas lunch was the easy part. It was when uncles and cousins came for the evening drink that, historically, things got tricky. Their back garden had witnessed many a good knock down the years. It's how the men tended to settle their differences.

Leonard patted his brother's shoulder. 'You have time to talk shop?' Vincent nodded as he dried the last of the wine glasses and followed his big brother to the heat of the sitting room fire. He lifted two tumblers from the cabinet.

'Francis Nelson called yesterday. His fighter, Kevin Neary, is off the card. He hurt his thumb in sparring, so a replacement needs to be found and soon'. Vincent looked up from his single malt as Leonard swirled his. 'Danny has been preparing for Murray, and he's fighting Murray.'

Leonard shook his head and downed his drink. 'Did I mention Danny? Relax, brother. Danny is fighting Murray. There is no change there, but Simmons can't be bumped from the card. He is a name fighter and without Neary, he needs an opponent to look good against.

Vincent downed his drink and poured them both another measure. He reached for the poker and stabbed at the peat fire. His left forearm leaned into the mantlepiece. Above it hung a picture of a family fishing trip. The brothers were barely teens. They held brown trout, and their shoulders were dwarfed by their father's shovel-like hands.

'Why should it matter to us who Simmons fights?'

'You want the big fights for Danny, don't you? If this card falls flat, what do you think happens to the TV deal? No TV deal means no tournament. And that means no big nights coming here. Try and see the big picture, Vincent.'

Vincent stabbed again at the fire. 'My concern is my fighters. Danny and McGinty have their opponents, and their purses are agreed. Anything else is Nelson's domain.'

'Exactly. And that means fleshing out the card and giving the tv brass three good fights. He needs an opponent for Simmons. I was thinking Paddy Hughes.'

Vincent turned away from the fire. His face was bright with amusement. 'You aren't serious! Paddy Hughes is a welterweight!'

'Aye, a big one. And he's strong.'

'Jesus, you are being serious. He's not had a proper fight in two years. He'll embarrass himself.'

Leonard sat forward in his chair. 'Are you sure about that? You don't think he's good for a few rounds? Think it through, Vincent. He gives a good account of himself, takes a loss and goes back to welterweight. Paddy gets a payday and it sets up a rematch between Danny and Simmons.'

Vincent let out a deep sigh. I'll talk to Fitzy about it. If he's on board then alright.'

#

Ela Bond was back in Shamrock Hills. It was 2pm. She dabbed her eyes with a tissue as she left Serenity House. Eileen Breen wasn't an old woman. Her bones were strong and her hair, though allowed to grey, was thick and glossy. Her face was as pretty as ever. But her eyes, once dazzling, were dulled and sunken, sedate with the effects of her medication. For Ela, that's what was most heart-breaking. Not the dementia, not the limited mobility but the sadness in her gaze.

She pulled her woolly hat over her ears as a bitter chill whistled in from the coast. A short-haired woman was still a rarity in Shamrock Hills. It hadn't been in Dublin where Ela had lived for years. Now, she was home. Looking in the direction of the Harbour path, she knew she'd eventually run into Dee. As teens, they worked the same shift pattern at the Harbour chip shop.

Ela's heart thumped in her chest as she entered that evening, but her best friend from school wasn't working the fryers. The owner, Archie Dougan, insisted there were shifts available. She only needed to ask. Archie was good like that. She stepped out for a cigarette and took in the sights and the smells. Memories flooded back, from camping along the embankment to smoking on the Harbour path... to the walks home from school with Dee and Danny.

She remembered wrapping herself a cowboy supper after her evening shift and walking in the direction of Cloverhill where Danny waited. They were only kids, and Danny was a shy boy. He'd never kissed a girl before.

'Number 24. Two fish suppers and mushy peas, one cowboy supper.'

Ela stubbed out her cigarette and took a deep breath of wintery air before picking up her order. She selfishly walked the long way home. It would chill her parents' dinner, but they wouldn't want to see her cry.

#

In Liverpool, the staff of Nelson Ring Promotions were working late. They didn't need to be asked. They understood the stakes and the race against time. The office phone rang, and Vincent Grant was patched through to Francis. 'We would like Paddy Hughes added to the card. He's not a natural 160 pounder, but he's strong and durable. He'll give a good account of himself against Simmons.'

Nelson pumped his fist and gave a thumbs up to his staff. His team were due in Shamrock Hills in a matter of days. The new kids on the block weren't looking for favours, but no one anticipated such a struggle to find Neary's replacement.

'Once we get him his boxing license, we'll be good to go…'

Nelson's jubilation was short-lived. 'I can't announce a fight card with an unlicensed boxer sitting behind me. If that gets out, we'll all look like shithouses.'

'He'll have one by Friday. We have our ways here, Francis.'

'You bloody well better because the presser is Saturday.'

Nelson put down the phone. His temples were pounding. The boxing business was like no other, and he could feel the toll it was taking. Still, he had his card. The next stop was showcasing the event to the public and making sure the Wolfhound was a sellout on the night. Selling was his strength, and the thought pleased him. He swung open his office door. His team's work was done for the night, and the beers were on him.

#

In Shamrock Hills, Danny Breen was well into his third pint of ale at O'Leary's tavern, the busiest bar in Shamrock Hills.

The dog racing was on the TV. Fitzy waited excitedly for the last run of his four-race accumulator. 'It's my night, Danny boy. I can feel it in my water.'

Fitzy had lost too much to the Punt House over the years, but his dog, Norma Stitz, started well and after the first bend was holding third. Norma Stitz was closing in on Norfolk and Chance, Norma Stitz was up to second, Norma Stitz and Norfolk and Chance were neck and neck coming into the final bend. It went right to the wire. Norma Stitz won by a nose, and Fitzy went wild as if he'd bred her himself.

'Yes, you lovely bitch! Yes! Yes! Get them in, Danny!'

Fitzy waddled to the toilets as Danny drained what remained of his pint. He chatted with Shane, the barman, as he filled another glass. He kept a good angle and skimmed the excess foam with a butterknife. 'I almost forgot to say, Danny... a lass was asking about you. I told her Wednesday night is your night.'

'A girl asking about me? What was her name?'

Shane topped up the heads on the pints and smiled affectionately over Danny's shoulder. It took him a moment. Maybe it was the hair. It could have been the dim lighting, or perhaps the ale had slapped harder than usual. Shane lifted another pint glass. 'Shall I make it three pints or what?'

Danny looked to Ela and back to the bar man. 'Aye. Stick it on Fitzy's tab,' he said.

'Oh my God... is Fitzy here?' she asked excitedly.

Just then a heavy weight wrapped itself across her shoulders. Turning, she buried her head in his chest. 'It's been too long, Fitzy.'

'It has, wee Ela. It has.'

Fitzy rarely looked a person in the eye. He did for her.

## Chapter 13

Ela's parents kept a tidy house. With two of them, little mess accumulated, but now their daughter was back, and she'd invited her ex-boyfriend over for lunch. Her mother, Sandra, vacuumed the sitting room while Ernie cleaned the windows.

Ela sat in the sun room, picking at a new song on her guitar. She was determined to get her fingers nimble again and took pride in her newly formed callouses. Her Martin D-28 was dented and scuffed, but its sound remained rich. 'Are you going to change into something nice?' asked her mother, Sandra.

'I've already changed, Ma.'

'For the love of God...' Sandra muttered, returning to the kitchen. She could not help but fret. The pressure of hosting was deeply instilled. Ela's father, Ernie, knew the routine. Anything that involved the outdoors or a step ladder was his domain. He winked at his daughter through the sun room window. He thought she looked lovely.

In her youth, she had been something of an outlier, and she was pleased to be back in the threads her parents so kindly kept. That said, she didn't want her mother fretting any more than necessary, so she put on her good denim jacket over a Stone roses t-shirt. There was a knock at the door and Ernie wiped frantically at the last of the sun-room windows.

Danny had shaved his beard and run a comb through his hair. He apologized for his dress. Fight night was close and he was due back in the gym. Ernie slurped his tea. He always had, and after thirty years of nagging, Sandra had accepted he'd never change.

Such visits followed a common pattern. First came multiple offerings of food and beverages. Then the profuse apologies for the state of the house. A refill of tea and an update on who hadn't been seen at church. These were the safe topics, tried and tested, breaking Danny in gently before the inevitable bombardment of personal questions. It didn't bother him for he didn't know any different, but Ela had almost a decade of Dublin living under her belt and concealed her discomfort with another cream bun.

'I'll show you what I've done with the garage' offered Ernie.

Ernie had probably replaced the vice on his work table or sharpened his hatchet. Depending on his mood, it could take five or ten minutes. Thereafter, Danny and Ela could go for a walk along the embankment. She pulled on her lavender sweater and matching hat. Its sparkling brown tints complemented her freckled cheeks. In O'Leary's bar, Fitzy had helped fill the awkward pauses. During lunch,

Sandra had exhausted everyone else's news. It left Danny and Ela with only themselves to talk about.

'How's the weight cut going?' she asked.

'Not easy like it used to be. Not that you would know. You've not gained an ounce.'

'Not for long. Not how Mammy is feeding me.'

Danny asked about Dublin nightlife, which bands played where and the varying cost of a pint of beer. They were his safe topics. Ela asked if Fitzy was taking care of himself. She always had a soft spot for him. Fitzy, on the other hand, didn't have a reputation for softness. As a rule, the old trainer forbade his fledgling fighters from mixing with girls, but he took a liking to Ela when she first wondered into the gym in 1984. It helped that she often brought him something warm from the chip shop.

He never told Arthur Breen about the budding romance. Life was short, and there were worse things that teens could do than fall in love.

Dee Breen, as she was known then, disapproved. She had felt Ela slowly pulling away, making excuses not to meet after school and working different shifts at the chip shop. When she eventually confronted her, Ela, through tear-filled eyes, admitted she was dating her brother. It took Dee a while to overcome the rage she felt towards Danny for stealing her away, and it took significantly longer to overcome the sense of betrayal she felt towards Ela. Danny was her blood, but Ela was her best friend.

By then Jimmy, the eldest brother, was in college and working part-time as a clerk. He gave his wages to his mum, ensuring that she could afford the little bits and pieces that their father overlooked. Arthur, with each passing year, became more distant. He didn't talk about prison, and Jimmy cared little for boxing.

In all, Ela had been with Danny from schoolboy to man. She was there for junior championship wins. She was by his side when he signed pro. It was a sizeable chapter in the Breen family story, and it weighed heavily as they sat on the same bench where they shared their first kiss. Ela rolled a cigarette and wondered where the last fifteen years had gone as Danny watched a stray cat go by.

'I'm sorry, Danny. Going away was just something I had to do.'

Danny shielded her hands from the wind as she struggled to light her cigarette. In the mid-afternoon light he studied the wrinkles around her eyes and brow, wondering how such minor imperfections could make her so much more beautiful.

'Dublin offered you things that this town couldn't. I understood that. But you never came back to visit, not even for Christmas. And you stopped writing. You ended it without telling me it was over. That's what I never understood.'

'But Danny, you were the one who stopped replying to my letters. Mum and Dad said you were knuckling down in the gym and big opportunities were coming. I wrote to you about it… and many other things that I wanted you to know…'

Danny looked away as she ran a finger against the grain of his stubble before gently tidying his fringe. 'You need a haircut before the big fight.' He closed his eyes and gathered his thoughts. 'Nine years, Ela. Nine years since I last saw you.' He clicked his fingers. 'Sometimes it feels as quick as that… like it just happened yesterday, like nothing's really changed. Most things haven't. Same streets, same pubs, and I'm still scratching a living from boxing. But Da is dead and Ma doesn't know what day it is. Dee's raising her boys alone, and Connor's stuck in that house with a bunch of cats. Plenty changed for us.'

'I'm sorry.'

Danny threw a pebble at the nearest lamppost. 'Da died, Ela. He just dropped like a rock at the prison. Ma could barely stand at his funeral. I needed you then.'

'I'm sorry, Danny. I should have been there.'

'And now you're home. Home for good?'

'I think so. Danny, I wrote to you. I wrote many times.'

Danny pinged another pebble off the lamppost.

'It's not like I didn't know where to find you. Anyway, it's a long time ago. I have to get back to Fitzy.'

He made the short walk to the Celtic Fist gym alone. Ela stayed seated on the bench at the bottom of Cloverhill.

There was a good ninety minutes of sunlight left. Danny's words hurt, but she was wise enough to know that they needed saying. She reached for her rolling papers. 'I still love you, Danny', she whispered to herself.

#

Fitzy leafed through the paperwork. The show would soon be in town, and the race was on to get Paddy licensed. Fitzy wasn't much of a reader and his phone calls to Vincent went straight to voicemail. Thus, Danny's timely arrival felt like a gift from heaven. 'This has to be sent off first thing in the morning. Help Paddy with it. It's all Greek to me.'

The Ballywell brawler was napping. Three workouts a day required plenty of rest. Luckily for him, he didn't have to boil down to make the middleweight limit, and it showed. Paddy's sparring was on point, and he had no niggling injuries. Even Fitzy was beginning to warm to him. Still, inactivity was the curse of all boxers. Two years without a fight was far from ideal, especially going in against a boxer as seasoned as Peter Simmons.

The forms took the best part of an hour and covered every conceivable illness. Protocol was protocol, but so long as a cat scan came back clean, Paddy would get his license.

'That's it done. Won't be long till you're stealing the show at the Wolfhound,' said Danny.

'Aye, right. I know you all think I've no chance.'

Danny turned back and smiled at his stablemate. 'That's not what I'm thinking, and it's not what Fitzy is thinking either. But it doesn't matter what we think. You're the one fighting Simmons.'

Paddy smiled as he looked up to Danny, though his eyes didn't brighten. Danny understood. Fitzy once told him that boxing was 90% mental. Paddy was getting good at his craft, and with that came doubts. Some fighters were gym fighters, and others thrived under the lights. Some needed to hate their opponents, while others needed to stay out of their own heads.

'Who's more prepared for battle… you or Simmons?'

'How would I know?'

'Come on, Paddy, you know. You think he's hungrier than you? You reckon he's been training harder? Hitting harder? What?'

Paddy smiled again, and this time his eyes brightened. 'No fighter is hungrier than me.'

Danny broke into a shadowbox. 'In that case, you rock into the Wolfhound like you own the place. You give Simmons zero respect… and beat the absolute snot out of him!' The Shamrock Express threw flurries of punches as Paddy laughed for the first time in weeks.

'It's as simple as that?'

'Simpler than life out there. Believe me. And, for what it's worth, I think you have his number. He won't like the pressure you put him under, so bring the pressure right from the opening bell, and don't let up on him. Do that, and you'll emerge victorious.'

'Aye. I will. Thanks.'

Danny playfully jabbed Paddy's arm and returned to the gym to stretch out his hamstrings. He was good at appearing cheerful, but Fitzy could tell that something was off. That said, it didn't affect his boxing. Danny and Paddy gave each other some great work, and McGinty got in six rounds as well. Paddy offered his hand and apologized for the last time they sparred. He was beginning to understand what the Celtic Fist boxing club was all about.

## Chapter 14

The Wolfhound arena prepared for its biggest night in years. Workmen were busy constructing new bleachers as engineers tested the lighting and sound systems. The plastic seating had just arrived. Things were on schedule and beginning to take shape. Francis Nelson and his team were staying at the Hibernia House hotel. They ventured out to take in the sights and court the press. Leonard Grant invited them to the Quayside to meet local business men. They then spent the evening in O'Leary's bar. Rumours spread across town that Nelson downed twelve pints of Shamrock ale in one sitting.

Dermot Robinson of the Shamrock Gazette had followed the promotion all week, squeezing in interviews with fighters and other key players. When starting out as a journalist, sport had not been his first choice, but he threw himself into the culture and was more than willing to serve his time before moving into more serious journalism.

That had been the plan, but somewhere along the way his priorities changed, and sport became more than a means to an end. He had found fertile ground for his writing mind. There were intriguing characters, comeback stories and corruption aplenty. Boxing provided more than its share, and Francis Nelson, the new promoter on the block, was a sports journalist's dream.

Fanfare was building outside the town hall. The St Brigid's girls put on a line dancing show, and the Four-Leaf Clovers, the town's premier band, played a half dozen Shamrock classics. Inside, the fighters were seated at the top tables. The purple lace curtains provided a tasteful backdrop to a beautiful hall. The iconography of Shamrock Hills was everywhere, from ceremonial swords to poems engraved in the town's cedar wood. The press section was filled with writers and camera men, all ready and waiting for the show to begin.

The podium divided the top tables. On one sat the Shamrock fighters with Fitzy and Vincent. On the other were Peter Simmons, Ricky Murray and Ballywell rookie, Dylan Wallace. Danny shook hands with Simmons. They went back a while. He also bumped fists with Ricky Murray. They'd be fighting in a few days, but that was no reason not to be civil. Paddy chewed his gum furiously as Simmons cracked jokes and posed for photographers.

Francis 'Big Daddy' Nelson entered from the far side of the hall. He was a hulk of a man, dwarfing all around him, even the Grant brothers. He had dressed to impress and was looking sharp in a three-piece suit.

'Thank you everyone for attending this event, and thank you so much for your warmth and hospitality. We've absolutely loved our time here. Shamrock Hills breathes boxing and I'm delighted to bring a big show to the Wolfhound arena on February 24$^{th}$. The card opens with light heavyweight Gary 'Thunder' McGinty making his pro debut against Dylan Wallace of Ballywell.

Moving up the card we have Birmingham's Peter Simmons against middleweight debutant, Paddy Hughes. And topping the bill, it's the 'Shamrock Express', Danny Breen against the 'Clydebank Destroyer', Ricky Murray.'

Nelson then unveiled the inaugural UBF title belt. 'We've waited too long for the big fights, and for too long our fighters have been overlooked. That ends now. This fight card is part of a journey. Both middleweight contests will be sanctioned by the UBF. That means the winners will be eligible to compete for this beautiful world title belt. I'll now take questions from the media.'

Dermot Robinson went first. He had earned the right and had done his homework, quizzing Nelson on rumours of gym wars at Mersey Gloves ABC.

'Dermot, you've been covering the sport long enough to know that what happens in the gym stays in the gym, but I'll confirm that it got feisty in there.'

Pushed to divulge more, Nelson looked to move on, but Fitzy, having tapped his microphone to check it was on, told Robinson, 'Let's just say, we came back from Liverpool with our tails up. Danny Breen is a class above those

Liverpool boys. We'll fight them home or away, but if Francis enjoys our stout so much, let's have the fights here. Danny can beat them both on the same night, and then we'll take Francis out for last orders.'

The remark brought a chuckle from Nelson and the press. Fitzy gestured at Dermot, inviting more questions. Danny giggled and pulled his cap down over his eyes. He'd sat with Fitzy for many pressers and knew the routine.

'Yes Barney, I have another question. Who forced you to put Paddy Hughes in with a highly ranked middleweight in Simmons? Hughes hasn't fought in two years, and he's jumping up two weight classes. If you're going to slaughter lambs for Nelson, can you not just cook him a stew?'

Peter Simmons let out a laugh as he leaned forward in his chair to get a good peak at Hughes. Fitzy took the question. 'Have you seen the size of Paddy? Tell me he's not big enough for the middleweight division.... and believe me, he's not here to make up the numbers. He's a hell of a fighter, and he will show it at the Wolfhound.'

Paddy pulled the microphone towards him. 'Three rounds. That's all I need. Simmons is a bottle-job and always has been. He had one good night against Danny Breen and thinks he made it. He's getting knocked out. I'm the best middleweight here and I'll prove it on the 24$^{th}$.'

Paddy reclaimed his composure for the face offs. He tried staring through Simmons, but the Birmingham fighter showed no sign of nerves. To him, Hughes was just a stepping stone to a rematch with Danny.

Ela Bond watched on from the balcony. As a lover of theatre, she enjoyed the drama that surrounded fight week. She returned on Friday to watch the weigh-ins. After making weight, Paddy grabbed Simmons by the throat, forcing Vincent and Leonard to wrestle him off. Breen and Murray then weighed in. The Clydebank Destroyer looked comfortable, more so than Danny at any rate. The latter had spent the morning shadowboxing in a sweat suit, working frantically to boil off the last two pounds.

## Chapter 15

Seats filled quickly on fight night. Riley from the paper shop worked the ticket desk. A mixture of foldout chairs and traffic cones were used to keep the crowd orderly. A couple of fist fights had already broken out in the parking lot. The rivalry between Shamrock Hills and Ballywell ran deep.

Fitzy was in in a foul mood. After testing the ring canvas, he threatened to pull his fighters from the show. Francis Nelson gave in and had his men remove a layer of foam padding. 'Good, now they'll have a ring canvas to move on and not a marshmallow!'

Gary McGinty's hands were wrapped, but he stood barefoot, still in his briefs having forgotten to pack his protective cup. His father sped through town to lift it from the Celtic Fist boxing club. Once on, Fitzy started the pre-fight ritual.

'Alright Gary boy. When you walk out there, fix your eyes on that ring. Trust me, son. Once that bell goes, all the nerves will work in your favour. Ok?'

'Yes coach. I'm ready.'

'Good. Sharp and quick, eyes on your prey. Forget the cameras and the crowd. It's just you and him in the ring. Relish the nerves. You're a fighter.'

Shamrock Hills' high society filled the ringside seats. In the bleachers, the punters grew restless as the smell of Shamrock ale and cheap tobacco filled the arena. McGinty walked out to a raucous reception. As the fight began, he quickly found a home for his body punches. Their force rippled through the soft gut of his opponent and forced him to take a knee. Dylan Wallace made the count at eight but cowered in his corner as McGinty threw unanswered right hooks. From the blue corner, a white towel was thrown into the ring, and the referee waved off the contest. Gary 'Thunder' McGinty of Shamrock Hills had made a winning start to his professional career.

The fight had been scheduled for four rounds, so there was time to kill on the GBT broadcast. McGinty interviewed well, relishing the attention and thanking his coach for believing in him. Dermot Robinson hurriedly scratched down notes before grabbing a soundbite from the victor.

Hughes versus Simmons was next on the card. Paddy paced the length of the changing room, rotating his large shoulders and bouncing on the balls of his feet. He glanced at the mirror, clenching and then stretching his jaw. His mind brimmed with anger, furious that he was being made to walk first to the ring, as if Simmons was the bigger attraction. Hughes meant what he said. He was the best middleweight on the card and was going to make Dermot Robinson eat his words.

But Simmons started well, unaffected by the partisan fans and showing 'One shot' Hughes that there were levels to boxing. He stayed one step ahead of the Ballywell brawler, negating his attacks and catching him with counter-shots. Paddy wasn't hurt but his size disadvantage was telling. As the bell sounded to end the third, Simmons was three points up and cruising. Paddy panted hard as he returned to his corner. Fitzy soaked him with a spray of cold water and tried summoning some urgency from his fighter.

'You're fighting his fight and making him look like a world beater in there. Box your way in and then unload. And don't let him tie you up. Rip your arms free and force him to work. You're three rounds down, kid.'

'I know what I'm doing,' snarled Paddy as his stomach muscles flexed with every breath.

Dermot Robinson was falling behind in his notes. His memory wasn't what it used to be. He recalled Paddy's three round prediction and wanted to work in a clever turn of phrase, something to serve as a cautionary tale for boxing braggarts. 'His three-round pledge diminished to parody as Simmons peppered him at will.' It needed work, but he could return to it later.

As the bell sounded, Robinson drew a line under his notes to mark the beginning of round four. He looked up just in time to see Paddy Hughes land a thunderous right cross on

Simmon's cheekbone. It drew a collective gasp from the crowd as the Birmingham man's body jack-knifed on its way to the canvas.

The referee didn't consider a count, dropping to his knees and removing Simmon's gumshield. Paddy ran for the nearest turnbuckle and thumped his chest. Dermot Robinson sat in shock, the screams of the fans ringing in his ears. He'd been to many live shows and had seen his fair share of knockouts, but the sheer velocity of the punch and the surgical accuracy with which it landed left him speechless.

'I told all of you that I'm the best fighter on this card. I'm a match for any middleweight that Nelson throws at me,' snarled Paddy, basking with vicious vindication.

Francis Nelson and Leonard Grant bunched in close to Paddy, making sure they were within the camera shot. 'Paddy has proven his doubters wrong. With that kind of power, he has a real chance against anyone.' Asked if a fight with Breen could happen in future, Nelson looked to Leonard, inviting him to take the question. 'They are part of the same stable, but put that aside for a moment... if you're asking me whether they'd match up well... after this performance I'd have to say yes. It would be a barnstormer.'

Vincent Grant watched on from ringside. Seeing the ease with which Leonard mixed with Nelson, he shook his head and stormed off in the direction of the fighters' pavilion. In the ring, Paddy Hughes nodded eagerly. 'I'm taking on allcomers. Tonight was about shaking off the rust and showing everyone that I'm the real deal. It's time for a new era. They talk about Luke Gibson here like he's still fighting. He's the past. It's time for a new champion, and you're looking at him.'

The interview stuck in Fitzy's throat, but he had no time to brood. Danny was now the priority and he made his way from ringside, ignoring the media and paying public. In the changing room, Dee checked they had everything. Gum shield, bandage, gauze, adrenaline, ice packs and mineral water. Vincent removed Danny's headphones. 'It's time to switch on, kid. Paddy knocked out Simmons in the fourth.'

Fitzy entered and quickly scanned the gear that Dee had so meticulously laid out. 'He needs to make a statement', said Vincent, planting his hand on Fitzy's shoulder. Danny could sense the stress in his trainer. 'What happened out there?'

'Paddy did a number on Simmons,' answered Vincent.

'That's good', replied Danny

'No, it's not. You're the headliner, Danny! You can't let Paddy steal the show. Come on, kid. Switch on!'

Vincent slapped his hands together. Till then, Fitzy had remained quiet. He set down the hand wraps and rose to his feet to face Vincent. 'I like a quiet changing room, so I need you to stop flapping your gums or leave.'

Vincent stepped in close, towering over the former featherweight. 'Are you confusing me with someone else,

Fitzy? Because no one talks to me like that. Now wrap his hands. We haven't got all night.'

'That's enough!' shouted Dee.

Vincent and Fitzy traded embarrassed looks. The former made to leave, frustrated but accepting that his presence was no longer benefitting his fighter. 'I'll see you out there, Danny. If you see the knockout, go for it. Make your Da proud, kid.'

As he rounded the corner towards the arena, he bumped into an old acquaintance and pointed her in the direction of Danny's changing room.

When she entered, Danny raised his head and returned Ela's smile. It was just like old times but for the absence of his father. Hammering his gloves together, he signalled to Fitzy that he was ready. Trainer and fighter entered the zone. Their connection on the pads was near telepathic. Dee's shoulders tightened. Try as she might, she couldn't make herself invisible. She watched her brother hit the pads, half-smiling through her nerves as the seconds passed like hours. At some point, Ela left without a sound.

Early in the fight, it was apparent that Ricky Murray wasn't the destroyer as advertised, but he was rugged and durable. Danny dropped him in the sixth round and wobbled him in the eighth, but he was unable to push for a finish. With four rounds to go, his legs began to weaken and his punch output dropped. It gave Murray all the encouragement he needed to press for an upset victory.

Danny absorbed sickening blows to his sides. In the tenth round, Murray cracked the rib that he'd bruised in Liverpool. It forced Danny to stand and slug for the last two rounds. As the final bell tolled, he felt he'd done enough. Fitzy lifted him off his feet as the home crowd serenaded their man. He looked for Ela but could not see her.

After the post-fight interviews, Dermot Robinson left the arena. It had been an exhausting week. He beat the traffic and got himself home to a bowl of Weetabix and a good night's sleep. He'd enjoyed fight week, and Paddy Hughes had gift-wrapped him the headline, the angle and the intrigue.

# Part 2

*The truth hurts*

## Chapter 16

As a spectacle, the Wolfhound card exceeded expectations. The venue was a sell-out, and three good fights satiated the public's bloodlust. Getting one over on Ballywell made Gary McGinty a popular man, and there was delight at seeing Danny Breen return to winning ways. But the story of the night was Paddy Hughes leaving Simmons spreadeagled on the canvas. 'Big Shot Hughes' was the headline in the Monday Gazette. It was a play on Hughes' boxing moniker and boastful post-fight interview. With one perfectly timed right hand, he announced himself as a major player in the middleweight division. And with one unscripted interview, he made himself a local villain.

This, in a perverse way, was good for him. The last thing a young fighter wanted to be was forgettable, and whether fans tuned in to watch him win or lose was of secondary concern, especially for Francis Nelson. It was a promoter's job to strike when the iron was hot, and Nelson saw the potential the moment Peter Simmons crumpled to the canvas. After the panic of Neary pulling out with injury, Nelson had a ringside view of the hottest prospect in Irish boxing. He leaned into Leonard Grant. 'Hughes versus Breen. That's a big fight, yes?'

'Potentially massive,' replied Leonard.

Leonard had pulled a lot of strings to stage the event in Shamrock Hills. He used his connections in the town hall to secure the Wolfhound arena, leaned hard on the boxing board to fast-track Paddy's license and worked tirelessly to secure sponsors. He hadn't crunched the numbers, but it was looking like the show would at worst break even. It was a satisfying outcome, though it strained important relations.

After Breen's hand was raised in victory, Francis Nelson put his arm around the younger of the Grant brothers. 'It's entertainment, Vincent, and this is what sells. Narratives and rivalries. Danny's a big boy. He understands the game.'

Vincent understood. He knew Nelson's job was to work the media, but he did not expect his brother to be swept along. 'They are stablemates, Leonard. What happens on Monday when they are back in the gym? Fitzy's pissing blood.'

Leonard only saw the money. Teasing a local rivalry increased the chance of another big card coming to Shamrock Hills, one that could turn a bigger profit for his various partners. If Leonard and, more importantly, Vincent played it smart, the rewards could be staggering. He placed his hand on Vincent's back. 'Was Danny the headliner? Did he earn a world ranking? Is he making better money than ever? You're looking for a problem that doesn't exist, brother. Nelson promotes fighters and events. That's his job, and he's damn good at it'.

'I don't trust him' replied Vincent.

'You don't need to trust Nelson… but you should trust me. You'll see, brother. In time, you'll see. This is just business. And like it or not, Paddy Hughes is big business now. You and Fitzy should be delighted that you've unearthed a diamond. Think of the leverage that gives you with Nelson'.

'Fair point.'

'Good. We agree on something. Now, get yourself home, brother. Let me deal with the media'.

When Vincent returned to his home in Cedar Heights, he reached for the whiskey. His brother was always the better talker. He knew how to cultivate relationships and had the patience to play the long game and win. Vincent was not cut from that cloth. He led with his heart and considered consequences after the fact. Because of this, he'd sabotaged more than a few ventures down the years… and some setbacks were less temporary than others.

#

Danny Breen spent the remainder of fight night in a hospital bed. Fitzy offered to stay but Dee insisted he go home and rest. She dabbed at the cut on her brother's cheek. She fluffed his pillows and gave him a sip of water. The adrenaline had left Danny's body, and he began to drift off. His mind was dazed from pain killers, and his body was exhausted from battle. He dreamt of his father. The night was pitch black. Danny powered up another steep hill as Arthur Breen followed in his Vauxhall.

*Push, son. Your rivals are sleeping right now and here you are, running in the freezing cold. And why? Because you want it more. Because you're a champion!*

Danny momentarily stirred. He was too weak to wake yet too weary for sleep. His mind was trapped in a feverish purgatory... his father fervently watching on, for every rep, every drill... every bead of sweat.

*This is what you're destined for. Suffer now and be remembered as a champion.*

Dee got home after 4am. Her little brother, Connor, was wrapped up warm on the living room sofa. It seemed a shame to wake him, and the least she could do was cook him breakfast. She'd find out then just how much grief his nephews had given him. She gathered the post and brought it through to the kitchen. Another month's wages from Ivan. Good. The rent was due in two days and the boys had quickly outgrown their school uniforms. Attached was a letter.

*Dear Dee,*

*I have good news and bad news. I've been offered the chance to stay on with the firm. The bad news is there won't be any break over the summer.*

*I'm sorry, Dee. This is the last job I'll take away from home, I promise. I hope Alex and Aiden are doing well. I can't believe how big they're getting.*

*Bye for now,*

*Ivan*

She folded it and slipped it back in the envelope. The news had not surprised her, and as she did the sums for the month ahead, she was accepting of her lot. She no longer questioned what really drove her husband to take such jobs, close enough to home to be acceptable to the family but far enough away to never visit. But he always sent money, and with Danny's fight purse on the way, she felt the pressure lift for the first time in months.

Jimmy Breen had watched the fight from the comfort of his pleasant four-bedroom house. His reputation as an accountant was well-deserved. He didn't rest on weekends, and he more than made up for the time he spent with his mother in Serenity House. He drove an Audi saloon. It was a fine car and in keeping with his profession. His bedroom wardrobe brimmed with tailored suits and Ben Sherman shirts. His kitchen was meticulously clean and well-ordered. In his home office lay leaflets on time shares and pension plans. He was a man in charge of his life, but the third and fourth bedrooms remained spare.

There had been girlfriends over the years, but his first love was work, and his main duty was to his mother. But as he watched Danny Breen labour to victory, with only the company of a Jack Russel terrier fast asleep on his lap, he felt loneliness for the first time in years. And while he'd never been especially close to Danny, something instinctive stirred within.

In Cedar Heights, Vincent Grant tossed and turned on the sitting room sofa, his mind swirling back to his prison days.

*Be fair to me and I'll be fair to you.*

It was the autumn of 1980 and a month removed from the gymnasium beating. Officer Breen kept his word. He was indeed a very fair man. He permitted Vincent to join the prison boxing club where he formed a bond with Barney Fitzpatrick.

'You could have been a boxer' praised the ex-fighter and trainer.

Prison was not where Fitzy wanted to carry out business, but a generous grant saw the Celtic Fist owner coach a broad church of delinquents on the sweet science of boxing during the 1980s. Fitzy loved talking boxing. His knowledge of the sport was encyclopaedic.

Arthur Breen, the block officer, rarely spoke to anyone including his own wife and children. But in boxing, he'd found something to interest him. Within weeks, he introduced Fitzy to his son, Danny. From that point, the men's lives were intrinsically linked by boxing. In time, they'd all come to believe that Danny Breen was destined for the top. The talent was undeniable. All they needed was the right strategy… and a bit of luck.

In the meantime, Arthur Breen kept an eye on Vincent Grant. Prisons functioned off favours, and the best he could do for Vincent was to pair him up with an agreeable cellmate. As convicted murderers went, Willie Dunne was as good as it got in the Shamrock Correctional facility. He was twenty years into a life sentence. He was a diminutive man, his woolly hat and long beard distinguishing him from the crowd.

'The top bunk is mine. I sleep better when I'm three feet closer to God. I take my shits first thing in the morning and again at lights out. The rest of the time, the bog is yours.' The terms were agreeable to Vincent. He'd already claimed the bottom bunk and was fairly free-spirited when it came to shitting. Dunne scanned his new cellmate's reading material.

'You like Joyce?'

'I can take him or leave him. You?'

Nah, he's no good, and I should I know. I'm a voracious reader. That's your new word for the day, Grant. Voracious.'

'I don't recall asking for homework.'

'Well, that's tough titties because it's just you and me now. Your eager ears and my soothing voice.'

Vincent lay tense in his bunk, tension that slowly evanesced with every passing paragraph. Willie's voice bordered hypnotic. They were an odd pairing, but after a few weeks' adjustment, Vincent had made his first friend in the big house.

He missed Willie every day, and he was grateful to Arthur Breen for bringing them together. He owed him for that. He owed him for a lot of things. Upon his release in the Spring of 1985, Vincent vowed never to return to that place, not to serve time, not as a visitor… not even to help Arthur and Fitzy run the boxing club.

Maybe he should have. He could have been there when Arthur's heart gave out and his body crumpled to the canvas. Fitzy held Arthur in his arms, but by the time the paramedics came, it was too late. The last words he uttered were, 'Take care of Danny.'

Vincent was trying.

## Chapter 17

Paddy Hughes packed away his belongings. The Grants had properties all over town, and they steered him towards a place on the waterfront. Vincent felt it was too much too soon, but Leonard insisted. Men with much deeper pockets now had their sights on Hughes. Whether he knew it or not, the Ballywell brawler had options.

Francis Nelson was first to show his hand. He wanted Paddy to compete for the UBF title. That meant a two-fight deal. The money was good. It would be great exposure for the Celtic Fist gym, and it heightened the chances of more big nights coming to Shamrock Hills. Hughes had earned his shot. In boxing it only took a split-second for a fighter's fortunes to change. Before the Simmons knockout, Paddy was an understudy to Danny Breen. Now, he was on the cusp of competing for the same world title belt and moving into a two-bedroom apartment in Shamrock Views.

It was quite the step up for the Ballywell orphan. As he stood on his balcony overlooking the Drumferry river, a regular man would have felt satisfaction, but Paddy was a fighter. He grabbed his gym bag and made for the elevator. Fitzy was already in the Celtic Fist gym. Paddy must have left in the middle of the night, he thought.

Danny Breen was still in bed. When the alarm went, he reached for his bedside table and yanked the radio lead from its socket. Dee would be over soon. He forced himself up and ran some bathwater. His arms and sides were still badly bruised. He rubbed his eyes. The bathwater passed his ankles as his reflection faded in the mist.

Later that morning, he and Dee walked the church grounds and enjoyed the first signs of spring. The groundsman was planting daffodil bulbs as two grey squirrels spiralled up a nearby sycamore tree. When they reached their father's grave, Dee's eyes began to water. 'I miss you every day, Da. I'm here with Danny. He's a world-ranked fighter and back to winning ways.' She encouraged Danny to speak, but it wasn't his way.

'He's going to be a world champion, just like you said he'd be.'

Alone, Dee made for the church door. She blessed herself and walked towards the candles. As she did so, a fresh-faced priest emerged from the vestry.

'Good afternoon, Miss. I'm Father Carrigan'

'Hello, Father. I was hoping to speak to Father O'Dowd'

'Father O'Dowd is actually on a short sabbatical.'

That was odd, Dee thought. He never mentioned it.

#

Pins and needles shot through Fitzy's tendons. Arthritis had been working on him for years. With his hip getting steadily worse, the day he couldn't train fighters was fast-approaching. Until then, he was still one of the best in Ireland. Paddy Hughes rattled off a six-punch combination, puncturing the silence of the gym. They'd built a good chemistry. Fitzy no longer barked orders or paused to correct him. He communicated with his body. A flick of a wrist and a roll of his shoulder signalled to Paddy the sequence of punches, their tempo and force. 'Time!'

The shutter went up. Danny was told to keep away for another week, but the days were long. Fitzy paced the ring as he fought for air. Despite it getting harder, he still enjoyed being between the ropes. Paddy leaned on the turnbuckle and raised a glove to his stablemate. 'I haven't seen you since fight night. How's the rib?'

Danny winced playfully.

'About that interview,' continued Paddy, 'the microphone was shoved in my face and the camera was pointing right at me. I didn't think about what I was saying.'

Danny let out a wry smile. 'Don't worry about me, but you owe the town an apology. I told you. Gibson is God to us.'

Fitzy's buzzer went. It was business as usual for the trainer, but he could sense what was coming. It was just a matter of time.

#

Peter Harrod of GBT Sports spent the morning at Nelson Ring Promotions in Liverpool. The television numbers were in for the show at the Wolfhound. Nelson had it all to prove when he first approached the network. Like all major broadcasters, boxing enticed GBT, and Nelson had talked a very good game. Looking up from his spreadsheets, Harrod voiced his displeasure.

'We weren't expecting miracles, but these numbers are dreadful. I have my bosses to answer to, Francis. I pushed this event hard, and I'm staring at a big loss.'

If boxing failed for Nelson, he had plenty to fall back on, but for Harrod, his days as a broadcast executive would be over. He leaned back in his chair and linked his fingers. 'The four-man tournament... are we settled on the name?'

'Yes', replied Nelson. 'The Celtic Four.'

'Okay, I like it. So... Breen is in. What about Hughes?'

'Absolutely. He's in 100%,' answered Nelson.

'And Neary and Hibbert fight in a month's time. Do they have opponents?'

'No, not yet.'

'So, we have a window of opportunity here. I propose we accelerate the schedule. The Stanley Hall card marks the start of the tournament. Neary versus Hughes and Hibbert versus Breen. That's something I can take back to GBT.'

Nelson thought for a moment. Liverpool was his town and tickets would sell like hotcakes, but Neary and Hibbert were a work in progress. He wanted them in warm-up fights before officially unveiling their place in the tournament. That said, while his pockets were deep, they weren't so deep as to turn his back on the television deal he'd worked so hard to secure.

Boxing was the theatre of the unexpected, and the Wolfhound card proved it. No one predicted the rise of Paddy Hughes, not even his own coach, so what was stopping Neary and Hibbert from achieving a similar feat? All it took was one punch. Nelson walked Harrod to his car before making the short trip to Mersey Gloves ABC.

Its owner and coach, Tommy Brown, was pushing his fighters hard. He screamed at Neary to breathe through the pain as he slammed a medicine ball off his abdominals. Meanwhile, Hibbert strengthened his neck muscles, his head bearing the weight of fifty-pound reps. Nelson flicked the gym light off and on. 'Not long till fight night, boys. Good to see you looking lean and mean. Tommy, a quick word, please.'

Tommy followed Nelson to his Bentley Continental. A group of youths had gathered around it but quickly dispersed when they saw the colossal Nelson approach. The two men slid into the back, a virtual living room on wheels. 'I'm here to tell you that Neary is fighting Paddy Hughes and Hibbert is facing Danny Breen.'

Tommy sat dumbfounded. 'Francis, you're gambling with those matchups. Breen would start as favourite against Hibbert, and Neary's thumb is still healing. He can't have a shootout with Hughes.'

Nelson leaned in. 'Let's get something clear, Tommy. I respect you. I respect what you've done in the sport, and I'm open to anything you have to say, but I'm the one calling the shots. Those boys are signed to a three-fight deal with Nelson Ring Promotions. Your job is to train them... and if you don't fancy their chances next month, say now and we'll find them another coach.'

Tommy held his breath. He knew the terms of the contract he'd signed, and of all the parties, he was the most dispensable. He was in line for some good money, but he held no veto when it came to matchmaking. He looked back at Nelson. 'You've already promised this to GBT, haven't you?'

'It's what we've agreed going forward. If you want out, fine. But that's not what I want. Those boys in your gym will fancy the job. Paddy Hughes caught lightning in a bottle that night. He's a crude brawler. And Danny Breen is shot at the weight. He's a six-round fighter now. Hibbert's got twice the engine and half the miles on the clock.'

'That's true.'

'Then grow a pair and back your boys, Tommy. They have home advantage. And before you ask, we aren't changing the date. April fourth, Stanley Hall. Liverpool will be watching. Don't let the city down'.

Tommy was one of boxing's good guys, and like his counterpart in Shamrock Hills, had no family of his own. The gym was his home and the fighters his sons. The short walk back gave him little time to resolve the conflicts that Nelson's news raised, but watching his boys toil as they pummelled tyres with forty-pound sledgehammers, the path ahead became clear. Sparring started tomorrow.

#

Danny Breen flicked through the Tv channels and pressed at his side. The pain was beginning to dull. He checked his face in the bathroom mirror and was pleased to resemble a civilian again. As he was making tea, his buzzer went. 'Who is it?' There was no answer. He peered through the peep hole and unchained the lock.

'This is unexpected.'

'You don't have a telephone, so you didn't leave me much choice.'

Ela undid her coat buttons and removed her scarf. Her cheeks were rosy from the cold, but her scent carried the freshness of spring. Danny took her coat and hung it against the door. 'I was just making tea.'

'You have anything stronger?'

'I do, but I can't partake. Doctor's orders.'

'I see. Then green tea it is.'

Ela was teaching English and Drama at St Brigid's School for Girls till the end of term. She'd already been sounded out for a permanent role. 'Even the sound of it is off-putting. Full-time. Such finality. I'm not sure I'm ready for it.'

'It seems a no-brainer to me,' Danny commented.'

'Maybe. Maybe not. I guess things have changed for me too.'

Danny swirled his tea and watched the leaves slowly resettle. 'What I said that day… all that stuff… it's a long time ago. Anyway, did you enjoy the fight?'

Ela took a deep drink of her tea. 'I saw the last few rounds with Mum and Dad. He was a tough one, that Scotsman. How are you feeling?' Danny lifted his t-shirt and pulled down the dressing. 'He caught me with some good ones.' Ela took a closer look, and her face twisted with unease. 'That can't be good for you.'

'No, it isn't. I don't know, Ela. I felt better than ever for the first few rounds… but by the end, I was hanging on.'

'Maybe it's time, Danny.'

He nodded and drained the last of his tea. 'Maybe… but I've got two fights left on my contract, and I need the paydays.'

Ela shook her head. 'You need your health more than you need money. Just look at poor Fitzy. What do you think he'd rather have?'

'Fair point, but I can still slip a punch. I'll be alright. It was nice having you back in the changing room. It felt like old times.'

Ela shifted in her seat and turned towards the only man she ever loved. 'That's why I'm here. To work out what is past and what isn't.'

She reached into her trouser pocket and brought out a small floral pouch. Danny remembered the ring well. It was a solid gold band embedded with red rubies. He turned it between his fingers. 'This was the ring I was going to propose with.'

Ela smiled as she watched the rubies glow from the light of the living room lamp. 'I know you were… but things happened. I loved Eileen.'

Danny closed his hand around the ring. 'She loved you too. She was heartbroken when you left.'

Ela touched his arm. 'It was me or boxing. That's why I left, Danny. I couldn't let you make that choice. All the training. All the pain. I couldn't be the reason you stopped.'

Danny smiled, but it was a feeble attempt at concealing the sadness in his eyes. 'I could have gone to Dublin with you and fought there. A few wins, a few losses… then I could have been a bricklayer. Or a barman. I wouldn't have been champion, but we'd have been together'.

Ela rested her head on his shoulder. 'You remember the cut in my fight against Collins?' he continued. 'Da was at me all camp. "You're not focused. You're thinking about her. Get your head in the game."

It was just like when I lost in the Ulster finals. "You're going soft. She's a distraction. You're destined for glory." I carried that pressure every day, and I could bear it because I had you. You were my life, Ela. You were never a choice.'

His fists were clenched so tight, his knuckles turned milk bottle white. His grip gradually eased, and he allowed her fingers to link his. 'I'm here now' she whispered, and before long, they started undressing one another.

#

Father O'Dowd sat in his rocking chair and watched the sun set over Glenwilliam Bay. His pipe lay packed on the window sill. He crossed his arms, warm in his beige woollen cardigan and feeling a world away from the Church of the Resurrection. The glow of the horizon spilled in through the window. It did him good. He'd arranged to go fishing at dawn. He reached for his pipe and enjoyed a last moment's solitude.

## Chapter 18

Dermot Robinson spent the morning at home to work on his story. He promised the editor it was his best scoop in years. Dermot knew Francis Nelson was a hell of a promoter, seeing it for himself in the lead-up to the Wolfhound card. He now understood the scale of his ambition and what it could bring to Shamrock Hills. The writer in him could feel it. Boxing could yet transcend the town's fortunes. As the wave of euphoria passed, he returned to the article at hand and cut three weighty paragraphs. He often got ahead of himself.

Leonard Grant had a day to get his brother on side, so he invited him for a morning of golf. Vincent had one of the best drives in the county. It always left Leonard playing catchup, and this morning was no different. 'Will you make the trip to Liverpool next month?' he asked as he lined up a putt for birdie.

Vincent refrained from answering till the ball had trickled past the hole. 'Yeah. We can make a weekend of it.'

Vincent proceeded to make birdie, leaving clear daylight between the brothers with five holes to go. Leonard took an impossibly long time on his next attempt, studying the curvature of the green and taking several practice strokes. His eventual attempt stopped half an inch short. Vincent smiled as they meandered to the next hole.

The nearby hawthorn trees were budding after a long, harsh winter. There was still a chill in the air, so the brothers kept their fleeces on despite the sun breaking through the clouds. Vincent's ball landed in the rough from a rash swing and a sure sign of complacency. He cursed as Leonard polished the head of his five-iron.

'What if we all went next month? You, me, Danny, Paddy?' Leonard asked. He measured the fairway as his eyes squinted against the sunlight. Vincent tapped a cigarette off his packet. 'That's a bit rich for your blood, no?'

'Aye, I suppose it is.' Leonard caught the ball sweetly, and its flight stayed flat before landing comfortably on the narrow fairway. 'You won't like what I'm about to say, but hear me out, brother.'

#

Paddy Hughes had never held a five-iron in his life. Growing up, the budget for extra-curricular activities didn't extend to golf. The orphanage had a decent-sized field for cricket and football, but he didn't take to either game. There were too many variables. Too many impediments to winning.

Boxing wasn't like that. Once in the ring, the difference between winning and losing was comparatively simple, and in a complex and menacing world, Paddy found comfort in simplicity. It made no difference whether it was a school hall tournament or a packed-out arena. As long as four ropes skirted a twenty-foot canvas and the gloves fit his fists, it was the fairest place he knew.

He studied his docket one more time. Newmarket. 3:30pm: Wayward line: 7 to 1. He looked around him. The Punt House was thick with smoke and thrummed with the noise of six televisions. Betters combed the race papers and studied the form. He told himself that he'd earned the right to have a flutter. The remainder of his fight purse was still to be sent. He wiped his palms on his tracksuit bottoms, not wanting to smudge the docket, and approached the counter.

#

Vincent tried for the sixth time. Francis Nelson had given him his personal line after Breen's win at the Wolfhound. While Vincent hadn't placed great value in the gesture, he now knew the true extent of its futility. 'Pick up you wanker!' Leanne tried to comfort her man. Her soft manicured fingers roamed over the rough stubble of his neck. 'The girls need picked up from swimming', she whispered.

Vincent raised the back of his hand and walked to the sitting room window, oblivious to the fading clicks of his wife's heels as she left by the back door. His phone sounded, but it was his brother, Leonard. 'No, he's not answering his phone. What do you mean give him time?' Vincent's voice strained with exasperation as his cigarette burned in the ashtray. He lit another. 'He's treating us like lackeys, brother.'

Dark patches had formed under the arms of his Burberry shirt. He checked his watch. No whiskey before

8pm. He promised Leanne. He hung up the phone, tossing it hard against the sofa, and grabbed the keys to his Alfa. He needed to speak with Fitzy.

#

Jimmy Breen parked his Audi and walked up the hill to the Cloverhill flats. He had been to see his mother. The visit had been cut short on the advice of her carer, Anne Simpson. Such occurrences were now happening daily. Still, Eileen Breen was in the right wing. It was good news for the family, and Jimmy made a point of visiting each of his siblings, starting with Danny.

He talked him through the latest set-up at Serenity house, the breakdown of costs and the new course of medications. He stacked the papers and returned them neatly to their binder. 'That's everything, and she's paid up for the foreseeable. Are you okay for money?'

Danny nodded. The remainder of his Wolfhound purse had cleared. It was the single best payday of his life. Jimmy stood to leave but lingered on the spot. He shuffled his car keys as his eyes scanned the apartment.

'I watched the fight. You put on a hell of a show.'

Danny's eyes softened, and his mouth curled in amusement. 'I took a battering, Jimmy. And that's the fight you watched?'

Jimmy smirked back. 'I haven't forgotten that bloody nose you gave Connor. You were due a good duffing up.'

Danny saw him to the door. Turning the handle, Jimmy paused, again grappling for words as he scraped at a smudge on the floor with the sole of his shoe. 'Visit Ma soon, Danny.'

Danny returned to his bed and took Ela in his arms. 'That was Jimmy. Says I should visit Ma soon.'

Ela slid from under him and propped herself on her elbow. 'When was the last time you visited?'

Danny didn't know where to look. The four walls of his bedroom reflected his shame of the truth. 'It's been a while since I visited Ma… but I visited Da the other day. He didn't say much. No change there.'

Ela held her pose and studied him intently. 'I'll go with you, if you think that would help.'

Danny kissed her on the forehead. 'I'll think about it.'

#

## SHAMROCK INVASION

*By Dermot Robinson*

*Chief Sports writer: The Shamrock Gazette*

*In a shock move by fledgling promoter, Francis 'Big Daddy' Nelson, Liverpool middleweights, Davey Hibbert and Kevin Neary, will face Shamrock Hills fighters, Danny Breen and Paddy Hughes.*

*Following hot on the heels of Breen's twelve round win against Ricky Murray and Hughes' stunning knockout of Peter Simmons, Nelson, in cooperation with GBT, has decided the time is now to crown the first UBF middleweight champion of the world.*

*Said Nelson, 'Why pad out the boxing calendar with meaningless fights? My boxers are raring to go. They had a good look at the Shamrock Boys last month and they fancy doing a job on them. Hibbert and Neary have Irish grandparents which adds another dimension to the event. They can't wait to show their Celtic warrior spirit.'*

*They are indeed good matchups and interest will soar at the official pre-fight presser. At the time of writing, it is set for next Friday afternoon at St Geroge's Hall, Liverpool. Those who follow the sport closely will raise an eyebrow regarding the respective fighters' training arrangements.*

*Both Breen and Hughes fight out of the aptly named 'Celtic Fist' boxing club in Shamrock Hills, while Hibbert and Neary ply their trade at Mersey Gloves ABC in Liverpool. Asked for his opinion on the situation and the very real possibility of stablemates progressing to the final, Nelson responded, 'This is the fight game and they are professionals. All they'll be thinking about is winning on April fourth.'*

*Nelson is never stuck for an answer, but one must wonder what the atmosphere in camp will be like as fight night creeps closer. In particular, Barney Fitzpatrick will have his hands full at the Celtic Fist gym. Paddy 'One shot'*

*Hughes made no secret of his ambition to face all-comers in a fiery post-fight interview, inviting the possibility of a local tear-up with Breen and disparaging the achievements of Shamrock Hills' favourite son, Luke 'Quick Hands' Gibson. Hughes has cut a frustrated figure since his move from Ballywell, overlooked by Fitzpatrick who has coached Breen since the amateurs.*

*And the intrigue does not stop there. According to a Liverpool source, Davey Hibbert and Kevin Neary have been on a collision course ever since their three days of sparring with Breen. Hibbert, the older and more seasoned of the two, was given what Neary described as a 'humbling' by the Shamrock Express. Asked on his own performance in sparring, he was quoted as saying, 'Hibbert made me look good.' The fighters' trainer, the esteemed Tommy Brown, was not available for comment.*

*It promises to be a fantastic night of boxing in Liverpool. I am tipping Paddy Hughes to finish Neary in five rounds. The former Ballywell man looks strong at middleweight, and I sense that this fight is coming a little early for Neary, though anything can happen when two big punchers collide. Blink and you could miss it.*

*As for Breen versus Hibbert, I lean towards the Liverpool man. He is the younger, fresher fighter, and while the sparring stories offer encouragement for Breen, my gut feeling is that the Shamrock Express will be derailed on April 4$^{th}$.*

Dermot checked his watch. The Gazette office closed in thirty minutes. He gave his draft one last read. 'Only in boxing', he said to himself.

## Chapter 19

Eileen Breen had been a sound sleeper since she was a little girl. As she entered middle age, she continued to enjoy a good eight hours per night. 'A clear mind rests well,' she often said. Arthur Breen was less fortunate. Switching between morning and night shifts made it all the harder to rest, and with four growing kids in a semi-detached house, he'd often return to work dead on his feet. As a rule, he wasn't the complaining type, though he unleashed the occasional tirade in Fitzy's ear as Danny toiled on the heavy bag in the Celtic Fist gym.

Eileen worried about Danny turning pro, but Arthur promised he'd take care of him. She believed Arthur and understood that boxing was his outlet. Eileen's was dancing. It had been since her primary school days… but there was a period when she'd stopped going to the halls. People wondered.

Whatever the cause, she would not have sat back while her son's girlfriend talked herself out of a leading role in the Saint Brigid's Girls' Christmas play. Ela Bond was a strong singer and capable actress, but she lacked a background in dancing. True to her nature, Eileen became a kind and willing mentor.

However, they faced a logistical problem. Given the size of their terraced house, the Breen family living room had its limitations as a place of learning. That and it was already a place of learning for Arthur and Danny.

Blocking their view of the television could not be tolerated now that Fitzy's fight videos had become vital study sessions. They studied all the greats. Jack Johnson, Mike Tyson, Harry Greb, Salvador Sanchez, Carlos Monzon… a never-ending library of fighters and their greatest nights. The bravery on display, the calmness of the fighters as they engaged in fistic battle, the ring canvas painted in fresh sweat and blood.

It was art to Arthur though he couldn't have described it as such. After all, he was a man of few words. The local YMCA hall, he suggested, was much more spacious, and Eileen and Ela were soon persuaded to stay on for the line dancing class. They attended every week until Eileen's stroke.

#

'Daddy!' Eileen screamed from her room in Serenity House. 'We'll be late for church!' Her carer, Anne Simpson, slowly adjusted the dimmer light. 'It's still a bit early for church' she said, calmly lifting a picture from the dresser. Eileen watched her suspiciously. Her duvet was tucked up to her chin, and her eyes slowly adjusted to the light as Anne perched by her bedside.

She rolled onto her side and studied the picture. She ran a long finger over the face of her father. 'That's me and my daddy at the dancing' she announced proudly, matching the beauty of the little girl's smile. Anne crept slowly to the door and gradually dimmed the light.

Danny too was having a restless night. A four-week training camp left little time to get primed for battle. He knew he was a better boxer than Hibbert, but sparring wasn't fighting, and the Liverpool man would be a different proposition at Stanley Hall. He told Vincent he'd talk it over with Fitzy when the gym opened. He re-plumped his pillows in a final attempt at sleep.

Across the estate, a cup of coffee sat cooling on the kitchen table. The morning edition of the Gazette was balled up and rammed into the waste bin. Fitzy had a month to prepare two fighters for their biggest night, and having the local sportswriter stir trouble was beyond the pale.

'We should pull them out, Fitzy. It's obvious what he's doing. It's set up for Danny and Paddy to lose. He's just playing the Irish card to build a bigger fight between the Liverpool boys.'

Fitzy invited Vincent to sit.

'I don't like this either', pointing at the Grant brother's copy of the Gazette, 'but Danny has two more fights in him, and this is the most money he's going to make. Two fights, two wins and he's world champion.'

Vincent shook his head. He was expecting more fight from the 'Irish Pitbull'. 'I warned Leonard that Nelson is a slimeball, but he's hitched himself to the idea that a big night is coming here. Nelson won't look twice at Shamrock Hills if he gets what he wants next month.'

'You're probably right' replied Fitzy. 'Nelson is just another shit talker in a business full of shit talkers...' He again pointed to Robinson's article. 'I didn't speak to him. Did you?'

'You know I didn't. What's your point?'

'I think you know what my point is. When I went to Liverpool, I knew there was more in the works than just sparring.'

Vincent shrugged. 'We already talked about it. My stake in the gym is part of Grant Enterprises. That's the only reason Leonard was contacted in the first place.'

Fitzy dismissed the argument with a shake of his head. 'We didn't know we'd be seeing Leonard in Liverpool, and I don't think that was an accident. And let's say you are right about next month, that the whole thing is rigged for the Liverpool fighters. It still leaves Danny with one more fight on his deal, and where else would the money be if not right here for a farewell showing against Hughes?'

Vincent's lip began to twitch as he again scanned the article. He looked up at Fitzy. 'You think Leonard fed this to Robinson, don't you?'

Fitzy shrugged his shoulders. 'Maybe. Maybe not. And really, what does it matter? It's done now. All I'm concerned about is Danny, and you should be too. This is all we need to know... Nelson will look to get the most out of Danny's deal, and we should do the same for Danny. I say we take the Hibbert fight. Beat him and Danny fights for the title. If he loses, he holds out for a fight with Paddy.'

Vincent looked at the framed picture of Danny and struggled to recall the year. He was fairly sure it was 1987. Arthur was still alive, and Fitzy looked healthy and considerably leaner. But Danny... for some reason, he saw the biggest change in him. He turned back to face Fitzy. 'You think Hughes is going to win the tournament, don't you?

Fitzy lit a cigarette.

'I asked you a question.'

'I heard you. Aye, if I was putting money on it, I think he blows them away... Danny included'.

'You don't think Danny could beat him?'

Fitzy flicked the ash from his cigarette and exhaled deeply. In his other hand, he tapped the edge of a coaster off his coffee table. 'I doubt he will get past Hibbert. Styles make fights, and at this stage of Danny's career, Hibbert is all wrong for him'.

'So, it's simple. We pull him out of the tournament and look at other options.'

Fitzy shook his head. 'There aren't any, Vincent. Danny's best years are behind him. He's a hard sale now. This tournament is as good as it's ever going to get. You have to trust me on that.'

Vincent tossed the paper to the floor. 'So that's it? We dance to his tune? How does that make us any better than Nelson?'

Fitzy looked beyond Vincent to the picture of Danny's professional debut. 'You didn't enter the game to become a good man, did you? Danny has two fights left. It's time we stopped dreaming. We do what's right for him, not what makes us good men.'

#

Oblivious to the storm that was breaking, Paddy Hughes returned to Shamrock Views after a brisk five-mile run. A black land rover occupied his parking space. Passing it, three short blasts came from its owner, Leonard Grant.

'You're a hard boy to get hold of. Rent is the first Monday of the month.' Leonard raised his sunglasses to his forehead. 'Not a problem, is it?'

Paddy was slow to answer as Leonard pushed open the passenger's door. The former orphan slid in, aware of his sweat-drenched back soaking the leather interior. Leonard chuckled as his hand slid over the steering wheel. 'I suppose you wouldn't know who owns the Punt House. Well, you're looking at him.'

Given Paddy's history in Ballywell, spreading his bets would have made sense, but he liked the Punt House, and after his first big win, he doubled down hard for another. The folly of his actions was only now beginning to dawn.

'I'm only joking about the rent. It's Vincent's property, not mine. He won't ask for a penny till next month's fight purse clears.'

Paddy glanced at him bemusedly. 'I don't have a fight date.'

Leonard smiled. 'You didn't read the paper this morning, did you? Well, I'm pleased to tell you that you've been added to the Celtic Four tournament. You'll be fighting Kevin Neary in Stanley Hall, Liverpool. April fourth. How does that grab you, son?'

Adrenaline coursed through the young fighter's body. He'd gone two long years without a fight. Now, he was two wins away from a world tile belt. 'I won't let you down, sir. I won't let any of you down. I know I'm a great fighter'.

Leonard slapped his shoulder. 'I see great potential in you, and so does Francis Nelson. He thinks you're a character. The press conference is this Friday, and then it's three weeks till fight night. You ready to give boxing 100%?'

'Yes… I was born ready.'

Good. And here. This is to tide you over.'

Leonard passed him an envelope. 'Nelson knows you've not been looked after in the gym. That's all about to change. Francis can't say it publicly, but he reckons you're the favourite for the title.'

Paddy flicked through the thick wad of notes. 'Tell him I said thanks.'

Leonard started the engine and pulled down his sunglasses. 'You can tell him yourself on Friday. He's looking forward to seeing you. Till then, Paddy, stay well clear of the Punt House.'

#

In Serenity House, Anne Simpson checked on Eileen throughout the day. She understood the condition, knowing it would leave her with no yesterday to remember and no hope of a better tomorrow. The first stroke confined her to a wheelchair where she strained like a newborn to form words. The doctor was confident she'd bounce back. Physically she did, but Eileen's mind would never recover.

After the second stroke, Connor was first to notice a more fundamental change. His mother accused him of hiding her money, moving the ornaments and plotting to sell the house from under her. It was too much to bear, and a family decision was made to move her to the care home.

Anne walked with Danny and Ela to Eileen's room. 'I'll sit in for the first few minutes. If she gets agitated, reach for one of the pictures on her dresser. She likes looking at them.'

Eileen sat by the window. She looked at Anne beggingly, gripping her wrist as the armchair slowly turned towards Danny and Ela. She scratched the arm of Anne's cardigan. 'He's very handsome', she whispered as her cheeks began to blush.

'Do you remember me?' asked her second-born son.

Eileen shook her head.

'It's Danny.'

His mother grinned. 'I have a wee boy called Danny. I have three boys and one girl.' She looked around the room, and her eyes suddenly filled with worry. 'Where's the children?'

Ela lifted a picture from the dresser. 'Look Eileen, here's a picture of you and your kids.'

Eileen studied the faces in the picture and looked back to Danny. She whispered to Ela, 'He can sleep on my bed if he's tired. I don't mind.'

Ela kissed her brow as Eileen's attention returned to the photo. Her finger stopped on Arthur. 'Oh, I know him. He took me to see the Swinging Chords.'

'That's right' replied Ela. 'You and Arthur are married, and you have four children. See them? There's Jimmy, Danny, Dee and Connor.'

Eileen laughed excitedly as Ela wiped the spit from her chin with a handkerchief. 'Is he your husband?' she asked, looking in Danny's direction. 'Does he work hard?'

'He's a boxer' replied Ela.

#

Outside, Danny heaved at the gate of the care home. His knees trembled as he struggled to catch his breath. Ela steered him to the nearest bench where he sobbed for the first time since his father died.

## Chapter 20

Francis Nelson spent the morning taking calls. The media wanted a piece in advance of the press conference at St George's Hall. His team worked furiously to get everything ready. The press passes had arrived, and the fight banner was ready for print. Nelson's switchboard again lit up with an incoming call from Peter Harrod of GBT.

'Is Hughes locked in?' he asked.

'We're almost there' replied Nelson

'Get it done. You've got till midnight'.

Harrod hung up. Nelson sifted through his address book as his free hand hovered over the dial pad. Pausing, he drummed his knuckles off the polished mahogany desk and pondered whether a local touch was needed. He dialled the number. 'Leonard, it's urgent. How far are you from Ballywell?... Yes, today... I'll fax you the details.'

#

Tension was rising in the Mersey Gloves gym. Hibbert and Neary had been on the warpath ever since the Liverpool

Chronicle leaked the sparring stories. Hibbert was adamant that Neary had run his mouth, and Tommy Brown was forced to bring in extra sparring partners. There was no way he was letting them beat lumps out of each other so close to fight night.

Gym rivalries were nothing new, and Tommy welcomed competition, but Neary and Hibbert were now rivals beyond the confines of Mersey Gloves ABC. If both emerged victorious in Stanley Hall, they'd face off for the middleweight championship of the world.

That was the position Francis Nelson had left them in, and it wasn't how Tommy Brown wanted to conduct his business, but for now he was trainer to both. He'd devised his best gameplans to topple the Shamrock fighters. Hibbert's job was to take Danny Breen into the latter rounds and drown him. Tommy was growing in confidence that Hibbert would emerge victorious so long as he showed some defensive discipline.

However, he was less sure about Neary's chances against Paddy Hughes. Much depended on his thumb holding up. Without his left hand working at full capacity, he'd be forced to slug, and that played right into Hughes' hands. Neary needed to be 100 percent fit, and with only three weeks till fight night, the signs were not good. There were only two reasons a fighter pulled his punches in sparring. Either he wanted to go easy on an opponent or he was trying to mask an injury. The sparring partner was walking through Neary's jab, typically the latter's signature punch.

Tommy immediately called an end to the spar and cut the padding and wrap from Neary's left hand. He pressed on the thumb from the face of the nail to the point of the wrist. Neary winced in agony. Tommy then submerged the hand in a bucket of ice. 'Keep it in there, kid. I've got a call to make.'

As Tommy waited to be connected to Francis Nelson, he saw Davey Hibbert enter the gym. He looked in superb shape as he passed the office window. Arcing his neck, Tommy noticed that Neary had abandoned the ice bucket and was shaking his head disconsolately. 'Give me strength', his coach muttered as the music cut out.

'Tommy, is this urgent? We're balls to the wall here!' snapped Francis Nelson.

'Kevin's done his thumb again. We haven't had it checked, but it looks like a break.'

An exasperated sigh crackled down the line. 'Then get it seen to. You're a trainer, not a physician.'

Nelson slammed down the phone and walked to the office window. It had been a rough week for the fledgling boxing promoter. The city council was taking him for a fiscal ride, charging through the nose for the use of Stanley Hall. He'd already pumped thousands into the promotion. To pull out now would be a fatal blow to the 'Big Daddy' brand not to mention a severing of ties with GBT. His switchboard lit up. 'Francis, I've been to Ballywell and spoken to Sammy Stewart. He accepts the terms.'

'That's good. I want him out here by tomorrow night.'

'Ok. I'll arrange it. And what about Paddy?'

'That's not your concern, Leonard. Hear no evil, speak no evil.'

#

In the Celtic Fist gym, Fitzy had doubts about Danny. He was the classier boxer and had a superior ring IQ to Hibbert, but there was no cheating father time. Hibbert was bang in his prime and fought like a wind-up toy, whereas Danny was the wrong side of thirty and coming off a taxing twelve-rounder. He could sense the weariness in his man.

In contrast, Paddy Hughes was training out of his skin. The extra poundage had given him more energy and considerably more weight on his punches. Neary was a decent fighter but far from the finished article. Fitzy expected Paddy to get the job done in style.

The aging trainer watched him shadowbox in the ring. He should have been elated for his fighter, but since Dermot Robinson's piece in the Gazette, Fitzy's resentment had steadily grown. The fighter he'd saved from the street had packed up and left without so much as a handshake, yet according to Robinson, Paddy Hughes was the one who felt discarded. He looked away from the ring. Seeing that Danny and McGinty had completed their circuits, his mind returned to the task at hand. 'Ok boys, it's time for sparring. Eight rounds. Easy on the power shots.'

Danny and McGinty raised their thumbs in agreement. Paddy's hands were already wrapped and, hearing talk of sparring, he came off the balls of his feet and turned to face Fitzy. 'What about me? Gary will be spent after eight rounds.' Fitzy kept his eyes on the timer. 'Ninety seconds left in the round, Paddy. Don't stop till you hear the bell.' Paddy stayed rooted to the spot. 'I need proper rounds too. I'm tired of you giving all your time to the golden boy.'

A firing rage lit Fitzy's eye as he stepped between the ropes. 'I'm the owner of this gym. *They* are sparring and *you* are hitting the bags!' Paddy spread his arms and presented his forehead, inviting the old man to meet it with his. Fitzy gripped Hughes by the throat and took aim at the bridge of his nose. McGinty and Danny quickly stepped between them.

'You're starting to believe your own hype, Paddy! You want smoke blown up your ass, go to the Gazette, but in here, you do as you're told!'

'I said nothing to nobody! It's not my fault the truth hurts, Fitzy!'

Danny hooked Paddy's arms and dragged him away. McGinty kept Fitzy pinned to the turnbuckle as the Ballywell brawler slipped between the ropes and out of the ring. Fitzy eyed his fighters. McGinty was barely a man. Paddy was a wild animal. Danny was the best prodigy to have graced his gym, but he now looked tired, drawn and every one of his thirty-two years. The Irish pitbull removed his stopwatch from around his neck. 'I'm done for today. Lock up when you leave.'

He sunk a meaty hook into the heavy-bag before ducking under the shutter and out of the gym.

## Chapter 21

The kettle came to the boil. Danny gripped the kitchen doorframe and allowed his weight to fall forward. He exhaled as the knots in his back popped and snapped. The faint scent of ginger and lemon reached his nostrils. It was not a flavour he cared for, but whoever made the tea chose the blend. Ela's face blushed with amusement. 'It's good for your immune system. It doesn't make you less of a man.'

Danny grinned and flexed his abdominals. She didn't like seeing him so lean. 'How was training?' she asked.

Removing his lips from the flowered scent of her neck, his eyes popped in faux alarm. 'Paddy got lippy and Fitzy flew off the handle and left.'

Ela mused a moment. Fitzy was known to lose it now and then but generally had skin like a crocodile. She blew on her tea. Her plump lips caressed the bridge of her cup. 'Maybe he's nervous. These next two fights are huge. Two wins and you're world champion.'

Danny smiled wryly. 'It's what Da always wanted. And Vincent… and Fitzy. You know, sometimes I wish

Fitzy wasn't there when Da died. Winning the title was my cross to bear, not his.'

'Or Vincent's…'

'Or yours. Do you remember after the Collins fight how close I was to packing it in? Maybe I should have. We wouldn't have lost those years. And who knows, maybe Da would still be here.' He drained the remainder of his tea.

Ela turned down the radio. 'I never told you this. I wish I had. After the Collins fight, your dad came to see me. He said it was best that I left you.'

'He said what?'

'He said that I was holding you back, and that if I loved you, the best thing was to leave and let you focus on boxing'.

Danny's mind raced back. He recalled the depressing grind of training in winter. His muscles cried for oxygen as his father pushed him harder than ever. He could still see the desperate urgency in his eyes.

'I'd already told Ma I wanted to marry you.'

'I know', Ela replied. 'That's why she gave me this.' She turned the ring on her finger. 'Your mum knew you wouldn't be giving it to me… but she still wanted me to have it.'

Danny studied the ring. 'Why are you telling me this now, Ela?'

'Because I was too much of a coward to tell you then. And to make you realize that you aren't fighting for him anymore. Or for Fitzy, or for Vincent. You're fighting for *you*, Danny. And whatever form that takes, whether it's in the ring or outside it, I am with you.'

Danny scratched at his scalp. His mind was in a whirlpool of doubt. His heart felt like it was drowning in the blood of old wounds. 'He had no right to do that. God forgive him. He had no right.'

Sleep eluded Danny that night. Memories of his father invaded his peace. The image of his mother, scared and alone in Serenity House, reappeared as the bedroom crept from pitch dark to grey. A sudden spring breeze brushed his blinds like a visiting ghost. The restlessness of the night had turned to anger by daybreak. Fitzy tried to keep them apart but was left with no choice. Paddy had been stalking the gym for days. He didn't need asking twice.

Danny gestured to the ring. 'You want the limelight, kid? You've got it. Just you and me'.

'Now you're talking.' Paddy replied.

Danny was an experienced pro and was wise enough to make his own decisions. The boxers skipped pleasantries and got straight down to business. Fitzy let the rounds run long. Sometimes fighters needed to fight.

#

Francis Nelson concluded his meeting with Sammy Stewart, flattering the Ballywell trainer with a three-night stay at the

Adelphi hotel. All remaining issues with the council had been ironed out. The final figure would still exceed the initial budget, but given where the numbers were a week ago, Nelson sat quietly satisfied. His receptionist knocked gently on his door. 'Mr Nelson, here is the report on Neary's injury.' Nelson slid the contents on to his desk. He could tell little from the x-ray so turned to the write-up.

- *MCP joint of left thumb.*
- *Metacarpal fracture (hairline)*
- *Splint cast (4 weeks)*

He reached for his phone and called Tommy Brown. It was a short exchange. His staff kept their heads safely behind their computers as 'Big Daddy' barked orders at the Mersey Gloves coach. 'No sparring or bag work till after the presser, and he's not to be seen out of the house with that splint…

… Shut up and get this through your thick head, Tommy. He's boxing on April fourth! He's the headliner! No excuses. This is the fight game we're in!'

# Chapter 22

High above Shamrock Hills lay thick woodland and blossoming shrubs. Years ago, a farmer made picnic tables from the wood of a fallen cedar, placing them in a clearing where his land ended and the forest began. They'd lasted well.

There was a choice of paths to the mouth of the Drumferry river. It was a seven-mile trek give or take. Vincent Grant was intimately familiar with the Applecross glen. As kids, he and his brother, Leonard, raced through the forest in their scrambler bikes. It was also a great venue for courtship. These days, a walk sufficed Vincent, and his company was the chirps of birds and the plume of cigarette smoke.

There was a particular lay-by he stopped at, securely fenced and skirting a steep drop. It overlooked a quartet of grey buildings. It was those he came to see, and where he stood was as close as he wished to get. He could still smell the mess hall, that sickly mix of bleach and boiled vegetables. He could still hear the echoes of steps after lights out.

He came not to reflect on the folly that kept him there for five long years but to remember the men he owed for his freedom. He thought of Willie Dunne and his life lessons. Willie was a talker, and each day, sixteen of Vincent's hours were shared with him in a ten-by-ten cell. Vincent didn't like yielding to anyone, but in Willie's case, playing the student to his master presented the path of least resistance.

'And what did Marcus Aurelius say of the mind, Vincent?'

'That we have power over our own mind and not outside events. Realize this and you will find strength.'

'And?'

'That happiness depends upon the quality of your thoughts.'

'Bravo. I'll make a gentleman of you yet, you terrible brute.'

Vincent laughed as he'd laughed then. They were the memories he wished to keep. It was Willie's voice that channelled his rage when the Gymnasium Four were moved to his block. 'I'm going to kill them,' he hissed in his prison bed, thumping the wall till the bones in his hand ached. Willie chuckled in his bunk, purposefully not settling till the pounding had ceased. 'Can you hear me, you awful brute? If your anger permits you, reach for that blue book.'

'I'm in no mood for a lesson, Willie!'

'Would you rather I talked all evening? Don't make an old man hoarse, you terrible brute.' Vincent rolled onto his feet. The squeaks of the bedsprings further grated his nerves. He reached the book to Willie.

'It's not for me. It's for you. Turn to the back.' A folded page was paperclipped to it. 'Go ahead. Open it.'

*My name is William Dunne, and I can read and write.*

*23rd of October 1969.*

'When I got here in 67, I couldn't spell my own name. I could have chosen to stay that way. I could have stayed thick and thran.'

'Why didn't you?' asked Vincent.

'Because even in the most terrible confinement, there is still a glimmer of light in the human soul. I chose to nourish mine with light.' He pointed to the cell block corridor. 'And if you go after those clowns that put a beating on you, you'll extinguish what's left of yours.'

A solitary tear broke from Vincent's right eye. He swiped it away as if the whole world had stopped to watch it drop. He dragged on the last of his cigarette and made his way back to the car. He had one more piece of business before the trip to Liverpool, but the Celtic Fist gym was locked up, and Paddy Hughes was not home.

#

Connor Breen was unpegging his washing when his brother, Jimmy, rounded the corner with an armful of groceries. He stumbled in the back door. Panthro lay snug on the kitchen top, nestled between the fryer and the bread-bin. 'Down, you wee shite!' spat Jimmy, dropping the bags onto the table. 'The meals are from Dee. Lasagnas, cottage pies and some other bits and pieces.'

He opened the freezer door and sulked at the sight of its contents. He fetched a chisel from the utility room. 'This is the last time I do this,' he vowed. Connor swept up the frozen debris. 'Is it faulty?' he asked.

Jimmy shook his head. 'No, it's just old. Stick the kettle on, would you? Black. One sugar.'

Connor brewed enough Kenco for two and poured out some kibble to keep the cats occupied. He scratched at his belly and picked the fluff from his navel. Jimmy took a deep breath and turned to watch the cats clear their trays. 'Do you know Ela Bond is back on the scene? I've nothing against the lass… but why revisit the past?'

Connor took his turn to watch the cats, smiling at Lyano as he stretched his back and hind legs. As always, he was the show-off of the two. 'I think it's nice Danny has someone again.'

The youngest of the Breens had a simple, unassuming view of the world that never failed to endear. It reminded Jimmy of their mother's sweetness… a sweetness that had never existed in him. She used to quip that her eldest son turned forty the day he was born. He must have taken after their father.

'Not long till Dad's anniversary', said Connor, as if reading his big brother's mind. 'Are we taking Ma this year?'

Jimmy repacked the freezer, dividing the savoury from the sweet and making space for Dee's dinners. 'No, it's just the four of us this year.'

He then bled the upstairs radiator before climbing onto the roof to adjust the tv ariel. The kettle clicked just in time for Countdown. Connor stroked Lyano and added more fur to his already filthy carpet. 'Why do you hate Danny?' he asked.

Jimmy kept his eyes on the TV. 'I don't hate him. I said I had a problem with him. It goes back a long time. Everything was about him. It was *his* training, *his* diet, *his* next fight. He never thought twice about what it was like for the rest of us, Ma included.'

Growing up, helping his mother was where Jimmy found his place in the family. Now, approaching forty years of age, he continued to visit Ma daily. Checking his watch, he realized it was visiting time at Serenity house. He readied to leave. Connor muted the television and followed his brother to the door. Lyano was tucked warm in his arms. 'The boxing got Da's time, not Danny.'

'At least he got something,' replied Jimmy.

#

The minutes passed slowly as Danny and Fitzy watched the appointment screen. Sparring was an occupational hazard, and niggles were par for the course, but with a fight three weeks away, Fitzy insisted they err on the side of caution. It was a fighter's job to be tough and a trainer's duty to observe. Fitzy could tell by how Danny was hitting the bags that something was wrong.

The doctor pressed on his side, checking each rib for the source of the pain. She saw the older abrasions, fading and browned, covered by the new like a rushed coat of paint. 'I don't think there is a break, but the bruising is a concern. I'll order a CT scan to get a better look.'

In the east wing of the hospital, Father O'Dowd stepped off the scales. The consultant asked whether he knew about the various meetings and groups. Out of good courtesy, he accepted the leaflets, knowing the coming months would be spent in solitude. He'd left his priest's collar in Glenwilliam, opting to blend with the crowd in jacketed tweed.

He was just another man with time to kill as he sipped a cup of tea. He rubbed at his chest, feeling the form of the crucifix in his breast pocket. *I can do all this through him who gives me strength.* He adjusted his flat cap and ran a hand over his beard. The last of the ginger had left his moustache. Glancing about him, he recognized the gait from their school days. He instinctively tucked the leaflets away and rose from his seat. 'Hello, Barney.'

Fitzy accepted his hand. It was big and strong like a bear paw. 'I wasn't sure it was you without the collar.'

Father O'Dowd smiled warmly. 'I'm taking some time away from the church.'

Fitzy looked him up and down. 'You've lost some timber, Michael. Is everything ok?'

O'Dowd nodded. 'I'm fine. I just had a bad bout of stomach flu. How are you keeping? I've read that things are testy at the gym.'

Fitzy rolled his eyes. 'When I see that scoundrel Robinson, I'll kick his arse so hard, he'll be wearing it for a hat.'

'I would urge you to turn the other cheek, but as you say, I'm not wearing my collar today.'

The two men happily reminisced. O'Dowd remembered the clobbering they gave each other on that cold Sunday afternoon after church. They were eleven and had their whole lives ahead of them. Now they were ageing men, Fitzy obese and one-eyed, O'Dowd wilting from cancer of the throat.

'What say you to a fishing day in Glenwilliam?'

Fitzy considered the offer. 'I fish to eat these days, not to relax.'

O'Dowd patted his arm. 'In Glenwilliam we can do both.'

They shook hands and parted ways. By the time Fitzy returned to his fighter, the extent of the damage was clear.

#

The man who'd inflicted it was sat in the lounge bar of the Adelphi hotel, cutting into a thick sirloin steak, cooked medium rare. Alongside him sat Sammy Stewart, Paddy's first boxing trainer. Sammy liked his steak well done.

They made quick work of them, neither man being well versed in the rules of fine dining. Paddy tilted his plate and funnelled the peppery juice into his waiting mouth. His head was freshly shaved, and his skin was a healthy glow bar the nasty swelling on his right brow.

'How recent was that?' asked Sammy.

'Yesterday,' Paddy curtly replied.

'Did you get the better of it?'

Paddy chewed hard on his steak as the muscles in his temples pulsated. 'I'd have him in a real fight.'

## Chapter 23

The final call was made for John Lennon airport, and there was still no sign of Paddy Hughes. Vincent Grant had a forty-minute flight to make up his reasons. The headline fighter not attending the presser was a terrible look, and as manager, the buck stopped with him. He had been told to prepare his fighters for a two-day promotional hoopla. That alone said much about the kind of money Francis Nelson was committing to the fight card.

He hadn't anticipated a stay in the Adelphi, but checking in to their rooms, even Fitzy, a man used to the rough side of life, felt considerably irked. Nelson, he mused, would have treated his dogs to better. After a quick look, Vincent agreed and made other arrangements.

He then checked his watch. The press conference was in a couple of hours. Reception arranged his taxi to the Dale Road and the office of Nelson Promotions. On the way, he leafed through his papers, checking he had the contracts, licenses and medical certificates. When he arrived, the office was thronging with people. Mr Nelson, he was told, was in a meeting with Peter Harrod of GBT.

#

'So, let's run through the schedule again' continued Harrod. The presser starts at 2pm and then we go to the Liver Bird Tower for the face-offs, and then back here for press interviews.'

'And tomorrow, we have the function room booked at the Adelphi for photography and video,' added Nelson.

'And about Ireland...we have one day to film there. We'd prefer to swerve this Ballywell place.'

Nelson raised his palms. 'We'll keep it in Shamrock Hills. Not an issue.'

Finishing their coffees, they made their way out of the office. Seeing Vincent Grant, Nelson grabbed the arm of a passing employee. 'Have Sophie take care of Mr Grant, and make sure Mark from Legal sits in.'

Vincent rose from his feet as the two men approached.

'Welcome to Liverpool, Vincent. Sophie will be with you now. We'll see you at the presser.'

Nelson had barely broken step before releasing himself from Vincent's hand. Vincent followed them to the elevator.

'Francis, there's an issue. Paddy wasn't able to make it today.'

Nelson gestured to Harrod to hold the elevator door and laid his other hand on Vincent's elbow.

'Paddy arrived in Liverpool a couple of days ago. He came early for some sparring. I assumed you knew. Well, no harm no foul, eh? Hope the hotel is ok.'

He slapped the Grant brother's back and made for the elevator. As its door closed in the face of an irate Vincent Grant, Sophie acted on cue and directed him to her office. She scanned Danny's papers, stamping them with the company seal and making up a receipt. She looked over Paddy's and paused. 'It says here that Mr Hughes is represented by Grant Enterprises. Odd.'

#

The St Geroge's hall presser was in a different league to the Wolfhound card. The GBT team, naturally, had pride of place. From the balcony, Fitzy surveyed the growing crowd. Upwards of three hundred fans had shown up and were already producing a cacophony of noise. He spotted 'Big Daddy' Nelson conversing with the President of the UBF. Fitzy studied the men and wondered whether he'd one day wear a tailored suit to a presser. He then saw Tommy Brown on the far side of the balcony, dressed like he'd just finished a gym session. In a sport that excessively courted razmataz, he was glad to see another man staying true to the old school.

When their eyes met, the Mersey Gloves trainer made his way over, bumping fists with Danny and squeezing the hand of his old coaching adversary. 'We go again, Barney. I hope you aren't as prolific with the pros as you were with the schoolboys,' he ribbed. He then rested a hand on Fitzy's back and leaned in. 'I've told my boys to keep it nice up there.'

'I'll do the same, but I might give you a good shellacking.'

'Chance would be a fine thing. It's just the fighters and Nelson up there. We're seated in row two.'

Danny assumed that Fitzy would be sat to his left. He had never graced such a stage and was only a showman inside of the ring. A rep from GBT took him to one side to explain the procedure. 'You'll be introduced first and will enter from the left. Walk to the middle, pose for the cameras, turn and sit on the far left. Don't tamper with the microphones.'

Fitzy checked his watch. He didn't notice Sammy Stewart enter. Down below, Vincent Grant bleated at the President of the UBF, Carlos Bernardi. His brother, Leonard, watched on.

#

Dermot Robinson of the Shamrock Gazette was seated in the same row as the trainers as Francis Nelson took to the microphone. 'We are delighted to present, on April fourth at Stanley Hall, Liverpool, the Celtic Four semi-final.'

The stage curtain went back, revealing the official fight banner. The faces of the fighters combined to form a four-leaf clover of fire. With much fanfare, the UBF president presented the title belt. It was a fine-looking bauble. Its face was solid gold, and the trim was dotted with gemstones. The leather was a rich Egyptian blue. Carlos Bernardi held it aloft. He had a showman's instinct... and he was a hell of a speaker. Made to wait longer than rehearsed, Francis Nelson looked slightly crestfallen.

Danny Breen stood by the stage. His throat was dry, and his forehead shone with sweat. The cameras flashed white as he entered, blinding his view of the crowd. The local fans greeted him with a tumult of boos. His opponent, Hibbert, came next, breaking into a shadowbox and pumping his fist. Then came Neary.

Francis Nelson hushed the crowd. 'And last, but certainly not least, he's come out of nowhere, announcing himself on the world stage with a devasting knockout of Peter Simmons. Please welcome the undefeated, the ferocious, Paddy 'One Shot' Hughes.'

Paddy entered the stage wearing a floral open-collar shirt and matching waistcoat. His wrist sported a new Cartier watch. He patted the UBF belt before taking his seat next to Danny. Fitzy's eyes darted between Nelson, Sammy Stewart and the boy he'd saved from the street. He leaned into Vincent and whispered, 'Looks like we've both been had.'

Paddy stole the show, vowing to take out Neary in two. Dermot Robinson asked about his relationship with Danny Breen and the Celtic Fist gym. 'The Celtic Fist was just a place to train. I've nothing more to do with the place or the people there. I'm back with Sammy Stewart, so forget this Liverpool versus Shamrock Hills talk. I'm a Ballywell man, and this tournament is about me getting my hands on the belt!'

Inside, Danny was hurting. He'd done his best for the kid, but there Paddy sat, attacking his gym and the coach he considered family. Out of respect for both, he did not stoop to his level. When asked to respond, Danny answered, 'I'm fighting Hibbert on the fourth of April. My focus is on him and him only.'

Later that afternoon, as the fighters posed at the Liver bird tower for pictures, Hibbert went at Danny. 'Your legs are shot. There's no hiding place for you on April fourth. You're entering the pit of hell,' he snarled. Danny stood his ground. He'd never bought into the pre-fight mind games. As far as he was concerned, fights were won or lost in the gym.

Paddy Hughes and Kevin Neary traded obscenities. The Ballywell man proclaimed he was ready to kill or be killed. Nelson and Harod kept within arm's reach of the fighters. The Celtic Four then posed as a quartet for photographers. Paddy, satisfied that he'd decimated the psyche of Neary, started on Hibbert.

'You're the one who can't hold a shot, eh? If Breen can wobble you, I'll flatline you. But don't worry. You'll be fine on the fourth. Breen's ribs are as weak as your chin.'

That evening, Vincent combed over the fine print of Paddy's contract. He grew in defiance, brandishing the document in Fitzy's face. 'It is food off our table, and I won't stand for it. When I see Nelson tomorrow, I'll speak a language he understands.'

Fitzy pointed an accusing finger. 'Danny's not to be used as leverage! You want compensated for Paddy… Ok, what you sign, I'll sign, but keep Danny out of it. It's nothing to do with him.'

'I agree, but they don't have to know that.' He again brandished the contract. 'Between this and Danny not being on the card, Nelson's ass will flap so hard, he'll call himself an ambulance. Just wait and see. All warfare is based on deception.'

The next morning, after refusing the offer of lattes, Vincent and Fitzy sat down with Sophie and Mark from Nelson's legal department. 'Our position is simple' stated Vincent. 'We expect to be compensated for Paddy's next two fights. This was agreed as part of our promotional agreement with Francis Nelson. If it isn't sorted, we will walk away from our obligations, starting with the Stanley Hall card.'

Sophie, having diligently made notes, smiled warmly at Vincent and Fitzy before rising to her feet. 'Thank you very much for coming, gentleman. I think I have everything I need and will liaise with Mr Nelson. I'm sure we will find a solution that's acceptable to you. Meanwhile, Mark will walk you through the finer legalities.'

Mark launched into legal jargon as the door closed behind Sophie. He insisted that a legal dispute was not in the company's interest, but in the event a case was brought to them, the document he passed to Vincent itemized the claims of their client, one Patrick Hughes.

- Inhospitable accommodation provided
- Insufficient financial support
- Failure to secure sponsorships

- Failure to secure prize fights
- Failure to provide a boxing license
- Inadequate training facilities
- One instance of physical harm
- Multiple instances of verbal abuse

Vincent looked to Fitzy who knew the battle was won before it was fought. Mark broke the tension in the room. 'As I said, we do not wish to pursue this matter through legal channels. I cannot speak for Mr. Nelson's motivations in signing Mr. Hughes, but from a legal standpoint, Mr. Hughes approached our company as a free agent. This contract you've presented, if I may speak frankly, will be laughed out of court.'

#

Danny was drained from the promotion, from the hours in front of the cameras and from interview after interview with journalists. He made sure Dermot Robinson was kept till last, but in the big scheme of things, Dermot was the least of his concerns. GBT had the fighters strip down to their trunks and pose for fight portraits. The welt on Danny's ribs was the size of a grapefruit. Seeing it, Hibbert smiled at his coach, Tommy Brown.

Paddy Hughes had been watching Neary like a hawk. He had known the minute he clapped eyes on him that something was amiss. It took him until the second day to figure it out, noticing the slightest of winces as Neary's coach fastened his gloves for the fight portraits.

That evening in the Adelphi hotel, Paddy cut into another thick steak with Francis Nelson and Sammy Stewart. His confidence was soaring. By contrast, the Shamrock Hills team cut sorry figures while they waited to board their return flight to Belfast. Vincent, in lieu of having Nelson to fight, turned on Fitzy, but the aging trainer didn't bite. They'd both dropped the ball with Paddy Hughes… and they knew it.

In a sense, Fitzy almost admired Paddy for walking away. And what difference did it make where he went? Fitzy had seen it all in his half century in boxing, and what transpired in Liverpool was just one more wound in the hundreds he'd suffered. Knowing that, Fitzy felt for Vincent. His deepest wound was yet to come.

## *Chapter 24*

A fountain pen, some blank sheets of paper and a dozen envelopes were tidily arranged on an old wooden desk. It had recently been given a fresh coat of varnish, but there was no disguising the woodworm or the blue stain of the ink well. For all Father O'Dowd knew, the desk was older than the man sitting over it. His cardigan was wrapped tight across his hollowing torso, and tufts of white hair half-covered his ears. Mid-morning was when he wrote, and he wished to keep some semblance of his old routine. He reached for his diary and browsed his notes before dating the first of the letters.

*Dear Dierdre,*

*I hope this letter finds you well. I am writing to let you know that I cannot attend your father's anniversary mass as I will still be on sabbatical.*

*I have left instructions with Father Carrigan who I am sure you have spoken to by now. I hope all is well with you and your family. While this is sure to be a painful week for you all, be assured that I am with you in prayer and fellowship.*

*Yours in Christ,*

*Father O'Dowd*

He was good with the pen. Men of his age tended to be. Amusement twinkled in his eyes as he recalled helping Barney Fitzpatrick with joined up writing. His old altar friend was a natural left-hander which was a mortal sin for its time. The priest let out a weak chuckle. His throat was dry and strained as he reached for a fresh page.

#

Jimmy Breen checked his watch. He had been in Serenity House for just ten minutes, and the realization affronted him. Inclination made him look over his shoulder, but it was just he and his mother in the room. Eileen faced the window and watched the birds flitting to and from the apple tree. 'What birds do you see today, Ma?'

She let out a dry tut. 'Blackbirds. All they do is squabble.'

He glanced at the pictures and wondered how his father ever stood a chance. Even in his twenties, he had the look of a haunted man. He reached for the picture of his college graduation and compared it to that of his father. The resemblance was uncanny. How could it be that father and son could look so alike yet have lived their lives barely knowing one another? Perhaps there was nothing to know. Maybe his mother was right. Maybe they were one and the same.

'What are you looking at, Arthur?' she asked.

Inclination got the better of him again, and when he looked over his shoulder, he saw Anne by the door, quietly scribbling on a notepad. He turned back to the picture in his hand. 'Just looking at you, Eileen. You look so beautiful.' She smiled in surprise. 'I still do, Arthur. I'm just getting on a bit'.

'Aye, so am I,' he agreed, returning the picture to its place on the dresser.

Anne covered her mouth. She'd had a busy morning, and the balls of her feet ached and burned. Elderly care was a tough profession, but every now and then, just when she thought she'd seen it all, something would bring a smile to her face.

#

In Cedar Heights, Vincent Grant stood in front of his living room mirror. He had been to the barbershop for a trim and a wet shave. His cologne stung the cuts on his neck as he again botched the trinity knot.

'Hold on, sweetheart. I'll do it for you', shouted his wife, Leanne, who blew at her freshly varnished nails. Burgundy was her colour for the day. It adorned her fingers, toes and the underwear below her silk gown. She crossed legs, and her hem climbed to mid-thigh. She slipped on her jewellery and made her way to the living room.

Vincent tried to disguise it, pretending that his sudden thirst was just a casual interest in the bottle's vintage.

Leanne looked him up and down. 'You always look good in a suit. Those big shoulders were made for them.' She turned up the collar. 'Rule number one. Never knot a tie with a folded collar.'

She stood on the tips of her toes, bringing her eyes level with his top shirt button. 'Rule number two. Know your ties. This one is made for a Windsor knot.'

'Don't be giving me a Windsor anything, Leanne. That's blasphemy', he joked.

'We can live with the knot,' she replied, working methodically at the tie. 'There. Tell me that doesn't look better.'

Vincent buttoned his waistcoat before puffing out his chest and widening his stance. 'Not bad', he proclaimed as Leanne wiped at the creases on his back.

'Turn, please.'

The belt of her gown was undone. As he turned, Vincent's nostrils filled with her scent. His previously worried eyes locked on hers. They were still as bright as the day he'd met her.

'I love you, Leanne.'

'Show me', she replied, unbuttoning his waistcoat as her gown slipped silently to the carpet.

#

Peter Harrod and the GBT team had reached Belfast. With interviews, gym footage and pan shots of Shamrock Hills to capture, time was of the essence. By sundown they'd be back in the capital for their return flight to Liverpool. For Harrod, the pressure was on, and the slightest rise in his voice shocked his team like an air raid siren.

At the Celtic Fist gym, Sammy Stewart had his fighter wait in the car. He and Fitzy went back a while, and he had no intention of ruffling feathers. 'I know as much as you do', he offered.

'You could have lifted the phone to me', replied Fitzy.

Sammy took a deep breath. 'I know.'

Fitzy smiled. 'It's okay, Sammy. We all need to earn a crust.'

When the GBT team reached Shamrock Hills, they quickly turned the Celtic Fist gym into a film studio, ordering the removal of fight posters and the screening of mirrors and heavy bags. 'Ok, I want the trainers in makeup now. Filming in fifteen minutes, so get the ring ready! Canvas, ropes, table, chairs!'

Sammy and Fitzy exchanged glances. There was a first time for everything, and, assured that it would be little more than a light dusting, they eventually acquiesced. Paddy Hughes soon grew restless as he waited in the car. He decided to pick up the last of his things from Shamrock Views. He walked at a fast clip to the waterfront apartment, buying himself time at the Punt House on the way back. It was the Cheltenham Gold Cup. It was only once a year.

Meanwhile, Vincent sped through the town in his Alfa Romeo, grinning like a cheshire cat alongside his beautiful wife. Passing Begger's Bend, he thought he saw the marauding gait of Paddy Hughes. Impossible, he thought. The boy had more sense than to be seen in Shamrock Hills. At the Cloverhill traffic lights, he then spotted the jogging figure of the Shamrock Express. 'Jesus, we really have cut it fine, Leanne. Even Danny Breen is ahead of us', he laughed.

'It was worth it', she replied. 'Enjoy today, Vincent. Be proud of yourself.'

But his sense of optimism soon escaped him as he tore into Peter Harrod of GBT. 'Your schedule is your problem. Paddy Hughes has no association with this gym. I don't care what Nelson told you.'

Leanne whispered in Fitzy's ear, and he nodded in agreement. Taking his keys, she slipped into the office. Only one person could mediate a situation like this. She dialled and waited for her brother-in-law to answer.

Leonard Grant was already enroute. He'd been tipped off that 'One shot' Hughes was betting big on the horses. He looked at the boy from Ballywell in his passenger seat. 'Did I not tell you, son? You lay a bet in this town and I'll know about it.'

'It was a one-off, Mr. Grant.'

'Aye, an expensive one.'

Pulling up to the gym, Leonard caught sight of his brother. His free hand gyrated in the face of Peter Harrod while the other pinched at a cigarette. He was right on the cusp. Paddy watched on from the passenger's seat as Leonard tried to calm him. It looked like he was getting somewhere until Vincent removed his waistcoat and threw it to the gravel. Then a classy brunette emerged from the gym, and Paddy laughed as she muscled her way between the men before letting fly with a thudding cross to her husband's shoulder.

Inside the gym, Danny brewed two cups of tea. He felt sorry for Fitzy, his trainer of twenty years, stretched out on a camp bed and rubbing at his temples. It was Fitzy's gym, yet he was hidden away in a back room while the cracks of Paddy Hughes's punches echoed through the wall.

'The boy can really bang', admitted Fitzy.

Danny reached him his cup of tea. 'And he can talk. But it's all hype. Just noise to put asses on seats. Paddy's too simple to know he's being used.'

Fitzy blew at his tea. 'Aren't we all?'

## Chapter 25

There was plenty in the coffers in Serenity House, yet Anne Simpson worked for minimum wage. She could claim the overtime, but she didn't go above and beyond for a pay bump. The time she put in came from a genuine place of care. She knew it, and so did her employer. Anne would always be good for an extra round, and at Serenity House, no good deed went unpunished.

Her tough night bled into mid-morning. She should have been tucked up in bed with a hot chocolate and a VHS tape. While physically exhausted, she still needed an hour of comfort before tapering off to sleep. Not this morning.

She found Eileen Breen strewn on the floor by the foot of her bed. Her nightie was wet with urine as she wept uncontrollably. She was a heavy woman, thick-boned and well-filled. Anne checked her watch. Most staff were either on breakfast duty or passed out in the staffrooms. It was breaking the rules, but she saw no alternative.

Jimmy Breen struggled to end the call on his new portable phone. It was a grey Motorola and was the size of a house brick. He squinted at the keypad before again lifting the speaker to his ear. His sister, Dee, looked up from their father's grave. 'You better go. I'll finish up here.'

When he reached Serenity House, his mother had exhausted herself to a state of relative calm. With Anne's help, he got her to her feet and into a walk-in bath. He rolled up his sleeves and removed his wristwatch as Anne sponged Eileen's back. Anne winked at him as he reached her the bar of soap. She was a pleasant woman. Her large round eyes lent her a girlish innocence, and her prominent front teeth added warmth. 'Thanks again for coming in', she said as Eileen was taken away for a late breakfast.

'That's ok. It's funny how things work out. I wasn't planning on coming today.'

'That's not like you. Is everything ok?'

'It's my father's anniversary. Speaking of which, I need to make tracks. The service starts in twenty minutes.'

'I'll sit with her if you'd like? During the service I mean.'

'Shouldn't you be getting yourself home?'

'One more hour won't kill me.'

#

The town was quiet. It was a week removed from St Patrick's Day, and the hangover could still be felt. The parade brought the usual splash of green jackets, orange beards and half-sober flute bands. The town's revellers had been blessed with blue skies and unseasonably mild air, and as the sun set over the Drumferry river, enough ale had been sunk to mitigate the drop in temperature.

That was last Friday. Fitzy shook out his umbrella before entering Riley's Paper and Post. He reached for a middling priced anniversary card and asked Riley for a half ounce of tobacco.

'Terrible weather, Fitzy. Just terrible.'

'It is. It's hardly worth getting out of bed for.'

'I don't know about that. Did you hear that Scratchcard Johnny won a grand on the cards? Well... give it a couple of hours and it will belong to the Punt House.'

Water was already pooling at the traffic lights. In Dana's kitchen, the final touches were being made to a family platter; an assortment of sandwiches, vol au vents and sausage rolls. Dana ran her finger down the contact list taped to her kitchen wall. She mouthed out the number as she dialled.

After three rings, she was through to O'Leary's bar. 'Shane, I'm just about done. But do me a wee favour, pet. Come and collect it. That's no weather for a lady.'

The downpour started to ease, but the clouds, if anything, were growing ominously darker. Cedar Park was abandoned, and the Luke Gibson Vista was a lake. The braver of the starlings swooped down for a drink while the rest fluffed their feathers and shook off the water. The blackbirds of Serenity House called a truce to their squabbles as Eileen and Anne Simpson sat by the window.

In the Church of the Resurrection, Father Carrigan was readying to begin the service as Fitzy, spotting an old colleague of Arthur's, feigned a kneel and slid in beside him. He negotiated the safe passage of his card to Dee. She looked back and nodded. Like the letter she'd received from Father O'Dowd, it gave her a timely boost. Jimmy arrived in the nick of time, pacing up the aisle faster than was customary.

'Loving father, grant comfort and peace to this family. May the memories of Arthur fill their hearts with love, and may the hope for eternal life be their strength in grief. Amen.'

'Amen.'

Only family attended the grave, and with the rain continuing to beat down, Father Carrigan kept his prayers brief. 'Eternal rest grant unto him, O Lord, and let the perpetual light shine upon him. May he rest in peace. Amen.'

'Amen.'

#

Whether in or out of competition, Danny kept his drinking to a minimum. Anything over four pints was a rarity. Vincent Grant, as he'd done every year since Arthur Breen's death, left a hundred quid behind the bar. He'd have stayed for a drink, but O'Leary's bar was one of many in Shamrock Hills that he was barred from. Fitzy and Ela were first to arrive. He gave her the half ounce of rolling tobacco as Shane pumped on the ale handle.

Shortly after, the Breen siblings came in from the rain. Connor lifted his raincoat over his head, exposing his gargantuan belly. The white polyester shirt was from his school days. Jimmy had the right outfit for every occasion. Despite the foul weather, he maintained an air of refinement. Ela was pleased that Danny had the good sense to own an umbrella never mind use one. He tipped his wrist at Shane who reached for four glasses. Danny's hand gently gripped the crown of Ela's head.

'Keep an eye on Fitzy. The food is for everyone. We're going to sit by the window. You'll join us?'

'Aye, we'll come over once you're all settled.'

Connor then approached Ela with three towering plates food. She got up from her stool and embraced him like a sister. 'Long time no see, wee Connor.' His cheeks blushed as his eyes darted between the beer mats. 'I have cats now. I keep two in the house and four more outside.'

'A woman is what you need', jibed Fitzy. 'That said, company is company.'

'What would you know about company?' ribbed Ela. 'And no, fishing and betting don't count.' She passed him a fresh pint, and they joined the Breen family by the window.

The day was hardest for Dee. Arthur Breen had been her world as a young girl. As she leaned on Danny's shoulder, her heart still ached for her daddy. She usually shared recollections while the brothers stared into their pint glasses, occasionally grunting in acknowledgment. Today, Dee kept to herself. Jimmy, if not the most sentimental of folk, was a man of duty, and aided by the ale, allowed the words to form.

'You're all too young to remember this one. Auntie Esther was staying with us during one of her blue spells. Ma was run off her feet, and it's the only time I recall her getting snappy with Da. So, he says, *'Tell me what I should do, Eillen, and I'll do it',* and she said, *'Read her the newspaper.'*

Danny snorted into his pint. This from a man who was too uptight to read to his own children.

'So, he starts at page one, and within five minutes he's bored the woman to death. She snaps and says, *'Just read me my horoscope, would you?'* I remember Da's face pinching up like a camel's ass in a sandstorm.

Anyway, he takes a deep breath and turns to the horoscopes. *"A sudden shock is in store for you this week. Best be prepared. Get your big fat arse home lest it be met with the toe of my shoe."'*

Fitzy had the goods on Arthur the prison officer. 'He took no shit from that lot. I remember him making Vincent drop and do fifty press-ups for not rinsing out the mop. He was tough, but he had to be. He was fair… and he was a good friend. May he rest in peace.'

Danny drained the remainder of his third pint, and Connor, forever the impressionable one, sank what was left of his. 'We still have some of your boxing tapes, Fitzy.' The trainer shook his head. 'I don't think so, Connor. Your da returned all that he borrowed from me.'

'No, some of them are still in the attic. Seven tapes. Marvin Hagler versus John Mugabe. Mike Tyson versus Pinklon Thomas. Barry McGuigan versus Eusebio Pedroza....'

He would have rattled off the rest had his brothers not interjected. 'What else have you got up there?' asked Ela, trying her best to keep a straight face as Fitzy spurted his mouthful of ale. Even Dee cracked a smile.

'Danny's boxing trophies and medals. Jimmy's math certificates. My jigsaws, a pile of Dee's Beano's and some of Ela's letters.'

Danny went for more drinks to hide his blushes. His little brother meant no harm. He never did, and regardless, the past was the past. But the letters held greater significance for Ela. When in Dublin, she'd written Danny many times with no reply. She'd often wondered, and now she knew. It was written all over Dee's face.

Ela took a deep breath and reached for her rolling tobacco. Today was not the day.

## Chapter 26

Team Breen arrived early in Liverpool. The stakes had never been higher. Win and Danny was one fight away from a world title belt. Lose and it was the end of the line. He felt fit and strong as he always did, but there was fit and there was fighting fit. He insisted that his rib was fine, but Fitzy made sure that sparring sessions focused on the chest up. The ever-willing Gary McGinty got his bell rung a half-dozen times. Danny was banging hard, and he needed to be. Stopping Hibbert early was his surest route to victory.

Word circulated Liverpool that Hibbert was in the shape of his life. Reports on Kevin Neary were comparatively mixed, with local journos suggesting he was carrying an injury. For Paddy Hughes, after stealing the show in the opening presser, the hype surrounding him had fallen off.

However, interest soon resurged when the pre-fight GBT documentary aired. It remained to be seen whether he'd walk the walk at Stanley Hall, but one thing was for sure, he generated strong opinions. The Liverpool boxing fans, by and large, took exception to his bravado, but there was a decided undercurrent of support for the Ballywell man and the hardest puncher of the four.

Danny Breen knew Liverpool well. The evening was dry and refreshingly cool. They were perfect conditions for his roadwork. He took in the richness of Liverpool's story as he sprinted along Castle Street. He'd be back in a couple of days for the pre-fight weigh-in. Taking in the majesty of St George's Hall at dusk, he breathed a huge sigh of relief that he only had another half-pound to lose.

#

In the Adelphi hotel, Vincent Grant was doing what all good managers did during fight week. He was fighting tooth and nail for his boxer. With it being such a high-profile card and with bigger riches awaiting the winners, it was no time for diplomacy.

*Don't start what you can't finish and not an inch will you give*

The family credo rang true in his mind and soul, even if it no longer did for his brother. Leonard Breen had long preached from a different book, one that stressed mediation, compromise and mutual gain. To each his own, decided Vincent. And while Leonard remained in Shamrock Hills to hob knob with sponsors, Vincent was in Liverpool, making sure Danny got to wear his preferred gloves.

After much rancour, Hibbert's team submitted to Vincent's demands. The next battle would be the referee's meeting. Despite neither boxer being overly aggressive in their styles, Danny was better versed in the dark arts of ringcraft, and neither Vincent or Fitzy wanted a touchy official.

It took Vincent a couple of weeks to make peace with 'Big Daddy' Nelson stealing Paddy Hughes from under his nose. Vincent hated being bested, and after Paddy's visit to the Celtic Fist gym and subsequent swagger for the GBT cameras, he promised he'd never be bested again. Back in his hotel room, he took a long shower. He then tried watching tv, but the extra satellite channels only aggravated his sense of restlessness.

He rummaged through his travel bag for the bottle of whiskey and came across a book. It was one of Willie Dunne's. Turning to the first page, he paused at his old cellmate's handwriting.

*The journey of a thousand miles begins with a single step.*

The scent of his wife's favourite perfume rose from the page and aroused a deep groan deep in his chest. Every prisoner missed that little something, and Willie Dunne was a perceptive man. He'd noted that the hours following weekly visits was when Vincent was most volatile. The ex-murderer had been a mainstay of Block B for twenty years, and he enjoyed easy relationships with the men in white. He'd quickly worked out the Gymnasium Four who'd laid a beating on Vincent. Every gang had a leader, and eyeing up Terry Tubbs, Willie muttered a verse from the book of Zechariah.

*Strike the shepherd and the sheep will scatter.*

#

Paddy Hughes had been in Liverpool for weeks. Good sparring was sparse in Ballywell, so Nelson's team made contact with a number of Merseyside clubs. On this visit there was no luxury stay in the Adelphi hotel for Paddy and Sammy. Instead, they took a black cab to a modest Bed and Breakfast in Kirkby. With the nearest gym five miles away, Paddy got his roadwork in early before the real work began. Seven days from the fight and the intensity of the training steadily tapered, ensuring that Paddy had time to replenish his strength before battle.

His sparring had been punch-perfect. He was breaking his personal bests on the tracks, and his weight was bang on the middleweight limit. Physically, he was more than ready, but with the easing of training, the evenings grew long as sleep escaped him. The city centre was only a six-mile run, and he hadn't had a flutter since losing three grand in the Cheltenham cup. Going in heavy on a nine-to-one outsider wasn't the smartest bet he'd ever laid, but it was the Cheltenham cup, he told himself, and horses weren't his game. Cards were.

He limited himself to two grand, his kitty for staving off boredom till fight night. Adorned in his running gear, he blended in well in the city casinos. He warmed up on the fruit machines, acclimating to the incessant noise and flashing lights. After two wins and a trio of losses, he was ready for cards.

By midnight, his two grand belonged to the house, having gone all in with three queens. Despite the loss, he jogged peacefully back to Kirkby and slept like a baby.

#

Vincent Grant was still awake. The pages of Willie's book had begun to blur, but he persevered, wanting to finish the chapter before attacking the rest of the bottle. He knew there was no utility in it, that there was nothing left to unpack, yet he couldn't help but fixate over every detail, wondering if there was anything he could have done.

In 1980, the year Vincent was sent to prison, Terry Tubbs, the leader of the Gymnasium Four, held the prison record for the bench press. Vincent got a little too close to breaking it, and for that, had three of his own ribs broken. It should have been adequate retribution, but as Terry Tubbs showered every morning, the bite mark on his calf served to remind him that Vincent had shown no quit. In the following spring, Tubbs was approached by Officer Breen and asked to join the prison boxing tournament. 'We need a replacement to fight Logan next month. Do you fancy it?'

'Yeah, count me in, boss.'

Every man and his mother knew that Terry was a born bully. Getting him to fight Logan was the easy part. The difficulty came in breaking the news to Vincent that he was off the team and suspended from training. For his own good, neither Willie Dunne or Block Officer Breen told him why. Secrets were notoriously hard to keep in the big house. When the week of the tournament came, Block officer Breen informed Vincent that his suspension was lifted. 'You've served your month. You're welcome back at the club when you're ready.'

Vincent turned to Willie. 'Don't look at me, Vincent. Logan's the man to talk to.' Willie lowered his book and gave Vincent a quick wink. The timing couldn't have been better for Logan. He'd spent most of the day shitting fear through the eye of a needle.

In the tournament final, Vincent Grant and Terry Tubbs went straight to war. Vincent had been in countless fights but had never landed a shot as sweet as the uppercut that caught Terry. It landed flush on the chin and sent him face first to the canvas.

'I'm telling you… you would have been a great boxer. That was straight from the textbook.'

It was high praise, and from the Irish Pitbull, Barney Fitzpatrick no less. Block officer Breen and Willie Dunne shared a fleeting grin. Another prison feud was brought to an end… or so they thought.

#

In Shamrock Hills, Dee was dividing a pot of stew into tupperware boxes. Three days was a long time to leave growing boys, and she made sure they'd not eat Connor out of house and home. She checked their bags and recounted the pairs of underwear and socks. She was looking forward to a long soak in the tub before the next day's crossing to Liverpool.

She should have been delighted to have Ela for company on the trip, but with the events at O'Leary's bar still fresh in her mind, her anxiety steadily grew. Maybe Ela hadn't noticed, she tried to tell herself. But it was beyond wishful thinking.

A woman could always tell.

## Chapter 27

In Liverpool, the fight hype reached a fevered crescendo. The final press conference at St George's Hall produced a gluttony of soundbites, and the UBF president, Carlos Bernardi, drew huge cheers when he draped himself in the red of Liverpool football club. Stanley Hall, a fourteen-thousand-seater arena, was sold out from ringside to the rafters. Five thousand fans were coming from Ireland.

The 'Celtic Four', the conception of Francis Nelson and the standard-bearer of GBT's maiden foray in bigtime boxing, was tantalizingly close. With the fighters only hours away from the public weigh-ins, the office of Nelson Fight Promotions was rich with optimism as the morning papers arrived. They knew Paddy Hughes was the 'bad boy' of the promotion, but stories of him splurging thousands on blackjack and poker was not a good look for the GBT network. The blame fell at Nelson's feet.

'This is news to me too, Peter. We had him set up in Kirkby, miles from any distractions.'

Peter Harrod gave it straight. 'He obviously needs looking after. We're trying to be the respectable face of boxing at GBT, and this kind of stuff alienates viewers.'

After the call ended, Nelson called Sophie into his office. 'Contact the casinos. I want to know how often he's been going and how much money he's burned through.' When Sophie returned having done her due diligence, her glossy, plump lips quivered as Nelson reached for his chequebook.

At 11am, the pre-fight weigh-ins began. Latecomers struggled to see beyond the wave of fans, their outstretched hands colliding in unison as their chants shook the foundations of St George's Hall. Danny Breen looked strong on the scales, and his eyes were brighter than they'd been in the Wolfhound. He flexed his eight-pack and stared beyond the partisan crowd. Seeing Ela, he blew her a kiss.

As his opponent, Davey Hibbert, squared up to Danny, the Merseyside fighter appeared the significantly bigger man. His lats and back muscles were befitting a light-heavyweight. He moved his head into Danny's and locked in his stare. He soon got bored and turned to the crowd. Their collective roar was deafening as they chanted his name.

*Hitman!*

*Hitman!*

*Hitman Davey Hibert!*

Paddy Hughes was next on the scales. His freshly shaved head caught the shine of the spotlights. Stripping down to his shorts, he looked in phenomenal shape. Vincent shouted to Fitzy that it was a miracle he'd ever made welterweight. Now a stone heavier, he was cut to perfection. Kevin Neary looked tense as he and Paddy stared off for the cameras. Paddy chewed fiercely at his gum before pushing Neary across the stage. A chorus of boos rang out followed by a chant that the Merseyside fans had made specially for the Ballywell brawler.

*He's bald!*

*He hates foldin!*

*He's shite at Texas Hold em!*

When leaving the stage, Paddy cupped his ear to the noise before thanking the crowd with a two-finger salute. It gave Dermot Robinson and the rest of the journos another easy headline. Undeterred by Sammy Stewart's protestations, Paddy then pulled on his running shoes and took to the city streets. Within minutes he was powering past the Albert Dock warehouses and the Liver bird towers.

Back at St Geroge's Hall, Peter Harrod of GBT was livid. All fighters were expected to stay for interviews. Danny kept his answers short. With Vincent and Fitzy marshalling him, there was little for the press to dig at. Fitzy was quick to deflect probes about injuries. He insisted that Danny was ready and reminded the men with pens that boxing was the hurt game and not a tickling contest.

While Fitzy worked the journalists, Vincent watched his brother mingle with Peter Harrod and the UBF president, Carlos Bernardi. His blood pressure surged at the sight of

Leonard being invited into shot with Nelson. He watched him drape his arm over the promoter's shoulder as they lapped up the attention from the tv cameras.

After a light lunch, Danny got back to his hotel where Ela was waiting in the lobby. 'Hold your nose, Breen. I'm carrying seven hours of ferry stink.' He planted his lips on her forehead as her hands crossed the hardened contours of his back. 'I could use a shower too, and it's a sin to waste water.'

They relaxed throughout the afternoon. Ela fell into a deep and restful sleep as Danny went over the fight plan. He visualized Hibbert feinting and blinding him with flicking jabs. He saw himself measuring Hibbert with hard counterpunches and stopping him early. 'I have to stop him early', he whispered to himself as Ela stirred.

'What did you say, my love?'

Danny smiled as he pulled her close and rested his chin on the top of her head. Her sandy blond hair felt soft against his stubble. 'Nothing, darling. Just thinking about the fight. I'm ready.'

'That's good.'

'What time did you arrive in Liverpool?'

'Just in time for the weigh-ins', she whispered softly.

'Was there much chat with Dee on the ferry?'

'Just the usual. You know how she gets before a fight. Anyway, we'd better shake a leg for dinner', she replied, patting his chest and rolling onto her feet. She slipped out of her pyjama bottoms as Danny sat up.

'Is everything ok with you and Dee?', he asked.

'Of course. Why wouldn't it be?'

'No reason.'

Danny watched her intently as she buttoned up her jeans. The musical cleft on her hip was new, and a film of flesh bunched around her waistline where it hadn't before. Her skin was as supple as ever, and her movements, languid and graceful, soothed Danny's soul. Even the smallest ripple in her peace, be it the tone of her voice or the speed at which she fastened the clasp of her bra, spoke to Danny. She never had been a good liar.

#

Fitzy bounced his weight off the ring canvas. He had forgotten more about boxing than most would ever know. He had a half century of experience that couldn't be bought, and it made him the calmest man in the arena on fight night. All the great trainers had that aura, and Barney Fitzpatrick was Ireland's best. A master strategist and a tactical savant was how Dermot Robinson once described him. But Fitzy cared little for plaudits. He knew his worth as a trainer and didn't need the awards or honourable mentions.

In what felt like the blink of an eye, he'd gone from a young up and comer to a respected sage of the sport. He'd been involved in countless big events but none on the scale of the Celtic Four. The whole city was gripped, and as he inspected the ring canvas, deep in the bowels of Stanley Hall, he felt nervous for his fighter. The fourteen-thousand black seats encroached like the walls of a bear pit.

Vincent joined Fitzy in the ring and walked the length and breadth of the canvas, surveying the various sponsors. By the red corner was the logo for the old Cobbler's End project in Shamrock Hills. 'Have you seen this, Fitzy? They'll be raising Lazarus next.'

Fitzy gave it a disinterested glance. 'I'm more concerned about these ropes. They are very slack.' Vincent rocked his weight against them. 'Aye, slack indeed. And have you noticed the ring walk routes? The away fighter's path bottlenecks at Section E.'

'Where our fans are?'

'No, our lot are on the opposite side. I told you. Francis Nelson is a scumbag.'

'Say it louder, brother. He can't quite hear you from the Adelphi.'

At the sound of Leonard Grant's voice, Fitzy checked his watch. 'I think I'm done for this evening. See you both tomorrow.' He slipped out of the ring and took the long way round to the exit. Leonard shrugged with indifference before ducking between the ropes. He looked around him. 'It's like the Colosseum, eh? Fourteen thousand screaming fans will be rammed in here this time tomorrow night. I don't know how the fighters do it.' He leaned against the turnbuckle and studied Vincent. 'What's been bothering you? I can smell the whiskey from here.'

Vincent surveyed the arena. 'Nothing you don't already know. This is the stage I wanted for Danny, but I didn't want it like this.' He turned to face Leonard. 'And I never pictured you on the other side.'

Leonard stepped slowly towards him. His loafers released soft puffs as they pushed off the ring canvas. Stopping a yard short of Vincent, he stared at him bemusedly. 'After all we've been through, and still, you think a handshake here and a picture there makes me the enemy. When will you grow up, Vincent?' He tapped the temple of his brother's head. 'The problem's in there. You root around in there looking for problems.'

Vincent slapped Leonard's hand away. 'You've been with Nelson from the beginning. Whatever he needs, you oblige him and that sleaze Harrod from GBT. Your loyalty is to them.'

The brothers squared up. Leonard was the taller by two inches. 'Who visited you every week when you were holed up in prison, eh? Whose money got you set up in the building trade? Who gave you a stake in the Celtic Fist boxing club? Me! And what thanks did I get? I never asked for thanks, but don't dare question my loyalty. I did everything I could for you, and all *you* had to do was bloody live your life in peace! But no, you just kept on being you, and to hell with the consequences for everyone else.'

'You'll never let it go, will you?' Vincent fired back. 'Is that why you're really here, Leonard? As a politician?

You get some free air time and a bit of interest in Cobbler's End…. is that your play?

Leonard grinned. 'Aye, maybe. Maybe I never stopped being a politician. And I'll tell *you* something you already know… you never left that prison cell. You lost five years of your life, and still you've learned nothing. If Arthur and Willie could see you now, they'd pity you!'

At the sound of his cellmate's name, Vincent lunged at Leonard, his bull-like strength slamming him against the turnbuckle. 'Take a pop, little brother', goaded Leonard as their panting breaths filled the silence of the arena.

Vincent shook his head.

'No. No I won't. We're blood and for that I'll forgive you this once, but if you ever breathe his name again, I swear it, we will not be brothers.'

## Chapter 28

Fitzy could still hear the clang of the ring bell. He could still feel the ring ropes chafing his back as Archie Buchanon rattled his rib cage. He still had the gloves he wore that night, mud brown and padded with horsehair. They were ugly, heavy things but tough and durable. The smoothness over the knuckles was the only sign of wear. They'd fetch a pretty penny at auction, but Fitzy didn't put a price on history.

Boxing was a brutal game, and Fitzy had the scarred eye to prove it. Archie Buchannon kept both of his, but like so many great fighters, the Scot fought on too long. Fitzy spoke at his funeral in 1982. One day, somewhere, they'd come out fighting for the seventh round, he said.

He still dreamt of that seventh round, over forty years on from round six. He and Archie, fit as butcher's dogs, circling one another, matching each other punch for punch till the horsehair padding rubbed against bone... and the light in his good eye dimmed to a shadow.

He woke with a start. It was 6:30am.

It was Fight Day.

Team Breen met for breakfast at the Adelphi hotel. The spread was to Danny's liking. There was porridge and wholemeal toast, boiled eggs, yogurt and berries. Dee had only coffee. The fight day butterflies negated her want for food. Fitzy took advantage of his 'all inclusive' stay with a Full English fry-up and an extra round of buttered toast.

The television showed clips from the weigh-in. 'The next time you have porridge, you'll be a household name,' said Fitzy. Danny pumped his fist as the table broke into cheer, their nerves momentarily washed away by an outpouring of pride. Vincent rose from his seat and gave Danny's shoulders an affectionate squeeze. 'Folks, if I can just have a minute, please? Tonight's a big night, and it's fitting that Danny enters Stanley Hall in style.'

He passed a white box to his fighter. Inside was a green and gold felt robe and matching shorts. On the robe read, 'The Shamrock Express.' Danny's cheeks blushed as he held them up for everyone to see. The hotel staff watched on. They'd taken a liking to Team Breen. It seemed many in Liverpool had, but it would count for little when Danny climbed into the ring to meet the local favourite, Davey Hibbert.

In Shamrock Hills that evening, O'Leary's bar was standing room only. Jimmy Breen had just purchased the fight on his living room tv. He was hosting his brother

Connor and their nephews, Aiden and Alex. He called his sister in Liverpool.

'The boys are grand. Aye, they'll have your stew tonight. Stop worrying. They won't starve. Ok, wish Danny the best from me. Bye.'

The sound of her big brother's voice helped ease Dee's nerves. Her fight night attire was freshly ironed and hanging in the wardrobe of her hotel room. The contents of her travel bag were laid out on the dressing table. Hair curlers, nail varnish, foundation, mascara. Looking at them, she wished she'd been born a boy as she rolled her shoulders and stretched the kink in her neck.

Keen to share Jimmy's well wishes, she walked to Danny's room. Ela answered, wrapped snug in a white bathroom robe. 'Oh sorry, bad timing. Where's Danny?'

'The boys went for a walk. They said twenty minutes, tops. Everything ok?'

'Yeah, fine. I just wanted to pass on Jimmy's well wishes. I'll leave you to it.'

'No, no. Join me. I could use some help.'

Dee returned five minutes later with her makeup and hair kit. Her hand was unsteady. Ela reached for a silver hipflask on the bedside table. Taking a swig, she passed it to Dee. 'A drop of brandy for the nerves.' The brandy warmed Dee's throat before settling in the pit of her stomach. 'One more of those and I'll be off my trolley', she joked.

Ela took a second swig and passed it back. The brandy went straight to work, reddening Dee's cheeks and leaving her warm and fuzzyheaded. Ela leaned in to put the finishing touches to her mascara. 'All done,' she whispered.

'Thanks, Ela.'

'We have to look our best for Danny's big night.'

'Aye, we do. It's been a long road. Win tonight and he fights for a world championship. Da always said he'd be champion.'

'Aye, he did', replied Ela, deflecting her eyes in search of something to hold.

'We only ever wanted what was best for him. You know that, don't you?' asked Dee.

'I know you wanted to talk on the ferry, but what good will it do? We're here to support Danny. When the time is right, I'll tell him everything.'

Dee's face turned scarlet. She got up to leave but the effects of the brandy dragged her back. 'You won't talk to me about it but you'll tell him everything? I did what I thought was right.'

'You did what your father wanted you to do, and deep down you know it, so please drop it,' insisted Ela. Her last words trailed as she ran out of breath.

'So, I take the brunt of the blame and the rest is put on a man in his grave. That's convenient for you. No one forced you to leave when you did, Ela, and you chose not to tell Danny you were carrying his baby, nobody else!'

'Dee, please…'

'Please what? You've had your say. I'm having mine.'

'Dee!'

She followed Ela's eyeline to the door of the hotel room where a hooded Danny Breen stood. His body was statuesque as black lines ran down the sides of Ela's cheeks.

## Chapter 29

It was five o'clock in the morning. Dermot Robinson's eyes burned with tiredness. He ran his hands through his thick, lengthy grey hair. His back was stiff from sitting all evening, and his ears still rung from the roars of Stanley Hall. There had been plenty of incident, so the journalist in him should have been pleased. If he wanted, he could flesh out a month's worth of articles. Would GBT abandon boxing? Might Nelson cut his losses?

Would the UBF president, Carlos Bernardi, ever grace the British Isles again? Being accustomed to the fineries of the French riviera, no one would blame him for staging his fights in the casinos of Monte Carlo.

'Once piece at a time', Dermot said to himself as he spellchecked his report on the Celtic Four semi-final.

### CELTIC FARCE

*By Dermot Robinson*

*Chief sportswriter: The Shamrock Gazette*

*In the most highly anticipated fight card in years, Francis Nelson's Celtic Four tournament descended into farce on Saturday night. Billed as an elimination tournament for the inaugural UBF middleweight world title, its president, Carlos Bernardi, departed the iconic Stanley Hall in a state of shock in what was a dark night for boxing.*

*At the time of writing, Merseyside police are investigating the breakout of violence in the 14000-seat arena. Said Chief Inspector Edward Flanagan, 'A number of glass bottles were thrown between rival supporters which quickly led to fist fighting. We are busy reviewing CCTV.'*

*The riot and ensuing delay caused major disruption to the GBT television broadcast. Fans were then made to wait over an hour for the co-main event, Danny 'The Shamrock Express' Breen versus Davey 'The Hitman' Hibbert. Speculation abounds as to what caused the delay with multiple sources suggesting that Breen's team considered pulling him out of the contest. At the time of writing, Breen's management were unavailable for comment.*

*As Breen finally made his ring entrance, he cut a distracted figure, failing to feed off the raucous atmosphere and looking sullen as he waited for Hibbert. The Merseyside man started fast as Breen struggled to find any rhythm, swinging uncharacteristically wild and off balance. His much-vaunted movement never left his dressing room as Hibbert peppered him to head and body.*

*In the second, the Shamrock Hills man managed some success, landing twice to Hibbert's ribcage, but the*

*Hitman answered back in emphatic style, landing five unanswered blows and opening a deep cut over Breen's left eye. In the third, Hibbert elected to box on the back foot, employing slick head and upper body movement, again making Breen miss wildly.*

*His trainer, Barney Fitzpatrick, had done a sterling job of stemming the cut, but as Breen came back to his corner, his eye was closing rapidly. The ring physician checked the damage and deemed Breen fit to continue, but Fitzpatrick waved a white towel, saving his fighter from further punishment.*

*In the main event, Ballywell's Paddy Hughes made short work of Kevin 'The Canon' Neary with a two-round demolition of the Liverpool man. Neary elected to slug the slugger and suffered a first-round knockdown for his troubles. He managed to rise at the count of four and tucked up well as Hughes unloaded a volley of heavy-handed shots. Neary bravely fought back, stunning Hughes with a looping right hook in close quarters which brought a thunderous roar from his Merseyside fans.*

*Their elation, however, was short-lived as Hughes upped the pressure in the second, overpowering the career middleweight who had abandoned his jab entirely. Forcing his man onto the ropes, Hughes slipped Neary's speculative right cross and countered with a crippling left hook followed by two ripping right uppercuts. The referee swiftly intervened and waved the fight off as Neary sagged against the ropes.*

*Said Hughes, 'Neary is a brave kid, I'll give him that. Those punches would have knocked a bull out. I'm twenty-five years old, I'm undefeated, I'm a natural born killer, and Hibbert has nowhere to hide. I'll destroy Hibbert and I'll do it right here, in his own backyard!'*

*Hibbert, not one to shy away from confrontation, re-entered the ring and faced off with Hughes for the cameras. Both men bored in with their heads, sparking a serious scuffle between the teams. In the ensuing melee, a GBT sound man was knocked off his feet. It was an unsavoury sight in what was an unsavoury night for boxing.*

*Francis Nelson, the mastermind promoter and self-appointed saviour of Liverpool boxing, could not hide his disappointment in what proved to be a lacklustre fight card and a poorly managed event.*

*'We don't condone that kind of behaviour, but let's focus on the positives. We provided a lot of exposure for local talent and we have set up the final for the UBF middleweight title. Hibbert versus Hughes will be an absolute belter.'*

At twenty-six years of age, Kevin Neary will come again. While he will be hurting over the manner of his first loss, he showed plenty of fighting heart as well as a solid chin. However, we may have seen the last of Danny Breen in a prize ring having now lost two of his last three fights.

As predicted, he simply did not have the gears to keep up with Hibbert, and more worryingly, it appears he no longer has the hunger for the fight game. In a career that promised *so much, the Shamrock Hills native failed to replicate the success he enjoyed in the amateur ranks where he won titles across three divisions. Despite the success, his legacy will be one of unfulfilled potential.*

*A new search now begins for the heir to 'Quick Hand's Gibson, while our great rival Ballywell has a champion elect in Paddy 'One Shot' Hughes.*

#

Sitting in his pokey hotel room and dreading the ferry ride back to Belfast, Dermot couldn't remember feeling this deflated after a sporting event. He again pictured Danny Breen. His face was torn and bloodied. His green and gold robe consumed him as he left the arena, flanked by the slouching figures of Vincent Grant and Barney Fitzpatrick.

Boxing could be very cruel, the journalist mused.

# Part 3

*As long as there's a why*

## Chapter 30

It was a hard pill to swallow for those who'd followed the career of Danny Breen. He'd been a professional fighter for twelve years. The sport promised nothing, and the fans understood that. Still, they believed Danny's day would come. They thought it would be the Celtic Four tournament.

But after his defeat in Stanley Hall, there wasn't a sinner left in Shamrock Hills who believed he'd box again. He was thirty-three years old. Fighters were never the same after beatings like that.

It was mid-June and two months removed from the Stanley Hall defeat. The sun beat off Danny's back as twenty-pound cinder blocks crossed his calloused hands. Working on the Grants' yard had been a steady side-earner throughout his boxing career. Now it was just work. He'd stopped making his porridge before bed, preferring breakfast on the construction yard where sausage rolls and bacon baps were common fare.

Vincent Grant pulled into the yard in his Alfa Romeo. His hair was freshly trimmed and his skin was bronzed from a fortnight in the Costa Del Sol. As he approached, his workers slid their beer cans behind their ankles. Vincent laughed. 'You can't bullshit a bullshitter, boys. I can smell it from the St Columb's Bridge.' He spotted Danny by the cement mixer and made his way over. 'Need you for an errand, kid. Be ready in five.'

Danny punched out and beat the dust off his jeans before climbing into the passenger seat. 'Just want to get your opinion on something', said Vincent before flooring his Alpha and beating the lights. Fifteen minutes later, they pulled into Shamrock Views. Danny threw him an inquisitive look. 'You showing me how the better half live?'

Vincent smiled. 'There's no harm in looking.'

There certainly wasn't. It was a fine apartment. It had high ceilings, parquet flooring and two bedrooms overlooking the Drumferry river. 'You have first refusal', said Vincent. 'It will fetch a lot more on the open market, but I'd rather see your fight purses put to good use.'

'Is this where Paddy Hughes stayed after moving out of the gym?'

Vincent nodded. 'Aye. We thought it would do him good. Well, Leonard thought it would do him good. Anyway, it's for sale. Have a look around, kid'.

Danny took in the view from the balcony. Shamrock Hills looked quaint from where he stood and not a town of forty thousand people. The Church of the Resurrection was the tallest building, and its tall spire scraped a passing cloud. Vincent peered out the window. 'You've earned this, kid. Twenty-eight professional fights and twice as many in the amateurs. Twenty years of graft.'

'And no world title,' replied Danny.

Vincent stepped closer. 'I wanted it for you, kid. You know that. And Fitzy wanted it too, but it's professional boxing. You have to forget about Stanley Hall. What happened that night, Christ, most men wouldn't have made it to the ring.'

Danny looked to Vincent. His eyes appealed for answers. 'I felt nothing in there. I still feel nothing. What am I supposed to do now?'

Vincent surveyed the view and pointed beyond the church to the Applecross glen. 'See those trees? There's a spot that I walk to every couple of weeks. It's where I wrestle with the same question... and I'm reminded of something a wise man once told me. He said that he who has a 'why' to live can bear almost any hour.'

Danny mulled over the words till the air in his lungs emptied. 'I'm not sure I understand.'

'Don't overthink it, and believe me when I tell you, the man was right. As long as you have a 'why', you'll be alright.' He passed the apartment key to Danny. 'I'll be back in a couple of hours. This is what good money affords you. Enjoy it, kid.'

Watching satellite tv in Shamrock Views was preferable to breaking his back on the yard, so Danny kicked off his work boots and got comfortable. Soon needing to piss, he made use of the ensuite bathroom. He studied the ceiling fan and tested its four settings. Before leaving, he pressed down on the mattress of the queen-sized bed. Looking around, he recognized the 12-ounce Everlast gloves in the back of the wardrobe. They were last worn by Paddy Hughes and property of the Celtic Fist boxing gym. Danny bagged them and locked the apartment door on his way out.

#

Fitzy loathed the heat of the summer and the influx of rowdy adolescents to his gym. A six-week headache awaited, but it was the only time of year that the gym turned a profit. His light-heavyweight, Gary 'Thunder' McGinty, would make a fine coach till mid-August. Rubbing at his eyes, he wondered who else he could rope into helping. Of his amateur stable, those over sixteen were going through an especially unreliable phase in their lives. Fitzy had seen it a hundred times over.

The shutter rattled, interrupting his game of solitaire. Looking up from his cards, Fitzy was glad to see his longest-serving pupil, a few pounds heavier and a healthy shade from working outdoors. He caught the bag that hurtled towards him. 'I didn't think I'd see these again. He had a strange understanding of ownership, that Hughes boy.'

Fitzy lifted the ring apron and placed the gloves neatly beside the rest. He turned back towards Danny. 'Do you fancy a game of checkers?'

Danny jingled the loose change in his pocket. 'What are we playing for?'

'I win and you help me coach the summer school.'

'And if I win?' Danny replied.

Fitzy laughed. 'You mean if I let you win. And, sorry, I can't today. There's too much at stake.'

It didn't matter the season or time of day. The Celtic Fist gym was a cavern all-year round, and the only light came from the ring lamp above them. Fitzy moved first having won the toss. Danny linked his fingers and studied the board. He built his attack with more foresight than usual. 'I should have paid you a visit before now, Fitzy.'

'It's alright, son. As long as you know you're welcome. Are you itching to train again?'

Danny's fingers drummed off his cheek as his breath warmed his palm. 'No, I can't say I am. I haven't been thinking about boxing. I haven't been thinking about anything.' He offered a piece to Fitzy and walked him into a double counter. 'It's not harming my checkers game.'

Fitzy raised an eyebrow. 'It's early days, son. Very early days.'

The old trainer was soon a game to the good, and Danny boiled the kettle during the intermission. As he reset the board, Fitzy waited for Danny to look up.

'What about you and wee Ela?' he asked.

'What about it?'

'You know what I mean. Why haven't you put things right?'

Danny lifted a checker. He made to play but hesitated. He drummed the small wooden disk off his bottom lip before abandoning the move entirely. He knew Fitzy was still looking at him. 'Ela and Dee were the two people I trusted most in the world. I thought I knew them. But you know what really nags at me about that night in Stanley Hall... when I entered that ring, I was a complete stranger to myself.'

'That was then. What about now?'

Danny ignored Fitzy's question and made the decisive move, securing victory and forcing a rubber match. Fitzy reset the board. 'You fancy yourself today, Danny?'

'Like you said, the stakes are high.'

The winner of the rubber match was never in doubt. Danny was always good for some coaching, and he left the Celtic Fist gym just as the schools were emptying out. The day was still warm, and the late afternoon sun gilded front gardens and baked the recently laid tarmac. From a distance, Danny saw his nephews, Aiden and Alex, leaving Dunhaven School for Boys. They were growing up fast.

He didn't want to keep Vincent waiting, so he walked at a swift pace. He took the shortcut through Glenview and passed the Bonds' residence. As he passed, he was unaware of Ela spotting him through the sun room window. Her heart thumped hard in her chest... but the love of her life kept walking.

## *Chapter 31*

Paddy Hughes functioned better when he trained. The hard sessions brought order to his day. Starting with a 6am run, his work didn't finish till the shock of a cold shower at sundown. That's how he spent the six days a week that he was permitted to train. A boxer's battery, like any other, wouldn't last forever, but Paddy was twenty-five years old. For a fighter, it was the age of invincibility.

He'd grown well into the middleweight division. His frame was naturally thickening as he developed his man strength. He was lifting heavier, running faster and honing new skills inside the ropes. Despite their proven pedigree, he made easy work of his sparring partners. Sammy Stewart kept him grounded as best he could, but privately, he couldn't in a month of Sundays see Davey Hibbert standing up to him in the Celtic Four final.

They were on standby for news of the fight date. The terms of the contract were already agreed, but Nelson Promotions wanted the juices to build. Hibbert was a big draw in his native Liverpool, and Paddy Hughes was a fighter on the up. The latter had embraced his role as master provocateur, but the GBT crew needed fresh material. For that, they were compelled to dig deeper. With his mother out of the picture and his father having never been in it, Paddy's story started at St Mark's Orphanage for Boys.

Paddy looked around the orphanage. Nothing had changed bar some chipped paint and a slightly stronger whiff of damp. Most of the sisters remained. Their faces were marginally more ashen and drawn since he'd last seen them. He spoke to the GBT cameras about the care he'd received at St Mark's. He had many fond memories of the place. Yet the more eyes he looked into, of boys who'd never met their mothers or fathers, the more Paddy's mind went back to the day he first arrived, aged eight.

He saw himself, waiting at reception, wearing a freshly ironed shirt tucked neatly into his shorts. His pudgy fist gripped a figurine of Optimus Prime. His mother was thin and haggard. Paddy recalled her promising time after time that she'd visit. She never did.

The GBT crew were taken aback. The plan had been to stay for lunch and film the Ballywell brawler enjoying a kickabout in the old playing field. But Paddy Hughes was already breaking into a jog as he crossed the orphanage grounds. Word soon reached Peter Harrod who was spending the week in Liverpool with Francis Nelson and the UBF president, Carlos Bernardi.

Nelson had survived his first year as a boxing promotor. He knew how expensive it would be, and he was willing to put his money where his mouth was. What he hadn't envisaged was the tripartite power to which he was now beholden. Nelson was the promoter, GBT was the broadcaster and Carlos Bernardi brought the UBF belt. Nelson needed them on side. It was the only way to deliver a world title fight.

Chinatown, on the aptly named Nelson Street, was where they stopped for dinner after an afternoon of golf. Carlos Bernardi had kept conversation light through the back nine, but now, settled in a private booth and dousing his dumplings in soy sauce, he wished to discuss the semi-final.

'The UBF did not form overnight, gentlemen. It took many years of work and countless setbacks, the like of which you can't possibly imagine.' He paused to eat, applauding the food with a wave of his chopsticks. 'The road ahead is long, and every step is crucial. Every step brings us closer to the UBF title being recognized as a major sporting title. Now, what happened in April was a misstep to put it mildly. My organization cannot afford, nor will it accept, another.'

Nelson listened intently, but inside, he cared little for Bernardi's regal air. By contrast, Peter Harrod of GBT matched the UBF president nod for nod and dumpling for dumpling. Peter's hands, as far as he was concerned, were clean.

Bernardi continued. 'Let's first discuss the telecast. I watched the recording when I returned to Monaco. Till then I had assumed that GBT had a studio somewhere in the arena. Presenting solely from ringside made the show look decidedly amateurish.'

Harrod could do little but swallow hard and wait for the attention to turn to Nelson. 'And just as GBT should have a contingency plan for delays, so too should the promoter'. Bernardi wiped his hands on a hot towel and ordered another plate of dumplings. 'I want assurances that security will be improved'.

Nelson made to speak but abandoned his sentence after the first syllable. '... and the quality of the fights left a lot to be desired. This was a semi-final for a world title belt, and what I saw was semi-professional.'

The remark stung Peter as much as it did Francis. He had pushed for the matchups and brought forward the schedule. He did what needed to be done to serve GBT. But there was no getting away from it; the semi-final had been a shambles, and Harrod's job was hanging by a thread. As Bernardi paused to eat, Francis Nelson saw his window of opportunity. He was one fight promotion away from delivering on his promise... to bring a world title fight to Liverpool. He just had to sell it.

'Carlos, there will be no more missteps. Peter and I will re-crunch the numbers and ensure we have extra security, a proper studio, a deeper fight card and plenty of added content to support a superb main event. Hibbert versus Hughes in Stanley Hall. Halloween weekend. For the UBF middleweight championship of the world.'

By the end of the meal, the three men were in agreement. Despite the false starts and the negative press, there was a cautious optimism that the Celtic Four Final would make a real statement in the boxing world. It would cost Francis Nelson a small fortune, but he'd weighed the risk and decided it was worth the gamble.

In Ballywell, Sammy Stewart knew all about Paddy's gambling and was powerless to stop him losing two years of his career to it. He needed looking after, urged Francis Nelson, and Sammy was doing his best. He gave Paddy the run of the gym and the spare bedroom in his house. He had his wife cook specially as he trained for his shot at the title.

But Sammy could do nothing about cards. Ballywell was a small town, and it didn't take long for a game to find Paddy. He'd lost the last four hands, and the minimum buy-in was raised to five hundred pounds. Five hundred was all he had left. When he'd joined the game, he had six grand in his pockets. Paddy didn't think twice.

He went all in.

## Chapter 32

Eileen Breen still had moments that conjured hope. It was misplaced, but it was hope nonetheless. Ela Bond sensed a flicker of recognition in her eyes. There was a warmth. Maybe there was a recollection of the closeness they once shared. She'd filed Eileen's nails before laying out her collection of varnishes. Eileen's attention, limited as it was, focused on the sparkling band on Ela's finger. For a moment, Ela believed she'd remember, but sensing a sudden gust of bewilderment, she delicately reclaimed it.

'Let's go with the lavender', she said, taking Eileen's hand in hers. She always had warm hands. She began with the thumb, applying the varnish with dexterity and calm. Looking up, she was met by one of Eileen's signature smiles.

'A beautiful ring for a beautiful girl.'

Ela smiled back. Despite the fog of her condition, Eileen Breen still had a genial nature and a loving soul. When her nails had dried, her attention returned to the view of the sycamore trees. Ela, meanwhile, leafed through one of the Breen family albums. She stopped at one of her and Danny. He must have been sixteen in the picture, and he'd just won the amateur schoolboys' final in Cork. She remembered the fight. Danny was perfect from the opening bell.

When he boxed, most observers watched the eyes and the gloves, but for Ela, the fascination was in the feet. She enjoyed the intricate patterns, the gliding steps and the graceful pivots. It was the first thing she loved about Danny. He was only a kid then. He was a kid who just happened to box… and a kid who seemed unsure of himself despite the cheering crowds and the shoebox filled with medals.

When their relationship started, Ela understood that his boxing came first. So long as he was winning and smiling, Ela stayed supportive. But while the winning streak grew, his smiles became less frequent. After the age of eighteen, amateur boxing stopped being a game.

She recalled how Danny shrunk to nothing after losing the Irish amateur middleweight title. She remembered Arthur Breen towering over him as his breath filled the room with the smell of cheap whiskey. Only then did Danny utter the words, 'I am done with boxing.'

Not to his father or sister… but to Ela. He had given his youth to the sport, and, she was glad it was ending.

Vincent Grant had very different ideas for the Shamrock Express and offered Danny a generous stipend to turn pro. His recent lapses, Grant argued, was on account of complacency. There was nothing more to gain from the amateur code, and switching to pro would relight the fire in his belly.

Eileen Breen was terrified of the prospect. Danny had done enough, she argued. He'd done enough winter runs and suffered enough broken bones. He was tired of feeling tired, of having to push through the pain barrier time and again. Ela told her not to worry. Danny was done with boxing. She truly believed it.

But there were other powers at play beyond her understanding. There existed in every son a primal need to please his father... to prove himself worthy of a stiff handshake and the indelible words, 'I'm proud of you, son.'

As Arthur watched his son sign his first professional contract, his determination only intensified. With a regular stipend, he could afford to commit more time to training him. Danny would continue to box, and while she'd never fully understand why, Ela vowed never again to convince him otherwise. It was Danny's decision when to walk away.

He raced to nine professional wins and the Irish middleweight title. He was knocking on the door of a British title fight, and a strong showing against Finbar Collins would strengthen his claim. He moved into the gym for his camp, cocooned from the world's distractions... and the life that was growing in Ela's belly. Danny went on to win the fight, but it was the last fight he won with Ela by his side.

Time was her friend, Eileen had counselled. Danny had already been to see her about an engagement ring. She reached for her jewellery box and slid the ring over Ela's engagement finger. 'This is the ring I've saved for you. A beautiful ring for a beautiful girl.'

As she left Serenity House having returned the ring to Eileen's jewellery box, Ela rubbed her thumb across its indent. Only then did she truly feel its weight.

## Chapter 33

Aiden and Alex were approaching the age of worry. They were too young to take care of themselves but old enough to broaden their scope. Their mother, Dee, was too busy to fret. Her husband, Ivan, had mailed his usual amount and a reminder that he wouldn't be home for summer. Dee was an uncomplicated sort. She liked to cut through the nonsense and get down to brass tacks… for the most part. Since that terrible night in Liverpool, she hadn't lifted the phone to her brother or Ela. Had Father O'Dowd been in Shamrock Hills, he'd have taken her to task over Stanley Hall.

His replacement, Father Carrigan, was fresh out of Bible college. His southern brogue betrayed an absence of local roots. The more pious of the congregation hadn't taken to him. For them, the face didn't match the cloth. But lapsed members rejoiced. After years of Father O'Dowd keeping a close eye on attendance, anonymity was a beautiful thing. The kids liked him too. He was a keen follower of English football and a diehard Newcastle United fan.

He didn't follow boxing, describing it as one step from barbarism. Surveying the boys, bright-eyed and dapper as they renewed their baptismal pledges, it was a stretch to imagine any one of them throwing a punch in anger. Certainly not Aiden or Alex.

Maybe it was all the fight talk that had been filling the sports pages of the Shamrock Gazette. Despite Danny Breen being out of the tournament, there was still plenty of interest in the Celtic Four final, and most people fancied Paddy Hughes to capture the UBF belt with another signature knockout against Davey Hibbert.

In Liverpool, the team at Nelson Promotions were beginning to get excited about the Halloween showdown. The fighters' styles meshed perfectly. Hibbert was a high-volume boxer and Hughes was a heavy-handed bruiser. Peter Harrod of GBT was hard at work making sure the television optics were befitting a world title fight. As promised, Nelson dug deeper into his own pockets to strengthen the undercard. That left safety, and he wasn't taking any chances.

*Leave the fighting to the fighters*

He'd been pumping the slogan for weeks. He was doubling the number of security staff for the final and was working closely with Merseyside police. It was important work and doubly important to get the message out that Francis Nelson was taking the game seriously. He was one fight away. Stanley Hall was booked for Halloween weekend. He'd absorbed the worst of the London media blitz and was beginning to look forward to the promotion.

He doublechecked the advertising space. There were billboards, newspapers and morning radio plugs. His team had done well. He considered knocking off for the day as Sophie and Mark from the legal department entered.

'Not today, guys. I can't look at anymore fine print.'

'It's not about contracts, Mr Nelson. We received a call from the UK Boxing Board.'

'And?'

Typically, Sophie was the talker of the two, and Mark was the attendant to details, but the latter had never before seen such a look of appeal in her face. She signalled not just that he could speak but that she wasn't able.

'It's regarding adverse findings in David Hibbert's blood samples taken after his fight with Danny Breen.'

#

Aiden and Alex returned home for the evening. One had a bruised eye, and the other had a fat lip. Father Carrigan stood between them as Dee opened the front door.

'Things got a bit lively down at the old school field.'

His face was red from an interrupted run. Dee had never seen a man of the cloth in running gear. It took her a moment to react. 'I'm embarrassed, Father. What in God's name has happened? What did I tell you both about fighting, boys? I don't care who started it.'

'We weren't fighting each other', Alex protested. 'The McLaughlin boys have been teasing us all summer about Uncle Danny, saying he's a shit fighter and calling him a shithead. They had it coming.'

He'd barely finished speaking as Dee's palm cannoned off the back of his head. Aiden braced for similar impact. They made their way to bed, knowing better than to inquire about supper.

'I'm so sorry, Father. Will you come in for a cup of tea?'

Irish people had done it since time immemorial. A visitor was never turned away without the prospect of a pot of tea, a tray of sandwiches and a selection of fancy biscuits. The youthful priest had better things to do with his evening, Dee assumed. Still, it was only right to offer.

'Actually, a cup of tea would be lovely', he replied. He ran his hand through his curly brown hair before wiping it on the back of his shorts. Dee stood to the side as he entered. She then made for the kitchen and put the kettle on the stove. Supplies were low. She ruminated over corn beef and ketchup as an acceptable sandwich for a priest. Father Carrigan just happened to love corned beef. He seemed positive about most things. His easy grin was ever-present as he took in the Breen family photos.

'Your brothers aren't churchgoers?' he asked.

Dee came through with the tea. 'Not as a rule… and not that I have any right to judge. It can be hard to find time.'

'We should always find time for God. Nothing pleases him more, Mrs Breen.'

'Breen is my maiden name. Please, call me Dee.'

'Right you are, Dee.'

'Have you taken to Shamrock Hills?' she inquired warmly.

The priest sped up his chewing. 'It's a lovely town. Very earthy. And work is going well, though the oldies tend to avoid me. I suppose I can't blame them. They take one look at me and see an oversized child in fancy dress.'

'I'm sure they don't think that.'

'I'm not so sure. I think it myself now and then. Anyway, how is your brother, Danny? Aiden and Alex mentioned they haven't seen much of him.'

She offered the priest another sandwich. The sooner the tray was cleared, the sooner he'd be on his merry way. That her brother, Danny, had taken the loss hard was as much as Father Carrigan needed to know. She dressed it up with enough bells and whistles so as not to seem avoidant, and the young priest scoffed another sandwich as he listened.

'I have an older sister. We don't talk as much as we should. She's the bossy type. Danny's older than you, yes?'

'Yes, by a couple of years. I suppose I was a bossy sister too, but only about boxing. Da needed help keeping him focused. It's the way it had to be. It's a tough sport… and a very unforgiving one.'

'And has Danny forgiven you yet?'

'Excuse me, Father?'

Her arms froze. She didn't know whether to sip her tea or return the cup to its coaster. Seeing this, Father

Carrigan fumbled for words. 'I mean for all the training you made him do when you were kids. I'm sorry, Dee, I've said something wrong, haven't I?'

Seeing only sincerity in his plump, freshly shaved face, she composed herself. 'It has not been easy between us. We have our challenges as a family. Our mother isn't well, and our father passed away a few years ago. After he went, it was all left to me.'

'What was?'

Father Carrigan didn't know that Dee's father had worked in a prison and developed a fondness for whiskey. He didn't know that her mother was in Serenity House with advanced dementia. He'd only seen Danny from a distance and had never met Ela. Dee struggled to answer his question, simple though it was. Father Carrigan leaned closer.

'You can speak to me.'

She laughed nervously, as if what was tearing her apart was but a trifling matter. 'I'm sorry, Father.'

'It's Rory for now. Please, Dee, tell me what's wrong.'

As she burst out crying. Father Carrigan fumbled for a box of tissues. They talked long into the night. Before leaving, the young priest took her hands in his. 'The Good book says much about shame. *"Be not confounded, for you will not be disgraced... you will forget the shame of your youth."* I could quote you a dozen more verses, but it would do you no good.'

He kept a firm grip of her hands and waited for her eyes to look up. 'Because it isn't shame you are wrestling with, Dee.'

'Then what?' she asked.

'Pride', the priest replied.

## Chapter 34

Cobbler's End had been in the works for months. Dozens of meetings took place across the province. The details were carefully guarded, and the papers failed to find even a whiff of a story. Their day would come but not before the contracts were signed and the money was in escrow. Shamrock Hills had suffered too many false dawns. Talk of regeneration had bubbled for decades, but it was 1996 now, and no one on the streets thought about it anymore. They had no idea just how close it was.

Leonard Grant could almost taste it. He stood to make serious bank, but what was another million or two in a bank account containing several? His family's future had long been secured, and with fingers in so many pies, his money now made itself...but money only took a man so far. He spent more on his political campaigns than his opponents combined, but mud really did stick. The Grants were a notorious clan going back generations, their infamy recalled by many as they entered the ballot box. Leonard's cause was not helped by the local papers running a piece on his brother, Vincent, who only weeks removed from his prison release was back boozing in O'Leary's bar, the same bar where he'd beaten a man half to death.

Leonard never did confront him about it. What was there to say? The damage was done, and he was tired of the same old speech. It hadn't worked coming from their father and it didn't work coming from him. Vincent, for whatever reason, attracted trouble. Failing that, he went looking for it.

Leonard had spent a lifetime getting him out of it, and Vincent was still Vincent. The same Vincent who threw Leonard's five-pound trout back in the river when their father's back was turned. A memento of that day hung over the younger brother's fireplace. Their father was so proud of Vincent for reeling in a three-pounder. Leonard never did tell.

Their father lived long enough to see one of his sons make good while the other languished in a prison cell. The brothers rarely talked about their old man. In many ways, they had grown up with different fathers. Different fathers to different sons, for beyond a physical likeness and a knack for fighting, all they shared was blood.

Blood, however, was everything to a Grant. Family came first, and Leonard had done his brotherly duty. During Vincent's sentence, he never missed a prison visit. In 1983, he had Vincent's family moved into a five-bedroom house in Cedar Heights. When Vincent got out in 1985, Leonard set him up in the construction business and signed off on his investment in the Celtic Fist boxing club. When it was all said and done, Vincent was his blood, and he loved him.

He mused over his freshly ground coffee. It was only natural to feel nerves. He remembered those early meetings, being told time and again that the project was dead in the water. Leonard disagreed. Cobbler's End had failed not for lack of money but of vision. The forty-acre area had once been the hub of a proud working class with all manner of factories and plants. The communal playing field had hosted worker's football leagues and carnivals. It was where hundreds of men and women had cast their first vote. The land deserved better. Shamrock Hills deserved better.

#

In Liverpool, Francis Nelson and his legal team combed over the doping report on Davey Hibbert. They had fourteen days to launch an appeal, but it was anyone's guess how long it would take the board to act. Both blood samples showed trace amounts of an anabolic steroid, and Davey Hibbert was looking down the barrel of a three-year ban.

Nelson could do little but ease his nerves with a shot of his favourite cognac. Even if the appeal succeeded, Halloween weekend was closing in fast, and it would only be a matter of time till the press picked up the story. After another shot of cognac, he was ready to make his play. 'Forget the appeal', he said to Sophie and Mark, ushering them out of the office before lifting the phone to Peter Harrod of GBT. He needed him on side. With that, he needed to hear the truth.

'What a total disaster, Francis. Hibbert is under your banner. Do you have any idea how bad this is? The poster boy of your stable gets done for doping? My balls were already on the line!' Francis clenched his jaw. He was a working-class boy made good, and to him, Harrod was just another stuffed shirt, his private education grooming a view that the world owed him an answer.

'It is what it is and we need to stay ahead of it. Let's hold a press conference at the end of this week. Meanwhile, we need to choose Hibbert's replacement. Neary is ready to step in.'

'Neary?' gasped Harrod. '… who Hughes blew away in two rounds? No way.'

'I can still sell it', offered Nelson.

'Neary might bring the fans to Stanley Hall, but it's an awful fight for GBT and the UBF. It's a non-starter.'

'I've looked at the rankings and I know who are available. They are good fighters, but there won't be any local interest. I doubt we'd sell half the seats in Stanley Hall.'

'Well, you're a promoter, aren't you? Create the interest. Find an opponent, and sell it to me.'

The line went dead as Nelson fell back in his chair. As much as he disliked the man, Harrod was right. The Celtic-Four final was for the middleweight championship of the world. He needed a name. He again worked his way through the list of potential opponents. Doing so, he realized that for the Celtic Four final to succeed, he didn't need to sell a fight. He needed to sell a story.

He called back Harrod and floated the idea. The GBT executive took a moment to mull it over. To Nelson, it was an encouraging sign. 'It's an interesting concept, Francis, I'll grant you that. But it's based on a major presupposition.'

Nelson shook his head. 'He won't be able to say no. His pride won't let him.'

'Then get to work' said Harrod before abruptly hanging up.

Nelson felt that seller's rush. He looked at the calendar. The schedule was tight. He called his contacts in the media and told them to be on standby for a big announcement. Finally, he lifted the phone to Leonard Grant. It was time to discuss Cobbler's End.

## Chapter 35

In Shamrock Hills, tales of Vincent Grant's drinking were the stuff of legend. It only took a look, a grazing of shoulders or an innocuous comment. His energy would darken. His eyes would brood into his glass as the demons slid through his every thought. Once sober, he'd always regret it. He'd visit his victims and pony up for damages. Chipped teeth? Torn shirt? Never a worry. Vincent had it covered. But every town had its limits, even for a Grant.

His wife, Leanne, was familiar with the pattern. She had been with Vincent since she was fourteen. She married him at sixteen and had suffered without him for five long years, but not for one minute did her loyalty waver. Vincent was her man, and she knew him better than he knew himself. Soon, a bottle at home wouldn't be enough.

It went against all of his masculine instincts, of pride and self-reliance, but when it came down to it, he'd do anything for Leanne. At least they weren't in Shamrock Hills. They were both grateful for that. And when it came to his demons, Vincent was more a thinker than a speaker, but as he looked around him, he could feel the stories that had already been told. For the first time in his life, it felt right to just talk.

He began with his gypsy lineage. The support group laughed in amusement before gazing in wonderment. Vincent choked up as he told of the beating he put on Robbie Flyn. 'Why him you ask? He was big and within swinging distance... and it got me five years in prison where I could have all the fights I wanted.' Leanne rubbed his arm as he continued. 'But two men taught me that the real fights are in here.' He patted his chest. 'And up here.' He tapped at the shine of his forehead. 'The toughest fights of all.'

He sobbed as he spoke about Block officer Breen and Willie Dunne... one a mild-mannered stoic, and the other a flamboyant sage. Vincent pictured them by the ring apron after he knocked out Terry Tubbs. It was like it was yesterday. He could see that subtle satisfaction in their eyes, that gentle reinforcement of all that they wished to instil... that a calm mind and a steady heart were how men made their way in the world.

'After the fight, Terry Tubbs told me the better man won, and I thought that was the end of it... but a month later they got to Willie. They stabbed him eighteen times, and he bled out on my cell bed. I couldn't stop it, and neither could Arthur. A blade to the neck will stop any man from being a hero. If not because of me, Tubbs would never have called a hit on Willie. It was me who didn't walk away from a fight, and me who didn't have the good sense to lie down. Had Willie not taught me different, I'd still be in that cell today. He showed me a better way, but it cost him his life...

...Arthur was never the same. It's a hell of a thing what trauma can do to a man. There was nothing I could do about that, but I promised I'd get his son, Danny, a shot at the title. He was a hell of a boxer. He was fourteen fights into his career when Arthur died of a heart attack. I don't think Danny ever got over it... and it showed in his boxing. We believed in him. Maybe we believed in him too much. The Celtic Four tournament came from nowhere. I thought he was going to do it. I know nothing can bring back Arthur and Willie, but if Danny had won the title, I could have told myself it was all for something.'

#

Dee was working in the Harbour chip shop. Business was unusually slow despite the agreeable weather. Archie Dougan had been watching her intently. He knew where not to poke his nose, but he could feel the weight of the world on her shoulders. 'Dee, I've got a question for you. A real thinker.'

'OK. I'll do my best.'

'Think of your three biggest problems. Imagine writing them down on scraps of paper and putting them in a hat. I do the same and a handful of others. They get mixed around and we each pull out three.'

'Ok.'

He put his arm around her shoulder and leaned in. 'How relieved would you be if you got your three biggest problems back?'

Dee rolled her eyes in amusement. 'Very.'

Archie smiled. 'Do yourself a favour, Dee. Knock off early and go see who you need to see, and say what you need to say.'

Dee looked about her. She'd polished the counter to a perfect shine. She scanned the floor but couldn't find so much as a speck of dirt. Looking to the clock, she wondered whether it was too late to visit. As she considered how best to broach the topic, Archie was already unfastening her apron. 'I'll see you tomorrow, pet. Bright-eyed and bushy-tailed.'

Sandra and Ernie Bond were watching Coronation Street when their doorbell rang. Dee apologized for the chip shop stink and accepted their offer of tea. Ela was due back any minute, they said. She'd been tutoring guitar all summer. When she arrived home, she suggested they go for a walk along the Harbour path. They'd covered a mile before Dee found the courage to set things right. Their pace slowed to a gentle meander. The evening was mild and free of midges. The story was long, and time was their friend.

It had been easier for Dee to blame Ela, for getting involved with her brother, distracting him from boxing and breaking his heart. That Ela was the cause of the discord, that her father was right all along. When he told her to stay away, Dee did not question it. Not for a second. For what was Dee if not a loyal daughter?

Neither Arthur or Dee knew that Ela was expecting her first child. They didn't know that only days later, Ela visited the local hospital for a twelve-week scan. The embryo looked smaller than average, the doctor said. There should have been a heartbeat. It should have been the day Ela told Danny he was going to be a daddy.

She chose not to tell him. At the time, he was doubling down in the gym as he waited for word of a British title shot. The fight was eventually made, but a week prior to the opening bell, Arthur Breen died of a heart attack. By then, Ela was a resident of Dublin and Eileen had suffered a second stroke.

They both wiped tears from their eyes as they remembered those difficult times. Ela pointed to a bench at the bottom of Glenview where they sat and shared a cigarette. She took a deep breath.

'I never should have left Danny.'

Dee shook her head. 'You did nothing wrong. I'm so sorry, Ela. The letters… I thought I was protecting him. But I wasn't. I was protecting our father. Boxing became an obsession, and I didn't question it. It's all that was holding him together, and I never questioned it… not for a second. I chose not to, and I chose to believe that you were somehow the problem. I am just so sorry.'

Ela looked at her. 'I'm very sorry too, and I forgive you. I just want my Danny back.'

#

Dee walked Ela home before crossing the bridge to her own… to where it all began for her, Jimmy, Danny and

Connor. Her little brother was slow to answer the door. His cats weaved between his hefty legs, fussing for a stroke and a tickle. 'Those letters you kept in the attic. Can you fetch them for me?'

'Ok. Why?'

'They belong to Danny.'

## Chapter 36

In business, Francis Nelson learned never to waste a crisis. The Stanley Hall dream may have been dead, but he knew how to make something from nothing. It's what he did. He had no time to hurt, not from the fortune he'd lost, the good work that was squandered or the hammering he'd taken from the big city press.

The Celtic Four was a name that just came to him. It rolled off the tongue, was simple yet could be made to mean anything. Nelson could feel it. He always trusted his instincts, and from the wreckage of the Stanley Hall semi-final, there was much treasure to salvage.

Unfortunately, Davey Hibbert didn't stand to benefit. It didn't sit comfortably with Nelson, but he told himself that he was young enough to come again. With any luck, the board would be lenient. Still, people would always question his last performance. None of the experts picked him to stop Breen early. The Shamrock Express may have been on the slide, but he was still more than a challenge for the light-punching Hibbert. However, on the night, Hibbert was bigger, stronger, faster and sharper. It raised doubt, and Nelson saw the value in it. So too did Peter Harrod of GBT.

Within twenty-four hours, the narrative was set. Danny Breen had not been given a fair shake, and in the spirit of fair play, now had first refusal as Hibbert's replacement. The Celtic Four Final was coming to Ireland. It was Shamrock Hills versus Ballywell. Danny Breen, surely, wouldn't turn down the chance to face his old gym rival, Paddy Hughes, for the UBF middleweight championship of the world.

#

Jimmy Breen scoffed at the prospect of the fight as he folded up his copy of the Gazette. His brother hadn't thrown a punch in months, and unless Cobbler's End was sitting on a goldmine, it had no business in the business of boxing. He didn't know what was more ridiculous; Nelson suggesting it or Dermot Robinson reporting on it.

'What's got you bothered, Arthur?' asked Eileen.

'Nothing. Just something daft in the paper.'

Jimmy used to think that his mother could avoid such mistakes if only she focused harder. These days it was easier to play along. His acting was wooden, but lucky for him, the role of Arthur Breen wasn't too much of a stretch. Anne Simpson returned the paper to the coffee table and fanned out the magazines. 'It was on the radio too. And all to watch two men fight', she tutted.

Jimmy nodded in agreement. 'And they have the nerve to call it a sport. It's just a money-grab. Plain and simple.'

'Will your brother be bothered by this?'

Jimmy took his time on the question. How Danny was feeling hadn't crossed his mind. He hadn't seen him in a while. 'How could he not be bothered? Winning a world title was everything to him. He was meant to be our next great champion after Luke Gibson. It's sad. I'm no expert on boxing, but Danny would have beaten the brakes off Hughes in his prime.'

'What about now?' she asked earnestly.

'Things are different now. Danny's a beaten fighter. You know, he never really believed in himself. Don't get me wrong, he loved boxing and he was bloody good at it… but you have to believe that you are going to be a champion. Da believed it. And my sister, Dee, believed it'.

'Did you not?'

Jimmy peered out the window. His mother's grip loosened as her eyes slowly closed. 'I didn't think too much about it. I suppose I focused more on Ma.'

Redness rushed to Anne's cheeks and her eyes melted with warmth. 'You suppose? You're a mummy's boy, Jimmy. Believe me. I've seen my share.'

Her hand reached for where the crease of his neck met his freshly pruned hair. A spark, little more than a tickle, jumped between her fingers. After the briefest of pauses, she turned her attention to Eileen's bedding and re-puffed the pillows. Jimmy didn't need the window's reflection to know that her hand came within an inch of him. He'd felt the spark too.

#

Whether Jimmy Breen was for it or not, an agreement in principle had already been made. If Cobbler's End could turn a profit, the council would not stand in Leonard Grant's way. However, where his brother stood, Leonard was still to determine. He parked his land rover a hundred yards short of the construction yard. A leather-bound folder was tucked tight to his side as he entered the head office. He found his brother hard at work, discussing inventory with his foreman.

'What brings you, brother?' Vincent asked. He knew exactly why, but it wasn't often that Leonard needed him more than he needed Leonard. He made space on his work bench and pulled up a chair. Leonard sat down and reached for his cigarettes. 'I had a call from the council. They wanted a quote for a job.'

Vincent offered his lighter and helped himself to one of Leonard's cigarettes. 'What kind of job?'

'A twelve-thousand-seater outdoor stadium. You can cut the act, Vincent. You know what it's for.'

Vincent took a deep pull on his cigarette. 'Ok, I'll have it costed by this evening.'

Leonard passed the folder to Vincent and watched his brother's eyes grow wider. A forty-acre regeneration project. Cafes, restaurants, a business quarter, a tourist information centre, a new library. Halfway through the booklet, Vincent looked up. 'How the hell did you keep this quiet?'

His big brother's face took on a serious expression. 'This is years of graft, brother, and I am close. If I deliver a show like the Celtic Four final to Cobbler's End then this…', he tapped the folder, 'this is what comes out the other side.'

Vincent leafed through the rest of the project. It looked both other-worldly yet immaculately realized. There was Cobbler's End, tucked beside the church grounds to the west and opening on to the Applecross glen to the north. It was as if it always had been.

Leonard masked his satisfaction before standing to leave. 'We all stand to gain from it. Cobbler's End is worth millions to us if we play our cards right. It could be legacy-defining, and it starts with the Celtic Four final. I know we've had a bumpy road with Nelson, but he wants the fight… here in Shamrock Hills. After that, Cobbler's End is ours.'

'So, you want me to talk to Danny?' asked Vincent.

'I think you'd be doing him a disservice if you didn't. Other than the monster payday, he'd be fighting for the title in his hometown… just like Quick Hands Gibson. And just imagine if he won? You couldn't write a better script.'

Vincent mulled it over. 'It doesn't change what happened in Stanley Hall. I'll talk to him about it, but I wouldn't hold my breath, brother.'

Leonard smiled. 'That's all I'm asking for.'

He kept a steady pace as he left the work yard, but inside he was dancing. Vincent's poker face was improving, but Leonard knew his brother. If the money didn't swing it, sentimentality would. At worst, the odds were even that Danny Breen would take the fight.

Vincent had his misgivings and badly needed a second opinion before approaching Danny. He drove to the Celtic First Gym. As he neared the shutter, he noticed the padlock. Wedged tight between it and the chain was a folded piece of paper.

*Fishing in Glenwilliam. Back Friday.*

*Fitzy*

## Chapter 37

When Father O'Dowd arrived in Glenwilliam at the tail end of Winter, the darkness and the damp swiftly suppressed any sense of nostalgia. His memories of boyhood were those of the summer. He remembered how sticky his hands got from climbing trees. He recalled the smell of freshwater trout. He remembered evenings that were so long, he thought they'd never end.

The cottage had belonged to his grandfather. Nothing had changed… from the thatched roof and flagstone floor to the pot oven that hung over the crook, everything had stayed the same. It took the ailing priest the best part of a month to get back in the way of things. His early bread loaves would have chipped a beaver's tooth, and his butter was slicker than car grease. Now, they were as good as his grandmother's, and his fruit scones were arguably better.

He lit the fire every morning as his grandfather had. A good fire was everything to a cottage. For cooking, for bath water and for drying out the timber. It was also good company in the evenings. The fishing season was almost over, and the caravan parks had emptied out. O'Dowd knew that it would soon be time to move on. It was all the more reason to savour the moment.

He folded up some bread and a thick slab of bacon. He placed them in his fishing bag beside a flask of black tea. Sitting over his work table, he struggled with the flies. The medication had further slowed his once nimble hands. Inspecting his shadow, he noticed the sharp edges of his cheekbones. The cancer was either in remission or would be the end of him. That lay with the Lord and not the pipe in his hand. O'Dowd was a temperate man in most regards. A puff in the morning, one at midday and another before bed had sustained him for months.

Temperance proved more challenging for his good friend, Barney Fitzpatrick. Whether it was smoking, a fondness of chippies or betting shop flutters, he was inclined to life's excesses. The morning was only half done, and his cigarette box was already rattling. His journey to Glenwilliam was a pleasant one. The half-empty coach scaled the coastline, cutting through the fresh Atlantic air born from the crashing of waves off thousand-year-old rock.

At noon, as Fitzy walked past a hamlet of cottages, the smell of burning turf seeped from the chimneys. It made him smile. As he ambled up the narrow lane that led to the cottage, he wouldn't have known him had it not been for his fishing cap. Other than his boots, it was all that still fitted Father O'Dowd. 'Have they stopped biting for today?' Fitzy shouted.

'It's our time to bite. Give your hands a wash at the well and we'll get started on lunch', O'Dowd hoarsely replied.

Fitzy descaled the trout while O'Dowd covered the crock iron in hot coals. Baked potatoes in parsley butter would go nicely. They ate well and slept till mid-afternoon. Sharing the sole cottage bedroom was no hardship. Compared to their boarding school days, it was the life of kings. Suitably rested, they set out to find a good fishing spot. O'Dowd led Fitzy through the thick shrub. He had better eyes for ducking branches and blocking brambles. After a few short minutes, Fitzy suggested they stop for a drink of tea. The old priest was exhausted. They sat on flat rocks, pleasantly heated from the afternoon sun. The river gurgled and foamed as O'Dowd poured the tea.

'What took you so long coming here?'

Fitzy looked at his cigarette. It was almost down to the butt. 'I guess it's one thing knowing and another thing seeing.'

O'Dowd nodded gently and watched a grey heron skim the surface of the river. 'Time passes slowly here, so we'll have to make chat. We don't have the legs for an evening of Cowboys and Indians.' He refilled the cups. 'It's no fun getting old, my friend.'

'No' replied Fitzy. 'It isn't.'

Father O'Dowd set a leisurely pace on the way back to the cottage. He allowed Fitzy a generous number of smoke breaks. He was a shell of his former self, but he still had his pride. Reaching the cottage, they fixed a supper of fried eggs and soda bread. By then, Fitzy was ready to talk.

'Danny Breen's on my mind. They are trying to goad him into a big fight in Shamrock Hills.'

O'Dowd stuffed a pinch of tobacco in his pipe. 'Yes, I've been reading about it. But isn't that normal in boxing? One more fight. One last dance under the lights?'

'Aye, something like that.'

'What does Danny think about it?'

Fitzy tossed the last of his coffee and watched it spit and hiss off the white of the turf. O'Dowd struck a match off the table and fired up his pipe. The smoke billowed from his nostrils and twisted through his greying beard. 'And there was me thinking you came here to rediscover the joys of youth.'

Fitzy snorted. 'No, Michael, I just missed your sanctimony. Anyway, it doesn't matter. Danny's done fighting.'

'Danny's done or you are done?'

The question hung as Fitzy threw another turf log into the fire. Temperance was Father O'Dowd's forte. He patiently waited as Fitzy reached for another cigarette.

'Look at me, Barney.'

Fitzy removed his glasses and met O'Dowd's stare before pointing to his blinded eye. 'You think this is easy to live with, Michael? I don't want this for Danny. There's always one more fight.... Always! And title or no title, I promised his dad I'd take care of him.'

O'Dowd leaned across the table so his eyes came level with Fitzy's. 'Then why are you here?' he whispered. The priest gingerly rose from his chair and reached for his fishing box. 'You do the flies. I'll see you in the morning.'

Fitzy held his tongue despite his boiling rage. It was a mark of respect that went back to their school days. They were an odd pairing then. One was little and the other was large. O'Dowd was the son of a doctor, and Fitzy came from an orphanage. His estranged uncle never did say why he took such sudden interest, collecting him from the orphanage aged ten before enrolling him in Dunhaven School for Boys.

After that, he never saw him again... and the following summer was the first of several spent with the O'Dowd Family in Glenwilliam. They never made it feel like charity. They were the happiest times of his life, and in return, he always allowed Michael the last word. Moreover, it was still his grandfather's cottage. They were both mindful of that.

It rained heavily during the night, so the next morning they took a more domestic route to the river. They kept to a path well traversed by farmers and their various livestock. It was still the Glenwilliam of old. Men inspected their turf quotas from their Massey 35 tractors. In a nearby quarry, a family still made their living from cutting limestone. A mile to the east was the fairy field. It was called the fairy field for who could have stood such large stones but the fairies themselves? Fitzy and O'Dowd had long outgrown the myth, but like everyone else, still considered the field sacred ground. Glenwilliam hadn't changed, and they hoped it never would.

The river was high and running at a good clip. They flicked out their lines and kept close to the bank. O'Dowd reeled his in and watched Fitzy make his way further downriver. The priest pondered just how far he would go to avoid conversation. In the end, the riverbed decided, the sediment slipping under the weight of Fitzy's boot and dropping him onto the seat of his trousers. O'Dowd laughed himself hoarse. It was worth the pain.

Fitzy beat his clothes off dry rocks before spreading them over a whin bush. In the time it had taken, O'Dowd had caught another trout. 'If I offended you yesterday, I apologize.' He unhooked his catch and returned it to the river. 'I don't know Danny like you do, but I know the family.'

'Then you know enough. The last place Danny should be is in a boxing ring. It's life or death in there, and that Hughes boy is a killer. When he first came to the gym, I told Danny to only use one hand in sparring. That's how far behind he was. But a year later, he's beating up Danny in sparring. That's how fast he's improved.'

O'Dowd thought quietly. 'Maybe that's how fast Danny has declined. Or maybe he no longer has this 'fighting heart' that you talk about... yes?'

'It's 'fighting pride'… and it doesn't matter now. Even if Danny's head was right… and even if it was ready to burst out of him, Paddy would still have the beating of him. He's not a young man anymore. He could get seriously hurt.'

'I read the Hughes boy was an orphan.'

'Yes. I took him in when he had nowhere else to go. He's a hell of a fighter, but he's his own worst enemy. I did what I could for him, but once Francis Nelson flashed the cash, it was adios Paddy Hughes.

O'Dowd mused. 'I imagine he needed a father figure as much as a place to train and sleep,'

'Well, he got more than I ever did.'

Fitzy flicked his cigarette into the river and checked the progress of his clothes. They were dry enough, he decided. Pulling the t-shirt over his head, he allowed a deep sigh to pour through the fabric. With his back to O'Dowd, he looked up to the tips of the fir trees. 'My uncle never said it, but I knew. I always knew.'

O'Dowd stepped away from the river bank and towards his friend. 'And you kept fighting, Barney. And in all the time I've known you, you've never shied away from a fight. Don't start now.'

## Chapter 38

The UBF president owned a two-hundred-foot yacht, a fleet of sports cars and had penthouses in London, Dubai, New York and Hong Kong, There was wealth. There was generational wealth. And then there was Carlos Bernardi, the billionaire business tycoon and the latest major player in boxing.

His love affair with the sport began in the 1970s, with household names like Joe Frazier, George Foreman and the greatest of all time, Muhummad Ali. They fought in epic fights that spanned the globe, from Kingston in Jamaica to the heart of the Congo. They were the nights that encapsulated Bernardi's ambition. Not money, not fame, but the chance to make history.

He loved his homeland, Monte Carlo, but the prospect of a few hundred millionaires concerned more for their next scoop of caviar than the world's greatest fighters did little for boxing's legacy. No, to truly leave a mark meant building something from the ground up. It was every promoter's job to talk big, and Bernardi had listened to more than his share. But Francis Nelson spoke with genuine passion and zeal. He kept faith that the Liverpool man would turn things around.

Peter Harrod of GBT was a man of economy. He was economical with his time and his words. In essence, he was the polar opposite of a boxing promoter, and he couldn't spin the delay of The Celtic Four final to Bernardi any better than he could to his bosses. After three tries, he finally reached Francis Nelson. 'You have till the end of the week to get Breen over the line or we're through, Francis. I don't care how you do it. I don't care if you bankrupt yourself. Get it done.'

Francis had been decent till now, but Danny Breen's team had dithered long enough. By mid-week the Irish sports pages were brimming with speculation. Why weren't the Grant brothers delivering their promised boost to the local economy? Why had Barney Fitzpatrick, after twenty years of grooming his greatest prospect, suddenly lost faith in the Shamrock Express? And most scathing of all, why was Danny Breen depriving his late father a world champion son?

Leonard Grant couldn't afford bad press and was at a loss to his brother Vincent's newfound sense of calm. 'Danny knows what offer is on the table. It's up to him'.

'Is he holding out for more money?' asked Leonard. 'Because I'm telling you, he's risking the whole event falling through. Have you spoken to Fitzy about it?'

Vincent lifted his work phone and flicked open his order book. 'I have to deal with this, brother. Go and see Fitzy. You might have more luck than me.'

As if luck had anything to do with it, cursed Leonard as he charged across the building yard and into his Land Rover. Checking his phone, he saw four missed calls from Liverpool. He was past caring about Nelson. His own reputation was in the balance. A few minutes later, he ducked under the shutter and into the fresh stink of the Celtic Fist gym. Young Gary McGinty was doing bursts on the pads. His bare back was gleaming like a newly polished car. Leonard rested an arm on the turnbuckle and waited for Fitzy's stopwatch to sound.

'We're done in ten', Fitzy said without looking to Leonard.

'I don't have ten minutes. You understand, don't you, son?'

McGinty looked to Fitzy. He nodded at the trainer and made his way out of the ring. Fitzy wiped himself with a dry towel and joined Leonard in the office.

'What's so urgent?'

'You know what. Why is Danny stalling?'

Fitzy leaned back in exasperation. 'He hasn't trained since the loss in Stanley Hall. You know that. And he hasn't come asking about the fight. He's done fighting.'

Leonard fixed Fitzy with a menacing glare. 'Are you telling me that you haven't even sounded him out? His biggest ever payday and a shot at the title…and you haven't even sat down with him?'

'To discuss what? We all saw what happened in Liverpool. He doesn't have it anymore.'

Leonard scoffed. 'He had a bad night. Shit happens. But that doesn't mean you let him dismiss the opportunity of a lifetime. Liverpool is the past. I'm talking about here and now!'

'So am I!' Fitzy snapped. 'If he came to me wanting the fight, I'd be in his corner no questions asked… because I care about the kid. And when I was tending to his cuts in Stanley Hall, you were getting your picture taken with Francis Nelson.'

'So?'

'So don't stand here now like you care at all about what's best for him. Don't piss down my back and tell me it's raining, Leonard. I've nothing more to say!'

'Is that so?'

'Yes! That is so! Now, get the hell out of my gym!'

A thin grin crossed Leonard's mouth.

'But it's not just *your* gym, is it?'

Fitzy shook his head as he buffered the steam off his glasses. 'I've spoken with Vincent about the fight. It's Danny's choice. There is nothing more to say.'

'Aye, and I'm speaking for Grant Enterprises. You forget that it's my company that owns a stake in this shithole, not Vincent's. And I promise you this, Barney, if you don't get Breen in the ring against Hughes, I won't just come looking for my money back.' His eyes scanned the confines of the gym. 'I'll raze this place to the ground.' Before leaving, he leaned in so close that Fitzy felt the warmth from his breath. 'One more fight.'

It took a couple of moments to process the shock before Fitzy rose to his feet. Looking across to the heavy bags, he was relieved to see that McGinty had gone for a shower. He grabbed a brush and began sweeping the grit off the ring canvas. The shutter door rattled. For some reason, he assumed it was Danny, but looking up, he was disappointed by the weasel-like figure of Dermot Robinson. Fitzy threw his keys onto the ring canvas. 'When you're done, tell Gary to bring them to O'Leary's.'

It was a setback for Robinson. The McGinty interview was only a means of getting his foot in the door. 'Maybe I'll see you there later.' Fitzy shook his head. 'I'd stay well clear If I were you. You've done enough scribbling about me. And you've done enough scribbling about Danny. Let it be, Dermot.'

Fitzy trudged towards the shutter door. Dermot thought about following but abandoned the notion with a half-hearted bid. 'It wasn't personal, Barney. You know that.' Fitzy kept walking, leaving Dermot only half-sure of what he muttered in response. That was probably best.

Writing about Danny's career was a journey incomparable to Fitzy's, yet Robinson still felt, like he had that night in Stanley Hall, a profound sadness. When he got home, he described it to his wife as a sudden and suffocating realization that he, and not only Fitzy and Danny, was yesterday's man. She laughed off the notion and ran him a bath as he undid his shirt buttons.

'Vincent Grant called about an hour ago', she shouted from the bathroom.

Grabbing a handful of belly-fat through his yellowed white vest, he shouted up the corridor, 'You mean Leonard Grant, sweetheart.'

'No, it was Vincent Grant He said he'd call back in the morning to see if you're free for golf.'

Dermot nodded to himself and turned his back on the bedroom mirror. There were worse ways to spend Wednesday morning, and he needed the exercise.

## Chapter 39

In Shamrock Hills, a day of four seasons was rarely uncommon, and Danny Breen, like any mere mortal, preferred a gentle wind on his back during his morning runs. But after Stanley Hall, there was no fight camp on the horizon. There was nothing to preserve his body for, and for the first time in twenty years, he had no reason to run.

His eye healed well. The blood had seeped like a faucet that night, running off his chest and staining his green and gold shorts. Looking at the scar in the mirror, it said little of that night. The thin pink line was barely a memento. For the first couple of weeks, the post-fight pain in his bones proved a useful distraction. What followed was a fog thicker than any he'd faced in his morning runs.

A month after the fight, he returned to the work yard. There were no comforting pats on the back. No *better luck next times*. Enough days had passed. Danny was just one of the men, blending so well he could hide in plain sight. Yet something continued to nag. It shortened his breaths and twitched the fibres of his quads and thighs.

The next morning, Danny rose early. Stripping down, he felt an odd sensation in the balls of his feet. As his right hand felt the water climb slowly from tepid to warm, his left hand twitched... almost cat-like. He knocked the shower off. Returning to his bedroom, he opened his wardrobe and reached for his running shoes.

Before long, he was charging the hill to the Applecross glen and sprinting through Cedar Park where Luke Gibson stood like a titan. That morning, he gasped for air through burning lungs, through the searing pain of his hamstrings and the bile in his stomach. In that moment at least, the fog had begun to disperse.

Meanwhile, Francis Nelson and Peter Harrod were touching down in Belfast. By lunchtime, everyone on the yard would know. All of Shamrock Hills would know. The gauntlet would be thrown. Would Danny Breen fight his Ballywell rival in a final farewell or officially retire? When the news broke, Vincent Grant told him to take the rest of the week off. The last thing Danny needed was the company of half-drunken labourers and their sudden expertise on the sweet science of boxing.

He returned to his flat where he noticed something jammed in his letterbox. He was typically lackadaisical when it came to mail, but the envelope was especially weighty and thick. Turning it over, it wasn't addressed or stamped. Opening it, he recognized the handwriting. He shuffled the contents and noted the dates on the postmarks. Images began to form as if appearing through a thick mist at dawn... of his mother in a hospital bed... and his father's face, pale and withered as the lid was placed on his coffin. Danny saw himself crying on the ring canvas of the Celtic Fist gym. He recalled the suffocating ache of a young man and his loss.

The flat was eerily quiet. Every piece of furniture, every fibre of cloth and every speck of dust was suspended in time as Danny held the letters. He could return them to sender. He could burn them in his kitchen sink. Or he could read them. He could learn that Ela's love never wavered. That the son they never met had a name. That boxing tore his family apart.

The next day he walked to the graveyard of the Church of the Resurrection. 'Why did it mean so much?' Danny asked. It was mid-afternoon and the weather had taken a turn for the worst. The blue morning sky was now lost to a relentless grey drizzle. The church graveyard was drenched. He waited... but Arthur Breen's headstone provided no answer.

When he reached Serenity House, Anne Simpson brought him dry towels and a woollen cardigan. He watched his mum sleep peacefully as the rain ran off the window. Jimmy arrived shortly after. Anne had seen that look of unfeigned concern in hundreds of faces. Jimmy wasn't good with his feelings, but in that moment, he'd have taken any amount of pain to spare his little brother.

He walked Danny to his car and drove him to the Cloverhill estate. The rain fell hard and would likely pour all through the night. 'You don't have to prove anything to anyone. Ignore the papers and don't let the bastards get you down. If you need anything, let me know.' Danny nodded his thanks and made a run for his flat. The cardigan was warm and snug. It would have been a shame to let it soak.

Vincent visited him that Sunday. There was nothing to be gained from brooding, Danny said, and with the last of Ela's letters read, it was time to move on and return to work. If anything, some hard labour would help purge his mind before he visited her. His silence had punished her long enough.

'That's good', Vincent commented. 'She's a diamond, Danny, and it's time you moved forward.'

Danny nodded. His face was half-covered by the hood of his Everlast sweater. Vincent, for some reason, found it harder to say to Danny what he'd told a group of strangers at his first AA meeting. 'Did your da talk to you about a man called Willie Dunne?'

'Don't think so,' replied Danny.

'He was an inmate on his block, and he was stabbed to death in his cell. Anyway, you were only a kid when it happened. I suppose it's right he never told you about it.'

Danny shook his head. 'No, he didn't. He never talked about work. He didn't talk much about anything…'

'…except boxing', they said before sharing a dry chuckle. 'You probably hold Fitzy responsible for that', Vincent offered.

'Fitzy's tape collection, yes. Every evening Da had one of those tapes in the recorder. All the old black and whites. Ray Robinson, Joe Louis, Ezzard Charles. For all I knew, boxing was the only sport in existence.' Danny stretched the fingers of his right hand and massaged the dents in his knuckles. 'It was just a way of life.'

'And it was a way of keeping order on his block. That prison was one nasty place. And boxing became the outlet, for the inmates and the guards.'

Danny pulled back his hood. 'I was neither. I was his son. Anyway, what happened to Willie?'

'There were four men involved. Three were training in the boxing club on the far side of the wing. Your da was watching on when all of a sudden, they turned on him. And in the space of time it took to get things under control, Willie was hit in his cell.'

'Da blamed himself?'

'Of course he did. It was his block and Willie was his man. He'd always have held himself accountable. But the blame lay with me. Anyway, your father came to see me that night. I thought he was there to console me...'

Vincent took a moment to steady himself. 'I thought the world of Willie and so did your da, but what hurt him most was knowing that while Willie bled out, he stood frozen with fear in that ring... with a rusty blade cutting into his neck. He told me he'd never felt so terrified in his life. And he promised himself there and then, that if you continued boxing, he'd move heaven and earth to make sure you never felt that way in the ring.'

'He never told me that', replied Danny.

'I don't think he would have wanted you to know that… not as a boxer. He dealt with it by doubling down on your career… and I was with him all the way. I wanted it for him as much as I wanted it for you. Had he not died, we'd have got you there'.

Danny smiled. 'It only takes one fight.'

Vincent nodded. 'That's right. One fight. I've seen the offer. It's good. It's really good. But that should have no bearing on whether you choose to get in there. Neither should the title. You only have to ask yourself one question, kid. Are you a fighter? Only you can decide if you have unfinished business in that ring.'

Before Danny could contemplate one last fight, he had some visits to make. He started with the Celtic Fist gym, but Fitzy was still casting his line in Glenwilliam. He then walked past the Glenview in the direction of the Bond residence. He peered through their kitchen window. They had just sat down for Sunday dinner. Ela could wait till tomorrow. His legs felt strong, so he broke into a jog and kept a steady pace as he crossed the St Columb's Bridge.

Aiden and Alex met him at the front door and speared him with hugs for their favourite uncle. Dee remained rooted to the spot, knowing by now that the letters had been read, fearing the worst, oblivious to the fact that all she needed to heal was a hug from her brother.

Later that evening, Vincent Grant parked outside Leonard's home and blasted the horn. He came out and joined Vincent in his Alpha Romeo.

'Well?'

'He's going to take the fight. I'm sure of it.'

# Chapter 40

### COBBLER'S ENDGAME

By Dermot Robinson

Chief sportswriter: The Shamrock Gazette

In a further twist in the biggest sports story of the summer, the much-anticipated UBF middleweight world title fight between Danny Breen and Paddy Hughes is on the brink of collapse. A number of concerns surrounding the vested financial interests of local businessmen, Vincent and Leonard Grant, have been raised with the Irish Boxing Board.

The brothers (and co-chairmen of Grant Enterprises) are in violation of several rules pertaining to their management of boxers, the planned construction of a purpose-built stadium for the proposed fight and their involvement in an investment fund to regenerate the Cobbler's End area.

At the time of writing, Shamrock Hills Council confirmed that Grant Enterprises were overseeing the construction of an outdoor stadium in the once fabled Cobbler's End. While such a project is nothing new for the company, it presents a series of conflicts regarding boxing's governance.

Billed as the final of the 'Celtic Four' middleweight tournament, one is compelled to ask (as the Irish Boxing Board surely will) who exactly is financing the event? Typically, the costs of delivering an event fall on the licensed promoter- in this case, Francis Nelson of Nelson Promotions.

In addition, the Shamrock Gazette can confirm that Grant Enterprises continues to manage the career of Danny Breen as well as owning a thirty percent stake in the Celtic Fist gym where Breen has trained throughout his career. Such ties breach a multiplicity of boxing guidelines, and in the most dangerous sport of all, how can the Grant Brothers act in the best interests of their fighter when it is now clear that their ultimate interests are financial?

Speculation is rife that they are spearheading a significant investment group tasked with regenerating Cobbler's End, transforming it into a modern-day hub for business, tourism and cultural arts.

So, what are we to expect come Halloween weekend? Will we see a bona-fide world title fight between Danny Breen and Paddy Hughes? Or will we be attending a real estate launch courtesy of Grant Enterprises? One thing is for sure; the Irish Boxing Board will not allow the Grants to have their flag in both camps.

*This of course presumes that the event goes ahead. With no official press conference having taken place, and with the construction of the stadium yet to begin, the onus is now on Francis Nelson and UBF president, Carlos Bernardi, to take back control of the 'Celtic Four' final. It is for them to leave the Irish Boxing Board in no doubt that the fighters' best interests are served and that the integrity of the sport is upheld.*

#

Within minutes of reading the article, Leonard Grant charged into the office of the Shamrock Gazette and threatened litigation. The editor insisted that nothing went to print unless the facts checked out. Dermot Robinson's sources were solid. He was just doing his job. Giving up, Leonard sped across town and knocked on the door of his brother's home in Cedar Heights. Vincent ushered him in and poured them both a large measure of whiskey. Leanne gave her man a long stare and, feeling suitably assured, she left the brothers to talk.

Vincent laughed off the suggestion that Danny Breen had leaked the Cobbler's End plans to Robinson. 'The press dogged him all summer and he said nothing. Why would he speak now? He's got everything he wants.'

'Does he?' Leonard pressed. 'He's taking his time signing the contract!'

Vincent nodded. 'I know. He had things he needed to deal with, brother. Trust me, he's taking the fight.'

Leonard paced the length of Vincent's living room. Stopping, the net suddenly became smaller. Who else, other than Danny, would have sought out a two-bit sports journalist in Dermot Robinson? Who else knew the details of the fight contract? Leonard turned to face his brother. 'There's only one person it could have been.'

Vincent set his whiskey on the mantlepiece. He had yet to sample it. 'Who?'

'Fitzy.'

'Why would Fitzy want the fight to fall through? He would never go against Danny's wishes.'

Leonard looked to the ceiling before downing his whiskey. 'Unless he had an axe to grind.'

He recounted his visit to the Celtic Fist gym. He was usually the cool-headed one, but he'd reverted to the type of street tactics he'd long admonished Vincent for.

'What does Francis Nelson make of all this?' Vincent asked.

Leonard's sigh gave way to an agonizing groan. He reached for Vincent's phone and tried the promoter's private line. It went to voicemail.

'Maybe that's a good thing', offered Vincent. 'We ought to get our own house in order before reaching out to Nelson.' He led Leonard back to his seat and stood over him. 'All that matters is that the fight goes ahead. Danny wants it. We want it. Christ, the whole of Ireland wants it. To hell with Robinson and his sources.'

'But we now have bigger problems than Robinson. It's the boxing board that I'm worried about. Eyes are on them now, and we can't expect any favours.'

Vincent edged closer to his brother. 'Then we play by the book.'

Leonard set down his tumbler before it smashed in his hand. 'I will bleed that pig dry', he threatened.

Vincent nodded in agreement. 'Fitzy's day will come. But right now, we need him to get Danny ready for a fight.'

#

In the Celtic Fist boxing club, Fitzy kept a close eye on the sparring as the buzzer went to end the fourth round. Danny Breen was blowing hard. After three months of inactivity and just two months from his day of reckoning with Paddy Hughes, he'd left himself a mountain to climb.

'Up the tempo!' thundered Fitzy. 'Four more rounds! If you don't like it Danny, go back to mixing cement!'

The Shamrock Express rose from his stool and, at the sound of the buzzer, raced across the ring and into the chest of Gary McGinty. They shoved and grappled, competing for the same half-foot of space to unload bruising shots to the liver and thudding hooks to the nose bone and temples. Danny was not boxing to instruction, choosing instead to dog it out with a fighter a full twenty pounds heavier. It was a good sign. He was hungry again.

It amounted to a satisfying session in the Celtic Fist gym. Readying to close up for the night, Fitzy's problems felt like little ones as Leonard Grant's land rover tore up the gravel outside. He entered alongside Vincent, both full-chested and brooding. The family solicitor followed closely behind. The trainer looked to the younger of the Grants.

'What's this about?'

'A parting of the ways…' replied Vincent. 'We're here to sign our stake over to you. Our stake in the gym, in Danny… everything.'

'Why?'

'I suppose you haven't had time to read the paper', added Leonard sarcastically before signalling to the family solicitor. 'I communicated with the boxing board earlier today. Neither Vincent or Leonard can represent Danny Breen for the Cobbler's End fight. And from today, Grant Enterprises wishes to end its association with the Celtic Fist gym.'

Fitzy again looked to Vincent. 'You want me to buy you out? You know I don't have that kind of money.'

'Your cut of Danny's purse will certainly help. It's now doubled', Leonard interjected. He again looked to the solicitor.

'What we are proposing is that full ownership of the Celtic Fist gym and Danny Breen's management be signed over to you. As for financial compensation owed to Grant Enterprises, I think it is in everyone's interests that we mediate after the proposed fight on October 30th.'

Vincent stepped towards Fitzy. 'You said that we do what's right for Danny and not what makes us good men. Well, I'm holding you to that. I believe Danny can win. It's his shot at the title, and I'm not going to stand in his way. Are you?'

Fitzy sighed. 'You're not leaving me much choice, but I already told you, if he wants the fight, I'm with him.'

'And does he?' asked Leonard.

Fitzy nodded. 'Yes. He wants it.'

## Chapter 41

The big players had arrived in Shamrock Hills. Francis Nelson, Peter Harrod and Carlos Bernardi were airlifted from Belfast. Today was the point of no return. The town hall was filled to capacity, and hundreds more thronged outside. Leonard Grant was among the first to arrive. He'd bought a new suit for the occasion and had his teeth whitened. His speech was neatly folded and safe in his breast pocket. He was leaving nothing to chance.

Vincent and Leanne were still at home, eating into their hour of safety. The day promised champagne and glamour, and Leanne was dressed to kill. All the encouragement Vincent needed was a whiff of her favourite perfume. In Cedar Park, Father Carrigan was walking his pug. After his 11am service, he had a wedding to bless. It was the first of his tenure in Shamrock Hills.

Sammy Stewart ruminated all night and all morning. He kept a small circle, and to those select few, there was no moral quandary. But Sammy had been down this road before with Paddy Hughes, and it only made his decision harder. He looked at his fighter in the rear-view mirror. He would soon be eyeball to eyeball with his old stablemate and mentor. It was Shamrock Hills versus Ballywell, and today was a declaration of war.

Danny Breen let himself into Fitzy's apartment. His trainer was finishing his third cup of coffee. He wiped the crumbs off his shirt and reached for his jacket. The town hall was twenty minutes on foot. Danny took a deep breath as they turned the corner and made for the Harbor path. Fitzy could sense his unease.

'You nervous?'

'Wouldn't you be?' replied Danny.

Fitzy pulled a bemused face. 'It's just another day, and you're just another bare bum in the shower.'

'Thanks. I'll remember that when I'm up there.'

'Good lad', replied Fitzy as he playfully patted Danny's backside.

In the Shamrock Hills town hall, the UBF title belt took pride of place just like it had in Liverpool. Again, Paddy 'One Shot' Hughes gave it an affectionate pat before sizing up his opponent. Fitzy leaned into Danny. 'That's not the swagger of a confident man. It's an act. This time last year he couldn't land a glove on you. Don't forget that. He's a crude slugger… ten a penny.'

The UBF president, Carlos Bernardi, was first to the pulpit. 'Ladies and gentlemen, it is my pleasure to be with you today.' He raised his fists. His left extended to the crowd, and his right stayed a half-inch from his jaw.

'It is boxing that brings us here. Boxing…. the noble art, the purest form of combat… and the greatest sport on earth.' He released his fists and squared his stance. 'For boxing is life. And in life…. we fight. We fight to be seen… to be heard. We fight for our family… and we fight for our pride.

These warriors…', gesturing to Hughes on his right and Danny to his left, '…they were chosen to fight. God lit a fire in them, and on Halloween weekend, we will see whose burns brightest. One of them will be crowned King of the Celtic Four… and the first UBF middleweight champion of the world!'

The hall erupted with cheers, but the multi-billionaire was just getting started. He gestured for decorum. 'And for flames to grow, the fire must breathe. Ladies and gentlemen, for many years I have dreamed of breathing new life into the sport I hold so dear, to provide opportunity, to inspire future generations… and to leave a legacy.

On October thirtieth, Danny Breen and Paddy Hughes will fight not only for their legacies but for yours. The UBF championship marks the beginning of a new chapter for Shamrock Hills. With that said, it is my honour to welcome onto the stage, Leonard and Vincent Grant, the pioneers of the Cobbler's End Regeneration Project!'

It was a hell of an introduction and, short of halos above their heads, the Grant brothers took to the stage like guardian angels. They kept their speech short and allowed the visuals to speak a hundred thousand words. It was a new

Cobbler's End for a new Shamrock Hills. It was thoroughly planned and fully costed... a perfect meshing of rich tradition and modern innovation.

It felt big and it was. Peter Harrod and Francis Nelson had yet to grace the stage. They hid their displeasure with plastic grins and half-hearted applause. It was not what either man envisaged, but this was the price to pay for needing Bernardi. At least Harrod had a sense of humour about it. Leaning into Nelson, he muttered, 'Luck of the Irish, eh?' That may have been so, but Leonard Grant had made his own luck, and Nelson, despite feeling eclipsed, could only respect his hustle.

The focus soon returned to boxing. The coaches were asked to speak. Sammy Stewart, a quiet man by nature, kept it simple. He gave respect to Danny Breen, highlighting his stellar amateur career and his signature wins in the professional ranks.

'But time is not his friend, and he's sorely lacking the one thing my fighter has in abundance... and that's momentum. Paddy Hughes has all the momentum going into this fight, and Danny knows it. He also knows that Paddy hits harder, works harder and wants this more.'

Fitzy grabbed his microphone. 'And he knows that Paddy Hughes has the boxing IQ of a pickled egg. And I know it, and you know it, Sammy.' He leaned forward to get a good look at Paddy. 'You're no phenom, son. You're a hype job, but I'm very grateful to you. Cobbler's End is sold out, and my boy is getting the biggest purse of his career. How much are *you* getting paid?'

Francis Nelson took a firm grip of Paddy's arm. The boxing establishment was waiting for another promotional fiasco, and Francis was not about to let Paddy serve it. He looked across to Fitzy and smiled as if it was all fun and games. 'Everything happens for a reason, Barney. Just look where we are now. We have two Irishmen in a stadium fight for the UBF title. You can dismiss him all you want, but Hughes is the real deal. He's been made the betting favourite by every major bookmaker in Ireland.'

Fitzy laughed. 'Don't tell Paddy that. You know how he gets.'

A mix of boos and cheers reverberated around the hall as Fitzy folded his arms with indifference. He had eight weeks to train Danny on overcoming Paddy's savagery in the ring. Till then, the verbal assaults were his domain, not his fighter's. Dermot Robinson watched on. Danny Breen had never looked so relaxed, he thought. Looking over to Paddy Hughes, he noted how the young fighter's rage had turned inward. As far as the fight presser went, Shamrock Hills was first to draw blood.

The fighters faced off for photographers. Danny stood tall, all six feet of him. Seeing the younger man's focus beginning to ebb, he smiled before turning to face the crowd. He looked for Ela in the balcony. Seeing her, his smile widened as he flexed his biceps.

As the town hall emptied, Fitzy brushed past Leonard Grant. The latter was preoccupied with photographers and journalists. Among them was Dermot Robinson. Seeing Vincent Grant leaving with his wife, Leanne, he winked at the younger of the Grant brothers.

Danny met Ela outside the town hall. She was wearing her favourite lavender t-shirt. Her skin smelled faintly of strawberries, and her golden locks caressed her neck in a delicate bob. 'You're the prettiest pixie I've ever seen', remarked Danny.

'Good enough to marry?' she asked.

'If you'll have me', he replied. He wrapped his arm around her waist and rested his hand on the small of her belly.

At Serenity House, Anne Simpson was readying Eileen. Seeing Ela and Danny enter, her face blushed with happiness. 'I'm sorry. I just love weddings.' She turned Eileen's chair away from the window. As she passed the happy couple, Ela spotted a tear forming. 'Just ring the bell if you need anything, and congratulations.'

Danny looked at Ela bemusedly. 'I didn't know we were so close.'

Ela jabbed at his ribcage as Eileen watched them contentedly.

'Who are you?' she asked.

Danny reached into his pocket for a photograph and kneeled by the arm of his mother's chair. 'That's you, that's

Arthur, that's Ela and that's me.' Eileen's eyes scanned the faces. 'I don't want you boxing anymore, Danny. It's a rough ole game.'

'I know, Ma.' He reached for Ela's hand. You always wanted me to marry Ela.'

'Did I?'

'You did. We are going to get married and start a family.'

Eileen looked up to Ela and back to the picture. Raising an arm, her warm palm rested on Danny's cheek. 'That's something worth fighting for.'

#

Ivan Young, Danny Breen's brother-in-law and best man, had been in town for three days. He was kept away from the public glare, taking up residence in the Celtic Fist gym and having his meals delivered by Dana and Shane from O'Reilly's bar. His main job was to turn up at the church before the maid of honour, Dee. Checking his watch, he decided to take a walk around the grounds. Doing so, he spotted the groom by his father in law's grave.

Danny struggled for words. They never had spoken much. Boxing had filled the void. The sun had risen and set with it, had sustained them through bitterly cold winters, along wet country roads… across the length and breadth of Ireland.

'I never did thank you, Da, and I'm sorry for that. I know how much it mattered and why you did what you did. I want to tell you I'm grateful… and I forgive you.'

He brushed a tear from his eye and filled his lungs with fresh air. 'I wish you were here today. I love you.' Turning, he saw Ivan a dozen grave plots away, his hands in his pockets, his wiry curls jiggling in the breeze. They looked towards the church entrance. 'Last chance to back out', quipped the best man. Danny laughed. 'Worry about yourself, Ivan. Dee might plant you with a kiss or a left hook, so keep your guard up.'

Eileen Breen arrived just before the vows, looking stunning in green and accompanied by Anne, a picture in pink. Jimmy rose from his seat to join them. Father Carrigan proceeded to the rings. Danny eased it along Ela's slender finger, and as it touched the rubied sparkle of the band once belonging to his mother, he couldn't help but kiss his bride.

## Chapter 42

The fire had been burning since daybreak. His breakfast of scone bread and jam lay untouched but for the interest of a passing wasp. He pushed open the living room windows and allowed the fresh September air to enter. The sunshine was warm against his bony hand. He packed the last of his belongings and sat by his desk.

Father O'Dowd's pen moved smoothly over the parchment. Each word flowed as if it were a signature. Eileen Breen was not long for this world, and as he penned his respects, he wondered when such a letter would be written for him.

At the Shamrock Hills hospital, the Breen siblings gathered by their mother's bed. Three nurses had come and gone. Eileen was comfortable, they assured. Dee's eyes were heavy. She'd sat up all night while Danny and Jimmy paced the halls. They waited till morning to tell Connor. 'She's had strokes before and got better', he insisted, his eyes wide and bright through thick-lensed glasses. Dee checked her watch and looked to Danny. 'Don't keep Fitzy waiting.' He rose from his chair and ruffled the hair of his younger brother. 'You'll keep Ma company till I get back, won't you?'

Jimmy reached for his car keys. Before leaving, he placed a kiss on the papery skin of his mother's brow. It had only been two days, but she looked half her size. It was strange what a hospital bed did to a person.

In the town, the shutter of Dana's kitchen hadn't lifted. Outside the Harbour chip shop, a trio of gulls picked at a half-eaten fish supper. At Riley's Paper and Post, Scratchcard Jonny fought to stay upright. Traffic was sparse on the St Columb's bridge. It was a typical Sunday in Shamrock Hills, and the brothers traversed its calm in silence, knowing their mother wouldn't live to see another.

Fitzy and Gary McGinty waited by the entrance of the gym. They each offered a hand to Jimmy before embracing the Shamrock Express. A hard spar was the best sanctuary they could offer. The familiar mix of fresh sweat and steam. The creaking of the canvas boards… the thuds of heavy leather punctuating time's passage to which they'd all one day succumb.

Fitzy watched Danny intently. They had four more weeks till fight night. The weight cut was on point, and if he kept to the schedule, he'd avoid having to boil down during fight week. He was too old to get away with it, and he needed every ounce of strength against Paddy Hughes. Thinking this, Fitzy blessed himself in a plea for forgiveness. He only wanted what was best for Danny and not the swift passing of his mother.

Every so often, Fitzy needed to remind himself that he was just the trainer, that readying Danny for a boxing match was, first and foremost, his profession. That while it felt like the biggest fight of their lives, it was only Danny who'd answer the opening bell. It was a boxing trainer's burden and it weighed on the very best, on Angelo Dundee, Cus D'amato, and the relatively unknown Barney Fitzpatrick of Ireland.

It stood to reason that Sammy Stewart would face similar conflicts. Had the fight been tomorrow, he'd have seen it through, confident of victory for his man. But the fight was in a month's time, and a month was a long time in the life of Paddy Hughes. As Sammy dialled the number of Nelson Ring Promotions, he shook his head in frustration.

Francis Nelson was banking hard on a Paddy Hughes victory. With it, he'd have a UBF champion under contract, a flagship fighter for his promotional banner and a launchpad to greater heights. A Hughes loss would hurt. A Hughes no-show was unthinkable.

'Get him to Cobbler's End, Sammy, and then you're free to go your own way. No penalties. A clean break. I'll pay you a fifty grand bonus if he wins… I'll have it drafted and sent tomorrow morning.'

'You don't understand, Mr Nelson. I know the boy, and I know the road he's on. I've done my best. I can do no more.'

The line was still hot when Peter Harrod was patched through. His GBT crew were due in Ballywell the following day. 'What do you mean *Hughes won't be there*?' he asked incredulously. 'The whole bloody promotion hinges on the rivalry between the towns. It's just one shitshow after another with you, Francis. So, what now? You'll find a trainer for him in Liverpool?'

'Yes…unless you have a better idea.'

He hadn't. Harrod had already hung up, and Nelson had no time to muse. He had Sophie make arrangements to pick up Paddy at John Lennon airport and have him taken directly to the Bed and Breakfast in Kirkby. 'Make sure someone stays with him tonight. He's not to leave his room. Not for a walk, not for a piss, nothing! I don't care if he has an aneurysm. He stays in his room!'

Nelson made for the elevator and was soon in his Bentley Continental. It was just another day in the life of a salesman. Just another day, and just another sale. He pulled up outside Mersey Gloves ABC and eyed himself in the rear-view mirror. He tidied his hair and removed his tie and jacket. On second glance, he lost his Rolex Daytona and turned up his shirt sleeves.

Inside the gym, the chief trainer, Tommy Brown was putting Kevin 'The Canon' Neary through his paces. After his loss to Paddy Hughes, Kevin had found solace in Chinese buffets, Bengali curries and doner kebabs, but after six weeks of hard graft, he was within six pounds of his fighting weight. As he eased into a shadowbox, he struggled to keep a straight face as Nelson made his pitch to Tommy.

'You know what Paddy Hughes is all about. You've seen him up close. He needs you', urged Nelson.

Tommy took a deep breath and blasted a whistle at Neary to get back to work. 'Davey Hibbert needed you, Francis. And so did Kevin.'

Nelson stepped closer. 'You know how the business works. We did what we could for Davey. It's out of my hands.'

Tommy shook his head in disbelief. 'You really do take me for a fool, don't you, Francis?'

The promoter took a half-step back and folded his arms. 'I don't know what you are getting at.'

Tommy shrugged his shoulders. 'All I know is that somebody gave Davey some very bad advice… and that his promoter threw him under the bus instead of launching an appeal.'

'I'll rebuild Davey after his ban. I'll make sure he gets his shot at the title. You have my word, Tommy.'

'I'll pass on the message. Anyway, I'm busy with Kevin. He doesn't have a fight date, but even so, I'm on his time.'

Nelson glanced at Neary and back to Tommy. 'Could Kevin be ready next month if an offer came his way?'

'I don't see why not.'

'So, we have an understanding?'

Tommy looked up to the Liverpool promoter. 'Do right by Kevin, and I'll do right by Paddy Hughes'.

On their way to Belfast city airport, Sammy Stewart pulled into a petrol station to fill his tank. He then suggested coffee. Sitting at the picnic table, Paddy Hughes' fingers rattled off his mug like Morse code. His bouncing thighs were propped on the balls of his feet.

'Drink it while it's hot', said Sammy. 'Liverpool will do you good. Keep your mind on boxing and everything will be fine. One round at a time, son.' Paddy looked around him, to the price per gallon of unleaded petrol, to the spider abseiling from their picnic bench, and to the rip of smoke from a departing Ford Escort. Anywhere but the eyes of Sammy Stewart.

'I just lost my head. I'm sorry, Sammy.'

The aging trainer leaned in. 'You don't need my forgiveness, son. I'm just an old man with a nagging wife waiting for me at home. This time next week, I'll not give you a second thought. That doesn't mean I don't care, but life goes on…. and it passes quicker than you think.' He rested a hand on Paddy's arm. 'Cobbler's End is your moment. You might not get another one, so show them all the fighter you are.'

Paddy took a deep breath. 'I will.'

#

In the Shamrock Hills hospital, the stethoscope felt cold on Father O'Dowd's back as he exhaled one last time. He could read the concern on the young doctor's face. He'd lost seven pounds since his last weigh-in, and his bones felt brittle as he stepped off the scales. He wanted more than anything to be back in Glenwilliam.... for one more morning by the river... for one more evening in front of the fire... for one last prayer before meeting his maker.

## Chapter 43

Jimmy led the walk to their mother's grave. Danny placed a hand on Connor's shoulder. Aiden and Alex laid a wreath by the foot of their grandmother's headstone. They had said little in the month since her funeral. Ivan pulled them in close as Dee rested her head on his shoulder. In the midst of worry, she breathed a sigh of relief that Ivan was there to share its weight. The marble was perfectly smoothed, reflecting the sun like a new pane of glass. It made relics of neighbouring slabs eroded by damp and devoured by moss.

'Eternal rest grant unto her, O Lord, and let perpetual light shine upon her. May she rest in peace.'

'Amen.'

Dee stayed behind to converse with Father Carrigan. By now the town knew that Father O'Dowd was unwell, though it was not Father Carrigan's place to confirm. 'I just want to know that he's alright', offered Dee as they began the short walk back to the church. 'We will pray for him', the young priest replied.

In Shamrock Views, Ela prayed for the morning sickness to pass. As Danny returned to their new home, she made another dash to the bathroom. 'Did you remember the crackers?' she asked weakly.

'Yes, got the crackers. Got the pickles too. And the ice pops.'

She lifted her head out of the latrine. 'The pineapple ones?'

Danny looked at the sticker on the box. It read 'Orange Burst.' He checked the freezer compartment, and by stroke of luck, found a pineapple pop nestled behind the meals Dee had prepped. He had one more week of plain chicken and rice. He tiptoed into the bathroom and on to the scales. Taking off his shirt, he flexed his arms and abdominals. Every inch of him was sinewed and tight… and the thought of a Dana's 'Champion Burger' made his vision blur.

#

Paddy Hughes may have been the hottest prospect in boxing, but Tommy Brown's chief concern was readying Kevin Neary for his undercard fight against Peter Simmons. A good showing against Simmons, and any number of opportunities would open up for the Merseyside fighter. One such option was a rematch against Paddy Hughes. With both fighters tied to Nelson Promotions, it was an easy fight to make. So long as Paddy did the business against Breen, Neary would be in pole position for a shot at his title.

Neary was not intimidated by Hughes. That said, sparring wasn't fighting, and as the roughhousing started, Tommy called an end to it. Both fighters wanted more, but Tommy ran a strict gym. It was time to rest before journeying to Shamrock Hills. A minder watched on from ringside. He was making double his hourly rate, and his last job of the day was to get Paddy checked into the airport hotel.

Before Tommy locked up, the office phone rang.

'Call for you, Paddy!'

On the other end was Sammy Stewart. 'Just want to wish you luck, son. There will be a lot of pomp and ceremony, but when you strip it all back, it's just another fight. Has training gone well over there?'

'Aye. I'm ready.'

'Good lad. Your weight is on point?'

'Aye, bang on the limit.'

'You know where you are staying in Shamrock Hills?'

'Hibernia House. Why?'

There was a slight pause on the other side. Paddy thought he could hear the scribble of a pencil. 'Just making sure you're being looked after. Good luck, son.'

#

Paddy entered the Hibernia House Hotel a little before ten that evening. He looked fit and strong in his customized shell suit. It was sky blue and burgundy, the colours of Ballywell. A woman, no older than forty, had been waiting in the lobby. The black coffee she ordered lay untouched. The staff again asked if everything was okay. 'I'm fine', she insisted, before ordering another.

As Paddy turned from reception, she rose from her seat. Both she and the elevator were in his line of sight, but his stride did not break. His brooding gaze did not waver. She made for the exit, forgetting to pay for the coffee. She had been so sure of her words. Since learning of the fight, she'd recited an answer to every question. She'd pictured all manner of reactions, but hadn't for a moment thought that her only son wouldn't recognize her.

Shortly after midnight, the Hibernia House staff welcomed Shamrock Hills' most celebrated son, now well into his fifties and several shades darker from the Sonoran Desert sun. His dimensions had barely changed since his triumph over Alfonso Rodriguiez, yet he had an aura that made him walk ten feet tall. It was the aura of a champion.

Luke 'Quick Hands' Gibson had returned.

Upstairs, Paddy Hughes rose for a glass of water. He studied his face in the mirror as the tap water ran. In the blacks of his eyes, the woman's face glinted as the bathroom light flickered. He drained the glass and poured another. While it filled, something inside began to ache.

The next morning, as the breakfast hall slowly filled, whispers of Gibson spread. A little after eight, the whispers gave way to a rapture of cheers. Tommy Brown and Kevin Neary made their way over.

'Where's Hughes?' asked Gibson.

'Running', they replied.

## Chapter 44

To the people of Shamrock Hills, the hinterlands of Ballywell was a relative world away. One town made its name in glassworks and fishing, while the latter laboured in mining and farming. One was a coastal town, while the other bragged of its proximity to Belfast. Their respective football clubs languished at the bottom of the Irish league. Neither had produced an international player in years. It was a pitiful return from towns of their size.

In boxing, however, they punched considerably above their weight... but only one boasted a world champion. Cobbler's End was Ballywell's chance to even the score. It was also where Paddy Hughes stepped onto the scales on the morning of the fight. His body was hard as granite, and his face was taut and menacing. He made the middleweight limit, and the travelling fans roared as one.

Four-feet-high barricades kept Ballywell's claret and blue from the green and gold of Shamrock Hills. By dusk the stadium would be packed to the rafters. The ground on which they stood would sell for £300 a seat. The Grant brothers had campaigned hard to have the weigh-in on site, yet even they were stunned by the colour and passion as the morning sun crept over the ring canopy behind them. They smiled at one another as the home fighter stripped down to his underwear and made his way to the scales with Barney Fitzpatrick.

The noise from the home support was deafening, but as the Shamrock Express looked to his trainer and back to the scales, the energy of the cheers gradually gave way to a murmuring qualm. Those pressed against the railings could almost hear Fitzy curse the Irish Boxing Board as the MC announced that Danny Breen was two pounds over the middleweight limit.

In a fight of such magnitude, Fitzy had planned for every contingency. Danny was a young man but an ageing fighter. The last couple of pounds were the hardest to shift, and he no longer had the sap in his legs to run them off. A pregnant Ela watched on as Fitzy sealed her bathroom door to trap the steam from the running shower. Danny was buried under a mountain of thick cotton towels. After thirty minutes, Fitzy checked on his fighter and noticed the scar on his brow, now bright pink and bulbous.

'That will open,' he heard himself say. He shook the thought and told Danny to hold out for another ten minutes.

Back in Cobbler's End, the crowds had dispersed as the hired hands of Grant Enterprises cleared the barricades and arranged the seating. The brothers watched on from centre-ring. Vincent was pensive, and Leonard, sensing his unease, broke the silence. 'Two pounds is nothing. He'll make it. He's got the rest of the day to regain his strength.'

Vincent nodded. 'That's easy for us to say. We only have to stand in this ring. He'll be going to war in it.'

Leonard looked about him. He imagined the cacophony of noise from the bleachers, the glow of the floodlights, and the glimmer of the UBF middleweight belt. Arcing his neck to see past the ring post, he spotted Dermot Robinson scribbling in his notepad. He studied the diminutive journalist. His shirt tail was untucked, and his mop of grey hair flapped in the cool autumn breeze. The once hardest man in Shamrock Hills felt a sudden twist of modesty as he turned back to his brother.

'Did you get the paperwork sorted?'

'Aye. It just needs dotted and signed', Vincent replied.

Leonard nodded and eased his large frame between the third and fourth ropes. Pausing, he knew that if he didn't say it then, he'd regret it for the rest of his life.

'Da would have been proud of you, brother.'

'He'd have been proud of both of us', replied Vincent, holding back his smile till Leonard's legs had broken into stride. Then, as if by the divine hand of providence, his wife's loving fingers slid between his.

'Have you chosen the reading yet?' she asked.

'I narrowed it down to three. I told Luke Gibson to read the one that feels right'.

'Which do you think he'll go with?'

'I don't know. I wish I could ask Willie'.

#

Paddy spent the afternoon of the fight in the Hibernia House Hotel. He'd eaten a large lunch of pasta, cottage cheese and garden salad. He tried on the robe that he'd wear on his way to the ring. The woollen linen felt good against his skin and would keep him warm till the sound of the opening bell.

He paced the length and breadth of his room, slipping punches, catching jabs and parrying crosses. He saw Danny Breen, up on his toes, drifting left and right, herking and jerking, creating every conceivable angle to keep his head off the line and his back off the ropes. He could run but he couldn't hide. He could bluff his way through two or three rounds, but sooner or later the boxing would stop and the fight would start.

Shortly after 4pm, Francis Nelson came to Paddy's room. Apparently, Breen looked like death as he weighed in a second time. 'Hammer his body, Nelson advised. 'Attack the body and the head will fall…this is just the beginning,' he continued. 'You'll be a household name this time tomorrow. We'll get you help for gambling. We're a family at Nelson Promotions. You are hours away from being crowned middleweight champion of the world'.

Nelson left Paddy for an early dinner with Peter Harrod and Luke 'Quick Hands' Gibson. After the Stanley Hall debacle, Harrod insisted they employ Gibson for the pre-fight pageantry and "blow by blow" commentary. It was sure to impress UBF president, Carlos Bernardi.

Unfortunately, it wasn't enough to sway the top brass at GBT. Come Monday morning, Peter Harrod would be out of a job.

'It's a brutal business…' Gibson opined. '… and a fickle on, so don't be surprised if this time next week, they're begging you to come back.'

'They can beg all they want,' Harrod snorted. 'I'll be in Tenerife sipping margaritas through a big curly straw'. He raised his glass. 'To life after boxing.'

It was a shame, thought Nelson. He'd just started to like Peter.

#

The first fight of the Cobbler's End card saw Gary 'Thunder' McGinty stop a journeyman from Romford, East London. He was now three wins into his pro career, all by way of stoppage. He lapped up the applause from the growing crowd. His trainer, Fitzy, wanted back to the changing room and away from the growing fanfare. Away from the blasts of the bass amps, the fights in the beer tents and the stench of the portaloos.

Cobbler's End was up and running, and Leonard Grant worked the crowds. Vincent Grant made his excuses and jogged towards the fighters' pavilion. Catching up with Fitzy, he handed him an envelope. 'When Danny gets here, look it over'.

'What is it?' asked Fitzy.

'We've signed our stake in the club over to Danny.' He offered his hand to Fitzy. 'It's been emotional, Barney. Win or lose, we did right by Arthur and Danny.'

Fitzy gripped his hand tightly. 'You're leaving boxing a good man. Thank you, Vincent'.

## Chapter 45

Big fights didn't come along often. That said, a full card of boxing was a slog for the average punter. When the first bell went for Neary versus Simmons, half the seats were empty. By the end of the fourth round, Cobbler's End was filled as the crowd watched Simmons deliver the performance of his career.

Asked post-fight who he was tipping in the main event, Simmons answered, 'It's boxing, and on a night like this, with so much electricity in the air, anything's possible.' Pressed for a prediction, he replied, 'Danny Breen.... just.'

Tommy Brown consoled his fighter in the corner. Neary had put his heart and soul into the training camp. Simmons was meant to be a stepping stone to better things, and maybe he still would be, but fighting the winner of Breen and Hughes had been lost in the ether. A major payday had slipped through Neary's padded gloves, and with it a shot at the title. The realization hit harder than every punch Simmons landed combined.

In the home fighter's changing room, Fitzy stood to one side as the Breen siblings wished Danny well. 'You've earned this, Danny. Go out there and enjoy yourself', urged

Jimmy as he patted the cheeks of his little brother. Connor fist-bumped his green and gold Everlast glove. 'I just know you are going to win. And I know Ma and Da will be watching.'

They made space for Ela. Danny's wiry arms rounded her waist. He rested his head on her belly as her hands ran through his thick wavy hair. She serenaded him with kisses before whispering in his ear, 'I am so proud of you, Danny.'

Dee kept her emotions in check. While her father had worked the corner of Danny's first professional fight, she was working what would surely be his last. In all that ensued from that night to this one, there was no higher honour. Thinking this, there was a gentle knock on the changing room door.

'For the love of Christ', cursed Fitzy. The last minutes between fighter and trainer were supposed to be sacred. He didn't want them squandered by hype men, hangers-on or well-wishers. But when he opened the door, he saw an old and very dear friend standing before him. Fitzy was willing, just this once, to make an exception.

With the youthful Father Carrigan by his side, Father O'Dowd had made the short walk from the Church of the Resurrection. Seeing him, Dee dropped a vial of adrenaline. Danny and Ela looked up from their embrace. The once bull-like priest was all skin and bone, but his eyes spoke of a man at peace with himself and what remained of his life on earth. Team Breen ambled together, forming a circle around the priest and the prize fighter. Together, they bowed their heads in prayer.

While Luke 'Quick Hands' Gibson was a natural on the microphone, the quiet life on his Arizona ranch hadn't prepared him for such strict time constraints. He made a quick dash for the fighter's pavilion. It had been his intention to visit Danny first, but peeking through the door, he swiftly changed course and headed to the away fighter's dressing room. Inside, he found the Ballywell brawler alone.

Paddy looked up from his hand wraps. 'I think you've got the wrong room.'

Gibson chuckled. 'No, I haven't, but if you tell anyone about this, it's my word against yours.' He pointed to Paddy's wraps. 'You should wait for your trainer to do that.'

Paddy shook his head as the tape rounded his wrist. Gibson cringed before pulling up a stool and grabbing the scissors. He unwound the tape and threw the wrapping in the bin. 'Padding first', he said, pressing it over the back of Paddy's hand, a half-inch above the knuckles. 'Padding, wrap, and then to wrist, knuckles, thumb and back to wrist. How does that feel?'

'Better.'

'I used to wrap my own hands too. I was superstitious like that.'

'I'm not.'

'Then you're lucky. I wore white shoes in the ring. I believed that the lighter the colour, the lighter my feet would feel.' He looked down at Paddy's charcoal shoes and smiled. 'I'd have been damned in them'.

Gibson finished the second wrap, snipping the tape and sealing it tightly before checking his watch. He reached into his breast pocket and unfolded the three pages that Vincent Grant had given him. Musing for a moment, he handed one to Paddy. 'Good luck kid', he said before exiting. Paddy turned the page over.

Out of the night that covers me,

Black as the pit from pole to pole,

I thank whatever gods may be

For my unconquerable soul,

In the fell clutch of circumstance

I have not winced nor cried aloud.

Under the bludgeoning of chance

My head is bloody, but unbowed.

Beyond this place of wrath and tears

Looms but the horror of the shade,

And yet the menace of the years

Finds and shall find me unafraid.

It matters not how strait the gate,

How charged with punishments the scroll,

I am the master of my fate,

I am the captain of my soul.

    The words echoed in his mind as he started the long walk from his changing room to the ring. They drowned out the chorus of boos and spattering of cheers for Paddy 'One Shot' Hughes, unbeaten in the professional ranks, concussive puncher, relentless aggressor, and the favourite to win the UBF middleweight crown. Having climbed the three steps to the ring, Paddy eyed every last soul in Cobbler's End before vaulting the top rope. He mounted the opposite turnbuckle and beat his chest at the Ballywell fans. They were four-thousand strong and ready for war.

    Moments later, it was the turn of the hometown hero, the former amateur standout, and the Fighting Pride of Shamrock Hills. Danny bounced on the balls of his feet as he neared the ring, Fitzy by his left shoulder and Dee to his right. He could see nothing but outstretched hands and the blinding glare of the ring light before him.

The canvas felt good as he stepped into the ring and circled its corners. While the MC thanked the various bodies and sponsors, Danny approached Vincent Grant. 'Thank you... for everything.' His former manager clasped both sides of Danny's face and kissed him on the forehead. 'It was always your stake, kid. This is all I ever wanted for you. This, right here. Now, go win the title!'

The referee ushered the fighters to centre ring.

'We went over the rules in the dressing room. Anything below here on Mr Breen will be ruled low. Anything below here on Mr Hughes will be ruled low. I want a clean fight. Stop punching when I call break. In the event of a knockdown, go to the nearest neutral corner. No rabbit punching, no headbutts and no use of the elbows. Protect yourself at all times and obey my commands at all times.'

Neither fighter had heard a word, but in the centuries-old tradition, they touched gloves and returned to their corners. Danny dropped to one knee and blessed himself. Paddy Hughes held his stare as Tommy Brown stripped him of his blue and burgundy robe. The twelve-thousand-strong crowd were suddenly plunged into darkness as the floodlights coalesced on the freshly laid canvas. The opening bell sounded.

Cobbler's End trembled.

## Chapter 46

The crowd returned to their seats as the fighters inched their way in. They flicked out jabs and studied the tells. The battle of the jabs was key, Gibson commented. He wanted to see the classier Breen establish his early and win Hughes' respect. 'He has to make it a boxing match.'

But it was Paddy's jab that found its mark first, speared fast and hard over the top of Danny's right glove. The Ballywell brawler was not there for the counterpunch, instead bouncing out of distance and back into his shell.

Danny resettled and looked for a fresh opening. He feinted with his head and lead shoulder before throwing a range-finding right cross. Paddy used to react to such probes, confusing them for an invitation to trade. This time, he stepped back at an angle and returned with a double left jab. The first blinded Danny's view, and the second landed flush on his mouth, pressing hard into his gumshield and tearing at the roots of his teeth.

The Shamrock Express shook his head as he made his way back to the corner. Fitzy kneeled by his feet. 'Settle down, son. You're thinking too much in there. He'll open up. It's just a matter of time.' Tommy Brown told his fighter he was one round to the good. 'The jab's working perfect. He's fighting scared. He'll burn himself out. Keep boxing smart.'

As the second round commenced, Danny rushed to claim the centre of the ring. It was one of the first lessons he learned in the amateurs. Take the centre and control the range. Neither Fitzy or Danny had envisaged Paddy ceding so much as an inch of the ring, and yet the supposed brawler was electing to box on the back foot. He was inviting the Shamrock Express to walk him down and onto a hammer blow right across. Danny was much too wily for that.

In the third, the crowd grew restless. Vincent and Leonard Grant sat pensively at ringside. Fitzy shouted at Danny to let his hands go, and the Shamrock Express obliged, rattling off a tidy three-punch combination and finishing with a stabbing jab to Paddy's solar plexus. It brought the crowd back into the fight and may have won Danny his first round.

'It's very cat and mouse', commented Gibson, 'but sooner or later a fight is going to break out, and I reckon it will be sooner. I have Hughes a round up but there are signs that Breen is warming to the task.'

Asked if he thought Paddy could box his way to a decision, Gibson replied, 'He's shown he can box, but he's not fooling me. His plan will go out the window once Breen lands something big.'

In the corner, Danny asked for water as Dee massaged the back of his neck. His legs felt strong. Fitzy was satisfied with his fighter's assurances. Despite the baying crowd and the world title at stake, in essence, they were doing what they'd trained a lifetime for.

In the opposite corner, Tommy Brown leaned over the turnbuckle and watched the opposition. Studying Breen, he noted how much water he consumed before whispering his instructions in Paddy's ear. The Ballywell brawler nodded as he arced his neck and spat into the bucket. Doing so, he caught a glimpse of Sammy Stewart four rows from ringside. He was sat beside the women from the Hibernia House hotel.

In the fourth, Paddy pressed the action. The fighters traded hard jabs and exchanged hooks to the body. Trusting his instincts, Paddy unleashed a second volley of punches to Danny's ribcage. Some caught his elbows and forearms, but two or three found their mark. Paddy felt the punches sink in deep and heard the expulsion of air from Danny's lungs. The Shamrock man momentarily sagged on the ropes, encouraging Paddy to headhunt. He landed a short right-hand cross on Danny's cheekbone. It was the best punch of the contest.

Danny bit down on his gum shield. He knew Paddy the fighter intimately well, and as his punches widened, Danny exploded with short, sharp left hooks. Their collective force backed up the Ballywell brawler and momentarily wobbled him. Cobbler's End shook once more.

Luke Gibson stood to applaud the action as Vincent Grant chewed his finger nails down to the nub. In a two-bedroom flat in Shamrock Views, Ela and Anne watched through shaking hands as Jimmy and Connor roared on their brother. In the bleachers of Cobbler's End, Ivan sat between his twin sons. He hid his fear well. To Aiden and Alex, their uncle Danny was unconquerable.

In the away fighter's corner, Paddy again glimpsed at the woman seated beside Sammy Stewart. Tommy Brown slapped his cheek and urged him to focus. He was the away fighter, Brown reminded him. He not only had to win but win emphatically. Paddy banged his fists in agreement and, coming out for the sixth round, immediately fired a pulverizing right cross. It cannoned off Danny's gloves and sent him staggering across the ring.

Dee readied the cotton as Hughes rag-dolled her brother from pillar to post. Having pinned Danny in a corner, he knocked him down with a razor-sharp left cross that tore open Danny's scar tissue. He rose to one knee and watched the referee's count. He got back to his feet at the count of eight.

'Are you ok to continue?' asked the referee

'Yes.'

'Step forward. Hold out your gloves.'

From ringside, Vincent looked to Fitzy. 'You can stop it, Barney! You can stop it anytime!' he shouted.

The referee waved Paddy in. Fitzy screamed at Danny to move, but all he could do was grapple and hold. Paddy was strong as an ox, ripping his gloves free and doubling his hooks to head and body. During the one-minute break, Fitzy pressed hard on the gash, but the blood continued to seep. Danny winced as his trainer applied the coagulant. 'I'm alright Fitzy. It's just a cut.'

'If it gets any worse, I'm throwing the towel in,' replied the Celtic Fist trainer.

Dermot Robinson of the Gazette had Paddy five points ahead. All but one of the rounds had been easy to score. That said, Danny was still in the fight. Through a bloodied nose and damaged eye, he'd risen from the deck and managed to survive the round. This was not the Danny Breen that surrendered in Stanley Hall.

Through the blood, Danny could still see plenty of Hughes but struggled to see the punches coming. He was once the master of 'catch and counter', smothering an opponent's jab before rifling in one of his own. Now, his only option was to fire first and keep firing. He threw caution to the wind and stepped in with a hard one-two combination that split Paddy's guard.

Feeling encouraged, he waded in with an arcing right hand, oblivious to Paddy having launched one of his own. Danny's punch partially landed, while Paddy's detonated on the point of Danny's chin. Danny's world went to black as his body crumpled to the canvas. Not even the glare of the ring light could penetrate the darkness.

'He's not getting up from that!!' screamed Gibson.

Fitzy looked to the white towel in his fist. He grabbed the third rope to pull himself up, but the diminutive arms of Dee Breen hauled him back down. With that, Danny's ears ceased ringing and the white of the referee's shirt came into focus. He rolled onto his side, but his elbow gave way from under him. The referee's count had already reached seven seconds.

Danny looked to his corner but couldn't make out Fitzy. The fans in the bleachers tilted and rocked as blood gushed from his nose and onto the canvas. He saw the bouncing charcoal boots of Paddy Hughes as the referee pushed him back.

Above the roar of twelve thousand fans, he heard a familiar voice from within. It was barely a whisper. It was the same voice that accompanied him on every morning run, for every bead of sweat and for every drop of blood.

*Suffer now and be remembered as a champion. We're proud of you, son.*

Danny Breen rose to one knee. With the referee's count at nine, he found himself back on his feet, hoisted by a force that carried no name. The referee took a close look before waving Paddy in. The Ballywell man was one hard punch away from world championship glory as the UBF belt glistened in front of the spellbound Carlos Bernardi.

To the surprise of all in Cobbler's End, Danny got up on his toes for the remainder of the round. His back barley grazed the ring ropes as he slid from side to side and negated the sting from Paddy's shots. He could barely see Paddy never mind time his punches, but his legs continued to carry him. 'Keep dancing!' screamed Ela. 'Just keep dancing!'

'Amazing powers of recovery', remarked Gibson. 'Breen has no right to be on his feet never mind up on his toes. Hughes must feel discouraged. He's thrown the kitchen sink at Breen and he's still in there!'

Another round went to the cards. Danny was past the point of tiredness. The broken nose no longer throbbed, and the torn eyebrow no longer stung. His breathing, like every part of his body felt even and warm. He smiled as he sat on his stool. In the opposite corner, Paddy Hughes batted away the offer of water. His leaden arms rested between the ropes, and his outstretched legs had turned to rubber. 'Pace yourself!' screamed Tommy. 'Get back to basics. Work behind your jab and stop winging your punches!'

The crowd no longer roared for one fighter. What they were witnessing transcended the rivalry that divided green and gold from claret and blue. For the first time in the fight, Breen was the fresher man, exhaling short blasts of air as he landed punches at will, touching Paddy to body and head and sending his sweat spraying. Paddy absorbed the punishment and came out for more in the following round.

The noise inside Cobbler's End reached a crescendo as Danny let fly with punches in threes, fours and fives, turning Paddy, pivoting left then right, outworking him up close and pot shotting at distance. His boxing was pure artistry. Paddy's legs quivered as he returned to his stool at the end of the tenth round. 'He's ready to go!' screamed Fitzy.

'Breen needs a stoppage', declared Gibson, 'Hughes has never been this deep into a fight, but he still has the power. It only takes one punch.'

In the penultimate round of the fight, both men dared to be great. Danny Breen rolled back the years and summoned all that was left in his thirty-three-year-old body. Paddy Hughes matched him punch for punch, proving that he too belonged on the grandest stage. Francis Nelson smiled towards Peter Harrod. They knew this night would never be forgotten.

Father O'Dowd kneeled by the altar in the Church of the Resurrection where he prayed with Father Carrigan. At ringside, Vincent Grant squeezed hard on his big brother's hand. Before issuing his final instructions, Fitzy looked up to the night's sky and wondered if Archie Buchanan was watching. 'One more round, Danny. You have one more round to fight!'

'One more round!' screamed the Shamrock Express as he rose from his stool and raised his glove to the sky. Paddy Hughes rose slowly from his and looked towards the woman sat beside Sammy Stewart. Doing so, he recalled the last words she uttered to him all those years ago.

*This isn't forever. Nothing is.*

Spitting blood through his gumshield, he turned to his army of Ballywell fans and pumped his padded fist. He looked across the ring to Danny, and the fighters smiled at one another. Paddy pointed to the centre of the ring, and the Shamrock Express nodded. Before the bell sounded for the twelfth and final round, they embraced. Only one could lift the title, but their names would be forever linked.

'Let's give them what they came for!' shouted the referee.

Twelve thousand souls stood to applaud the greatest fight they'd ever seen. The fighters touched gloves and waited for the bell.

They'd given their best.

All they had left was pride.

# Acknowledgements

To the fighters, thank you for inspiring me to write this book.

Printed in Dunstable, United Kingdom